The Strange Case
of Eliza Doolittle

The Strange Case
of Eliza Doolittle

Timothy Miller

SEVENTH
STREET
BOOKS®

For Sanna

Chapter One

I have perhaps left the impression among my readers (such stalwarts as remain!) that, when Sherlock Holmes retired to his villa in Sussex to pursue his avocation as a beekeeper, his extraordinary career as the world's first consulting detective came to a lamentable end. This was true in the main. But there were some few instances of such importance to the Crown that Holmes felt obliged to assist, even in his waning years. And there were certain cases, no more than a handful, of such bizarre aspect and puckered logic that he simply could not resist the temptation to wade back into the black cesspools of London's vast criminal underworld. I have hesitated to record, much less publish, any accounts of these latter-day adventures. My friend has begged privacy, and earned it. Yet there was one case so singular, so wholly outside the pale of human understanding, that even after all these years I feel compelled to set down at least a précis of the matter. Whether it will ever see the light of day, I cannot hazard to predict. When I have finished it, I shall place it among my personal papers, and leave instructions with my publishers in case accident should befall.

The story begins with my old comrade from Afghanistan, Colonel

Hugh Pickering. And a very odd place it is to begin such an odd story, for there was never anything in the least bit odd about old Pickering. There were those among his associates who swore that his uncanny gift for languages was the result of a compact with the infernal, but that was only japery, or jealousy, more like. In all other respects, he was a paragon of conventionality, with the mildest disposition of any man I ever met. Then again, were it not for that peculiar linguistic facility, he would never have met Miss Eliza Doolittle. Nor would Sherlock Holmes and I.

In the year 1912, it had been more than a decade since I had corresponded with Pickering. When last I had news of him, he was still traipsing about the subcontinent, ostensibly collecting scraps for a grammar of Sanskrit he was always threatening to publish. I thought it more likely a cover for his role in British intelligence. Pickering's reports, idiosyncratic though they were, were always widely disseminated at the Foreign Office, although of course his contributions were never officially acknowledged.

So I was both surprised and delighted that mild September evening when my housekeeper announced a visitor, and laid a card upon my table that read simply, "Colonel Pickering. 27A Wimpole St." Colonel! He had been a lowly subaltern when first we met in Kandahar. And a Wimpole Street address to go with the title. Pickering had evidently done well for himself.

As for myself, I was once again dwelling and practicing medicine in the flat in Queen Anne Street which I had taken after the death of my dear wife all those years ago. I had decorated the sitting room in a muted style meant to soothe the most anxious patient, with a portrait of Victoria Regina over the mantel and a marble bust of Admiral Nelson on a plinth by the door. The chairs were a compromise between Victorian rigor and modern indulgence: a patient might sit back in them, but never wallow. The articulated human skeleton hanging in the surgery gave some ladies palpitations, but it had been a gift from Holmes upon his retirement. I would not part with it.

It was evident when Pickering appeared on the threshold that he had not haunted Wimpole Street for any great length of time. (My years with Sherlock Holmes have taught me some few things about reading people.) He was still brown as a walnut from his years in the southern sun. He still sported an erect regimental bearing. Yet there was also that mild diffidence about him that westerners sometimes pick up from the Hindoo native, a certain philosophical equanimity.

"Wobbly!" he cried upon seeing me. "Pixie!" I returned—our old regimental nicknames, which I had long since forgotten, leapt unbidden to my mind. We shook hands warmly. I offered him a chair, a cigar, and a brandy, in that order, and soon we were knee-deep in misre-membrance of our gallant youth. There was a great deal of "Remember old what's-his-name?" and "When was it that droll thing happened?" but we pushed on through the gaps with the best will possible.

Eventually we ran out of halcyon days to memorialize. Pickering's brow clouded over. He set down his brandy and extinguished his cigar. "I'm looking for a fellow, Wobbly, a sort of human bloodhound, I've been told he is. And more, I've been told he's your particular friend."

The allusion was obvious. "You mean Sherlock Holmes."

"Sherlock Holmes! That's just the fellow! You do know him, then?"

Here lay further proof that Pickering had not long been stranded upon the shores of Albion. He was barely familiar with the name of Sherlock Holmes, and wholly ignorant of my role in chronicling the great detective's exploits.

"You're not in any sort of trouble, are you, Pixie?" I asked.

"Oh, bless me, no!" The corners of his mouth dipped. "At least, I don't think so. But I've come up against a sort of a puzzle, or enigma, or whatever. Damnedest thing. Could you introduce me to this fellow Holmes, do you think?"

"I'm afraid Mr. Holmes has long since retired from detective work."

Pickering's face creased in disappointment.

"Perhaps I can be of help?" I suggested. "I worked with Holmes hand in glove for many long years. I don't claim to share his natural gifts, but I'm as familiar with his methods as any man on earth."

Pickering brightened. "I'll be glad to tell you the story, old fellow. If you can squeeze anything out of it, you're a marvel."

Storytelling is thirsty work, and so is listening. I poured us both another bumper of brandy. He launched into his story, the tale of a distinguished phonetician, a girl of the streets, and a singular wager. It was indeed one of the strangest problems I have ever encountered, and I will admit without compunction that I could make nothing of it at all. I confessed it unabashedly.

Pickering put on a stoic face. "Well, I can't say I'm surprised, Wobbly. It's a preposterous tale on the face of it."

"It is indeed, my friend. So much so that I would have called the fellow who told it me a fabulist or a madman, were it not solid old Pickering. But in its very absurdity is its allure. I think even the great Sherlock Holmes would agree with that assessment."

"You mean you'll take my problem to him? By Jove, that's capital."

Pickering's excitement was infectious. "I'll do you one better. I'll take you down to meet him and let you plead your case in person."

Pickering clapped his hands upon his thighs. "Better still. Where can we find the fellow?"

"He has a villa down in Sussex, near Eastbourne. We can take the train from Victoria tomorrow. I'll wire him to let him know we're coming." I had surrendered to the demands of the modern age a few years ago, and had a telephone installed. Holmes had not.

Pickering left beaming, humming one of the old marches from our Kandahar days. My own spirits were considerably lifted in his wake, if only temporarily. But an hour of somber reflection left me in doubt that Sherlock Holmes would indeed take an interest in this case or any other. Pickering had described him as a human bloodhound; it had once been an apt description, but nowadays the old hound was as likely to be found lolling in the sun or stretched before a fire, dreaming of former glories. I had in my possession a whole dispatch box of cases meant for examination by Sherlock Holmes, clipped from a dozen newspapers—crimes that had baffled Scotland Yard, tangled mysteries and bizarre occurrences that would appeal to his yen for the baroque. I had never summoned the temerity to post a single one to him. Under scrutiny, none seemed really worthy of the great man's attention. I didn't know whether he even took the London papers anymore. He had been wont to pore over them like a Baptist with his Bible. Now perhaps they would only dredge up memories of a life deliberately abandoned. This was after all the same man who had ignored the French government's pleas for help when the Mona Lisa was stolen. His exodus from public life had been abrupt and was still unexplained.

I had even tried to soldier on without him, attempting to solve some of those cases myself, sitting in my armchair on Sunday mornings, applying his methods, mumbling his old aphorisms to myself. I had never got anywhere with a single one. Perhaps Pickering's mystery would prove to be another such disappointment. But even if the affair provided no more than an excuse to introduce two of my dearest friends to one another, I told myself, it would suffice. Had I any idea of the events which were about to be set in motion, I would have quailed at the thought.

Chapter Two

Sherlock Holmes's tumbledown old villa on the Sussex downs was the very *sine qua non* of a country squire. That squire was not Sherlock Holmes, who had made little alteration to the place since inheriting it from some distant relation. There was a quiet courtyard in front, undisturbed by visitors, and an overgrown garden in the back, red and white with clover, enjoyed only by the bees. There were rooms that Holmes swore he had never entered, for lack of any good reason to do so. Whether his housekeeper kept those rooms neat as a pin or whether they had become infested with field mice and black beetles was all one to him. His chief contribution had been to refit the old stable as an apiary. The drone of bees about the place seemed menacing at first impression, but gave way over time to a pleasantly soporific feeling.

The sitting room I was ensconced in with Holmes and Pickering was reminiscent of our old digs in Baker Street, where so many of our adventures had begun, save that the catalogues and scientific instruments which littered shelves and tabletops were now all devoted to the art and science of beekeeping rather than crime. But it was an airier chamber, with a high timbered ceiling, and the tall windows looked out not on the parade of unwashed humanity in Baker Street but on the wide green expanse of the southern downs, with white cliffs and a blue sea shimmering in the distance.

"So this is the great Mr. Holmes? All of London rings with your praises, sir," said Pickering, shaking Holmes's hand like a village water-pump.

"You do me too much honor." Holmes always pretended that compliments did not move him, though he basked in their glow as much as any man. "Please do be seated, gentlemen. Watson, I see the new chef at Simpson's meets with your approval." I blushed. He had noticed the weight I had put on since last we had met. Simpson's had always been one of our favorite haunts.

As soon as we were comfortably settled, Holmes's housekeeper shot forth from the kitchen with a pot of tea on a tray and some marvelous seedcake. The housekeeper was herself round and plummy as a Christmas pudding. She was obviously devoted to her baking, and nearly burst with pride when she saw how avidly we wolfed down everything she put in front of us. Holmes was an indifferent epicure himself; he accepted the tea with an air of noblesse oblige, but abstained from the seedcake. "Mrs. Plymouth used to cook for my brother, Mycroft, before his death. She has never adjusted," he said reproachfully.

"Holmes! My condolences!" This was the first I had heard that Mycroft had departed this world.

Holmes merely waved away the sentiment as if it were of no consequence. His saturnine countenance registered little in the way of emotion. He took a sip of tea, set the cup down on the arm of his chair, and settled back dreamily, his lanky limbs splayed out before him, his feet capped in carpet slippers, scuffed at the heel. His eyelids fluttered. I began to fear that he might doze off.

Then from those hooded eyes there flashed that quicksilver light that I remembered from so many previous interviews. "Now then, Colonel: the matter," he said quietly.

Pickering set down his own teacup. "The doctor has told you everything?"

"The details may have escaped my memory."

In fact, I had told Holmes very little, only enough to whet his curiosity. I had been half afraid that if I wired him all the details he would wire me back with his solution to the mystery and a remark or two disparaging my mental faculties. But I certainly had not expected this foggy-minded memory lapse.

"Well . . . the long and the short of it, Mr. Holmes, is I believe he's done away with the girl!"

There was a beat of wings and a black shadow dropped like a plumb from the rafters. Pickering gave a start as it landed at his feet. The shadow let forth a raucous cry, picked itself up, and sorted itself into the shape of a bird: a large raven with glossy purple wings and an unwavering golden eye.

Holmes ignored the bird. "That may be the short of it, but it can hardly be the long, Colonel," he said. "Who is the *he* you refer to, and who is the girl?"

Pickering had not heeded a word. His attention was entirely fixed upon the bird of ill omen at his feet. For its part, the creature seemed equally fascinated with him, glaring as if Pickering were a junior officer expected to give an account of himself. It let forth another gravel-throated cry.

"Moriarty!" Holmes scolded the bird. "He's not dangerous, Colonel, despite his namesake. I confide in him my thoughts; he does not publish them abroad as some are wont to."

He may have meant it as a backhanded reproach to me. I took it as an admission that he was lonely without me.

Moriarty advanced on Pickering, his eyes hard with suspicion. Pickering shrank back. "Perhaps if you start with your first meeting with Professor Higgins," I said, hoping to draw Pickering back to the subject at hand.

He took a handkerchief from his sleeve and dotted at his brow. "Most extraordinary thing! I mean, if it hadn't been for the downpour . . . but that's not really where it begins, is it?" he mused.

"Then pray begin at the beginning," said Holmes.

Moriarty paced the carpet back and forth in front of Colonel Pickering with the same nervous energy Holmes himself used to display when listening to the facts of a case. For his part, Holmes slouched back in languid repose.

"Yes, but what is the beginning, eh? Watson here can tell you that my military career was not made illustrious by bravery or skill, or the mind of a military strategist. But I was useful to the Raj almost from the beginning as a translator."

"Not merely useful, but indispensable," I said.

Pickering gave me a nod. "Thank you, Wobbs."

I cast a sidelong glance at Holmes, praying that he had not heard the name "Wobbs." He was a man who generally shunned society and had nothing but ridicule for school nicknames, club nicknames, or regimental nicknames. He rarely referred to me by my Christian name, and would have no more called me Wobbly than allow himself to be referred to as Sherry.

"Do continue," Holmes urged. If he had noticed the nickname, he mercifully let it pass.

"Oh, yes. After the Afghan campaign wound up I was chivvied about from place to place, all over the subcontinent. I had a natural ear for native dialects and was usually able to pick up a new variant within a few days. But there were so many that I was forced to start taking notes to keep them all from running together in my head. Over the years my notes piled up so thick they could have made a book. Which is exactly what I did."

"*Spoken Sanskrit*," Holmes said quietly.

Pickering was delighted. "I'm amazed that you've heard of it!"

"Astonishing, Holmes!" I said.

"Not in the least. There is a copy sticking out of your coat pocket, Colonel."

Pickering's cheeks turned pink. "Oh, yes, of course. One never knows when one might need it, you see." He looked down at his hands self-consciously, giving his nails a thorough inspection before he could go on. "Well then, a few years ago, I was posted to Bombay. Ever been there?"

"Some years ago, but only in transit, while journeying to Tibet."

Holmes had never mentioned any such journey to me. But then his wanderings between the fateful events at the Reichenbach Falls and his return to London were largely a closed book as far as I was concerned.

"Glorious city, if you don't mind the crowds. And the filth. And, well, the filthy crowds. What struck me most forcefully about the place was the amazing variation of dialect and pronunciation from one ward to the next, sometimes even from one street to the next. An absolute hotbed of languages. I thought there could not be another such polyglot city in the world. Then I came across *Higgins's Universal Alphabet*. Don't suppose you've read it?"

"The booksellers here in the country . . ." Holmes made a desultory gesture, as if the philistinism of local merchants was all that came between him and the joys of universal alphabets.

"Say no more. At any rate, Higgins's book opened my eyes to another such polyglot city—London itself. I was so impressed with his work that I felt compelled to seek him out without delay."

Holmes lofted an eyebrow. "You voyaged halfway round the world because of a book?"

"Sounds daft when you put it that way, doesn't it? But here's the truly astounding part: on my very first night in London, I attended the theatre—the American actor William Gillette. Tremendous stuff, had me on the edge of my seat. Who did I meet there, loitering about the porch of Saint Paul's in the rain as if he'd come there a-purpose to meet me? Henry Higgins himself. Ten minutes after we discovered ourselves to each other, he had invited me to come stay with him in his home. And that was the very same night we met Eliza. What are the odds, eh? I ask you, what are the odds?"

Holmes ignored the invitation to do the calculations. "Eliza is the girl he's done away with?"

"Miss Doolittle, yes. Or possibly no. She was selling flowers to the theatre-goers."

"This was how long ago?" he asked.

"Six months? No, nearer to seven. Where does the time go?"

"And you've resided with Professor Higgins since?"

"I suppose that seems odd? Two bachelors with similar interests living and working together cheek by jowl?"

I could not repress a smile.

"When did Miss Doolittle join the household?" Holmes asked.

"The very next day. She had got it in her head that she wanted elocution lessons. Determined to get them, wouldn't take no for an answer. Wanted to talk like a 'lady' so she could get a position in a flower shop."

"Professor Higgins is a bachelor, you said?"

Pickering nodded vigorously. "Confirmed. Anointed, you might bloody well say. If you'll excuse the camp talk."

"Is it customary for him to provide lodging to his students?"

"Couldn't say. Eliza's the only one of his students I've ever been acquainted with."

"The only student he's taken on in the last seven months?"

"Higgins caters to a very exclusive clientele."

"Yet that clientele consists solely of a Covent Garden flower girl."

"That's it in a nutshell! On the one hand he's the most sensible, logical man I've ever met. On the other hand, nothing he does makes the least bit of sense. It's enough to drive a fellow mad."

"What about the girl? Was there anything unusual about her?"

"Yes . . . well, no."

"Which is it?"

"She was the most ordinary sort of girl in the world, nothing to look at, certainly. But there was something . . . something *wrong* with her."

"Something? Could you elaborate?"

"Was it a cast in one eye? Or was there a swelling on one of her—perhaps her hip was turned—I know I sound feeble-minded, but there was something wrong with her, and I can't recall just what it was!"

"This something presumably has . . . gone away?"

"Well, there was the fit, you know."

"She had a fit?"

"I had a fit. Relapse, really. Malaria. Souvenir of my days in India. That's when the transformation occurred."

"You were transformed?" I asked.

"She was transformed. Am I getting things muddled? We both took ill. I was down nearly a fortnight. When I got back on my pins, I toddled down to breakfast. Same old Higgins, same old Mrs. Pearce—the housekeeper, you know—same housemaids in their snowy caps, same insolent footman. Different Eliza. No one offered a word of explanation. Acted as if nothing had changed. I thought I must still be awash in the dreams of my malady. Except I suppose you'd call this one a good dream."

"What had changed about the girl?" Holmes asked.

"Hard to pin down. She seemed taller. Straighter. More—what's the word?—*willowy*. And her features were far more pleasant. Sunnier. And then her language—well!"

"You've said she was taking elocution lessons. Would that not explain the difference in her language? Could not every change you've mentioned be accounted for by a new position, new wardrobe, a new confidence?"

Pickering pondered the question. He appeared ready to accede. Then: "No, by thunder! She's not the same girl! I'll stake my fortune on it, Mr. Holmes."

"Did you share your suspicions with anyone?"

"I discussed it with Mrs. Pearce, in a roundabout fashion. Mrs. Pearce is a most formidable woman. Like a tigress with her cub. And I talked to the doctor, same fellah who looked after me and Eliza both, don't you know, but doctors are such a close-lipped bunch. May as well talk to an oyster. No offense meant, Wobbly," he added.

"None taken," I assured him.

"But you did not take your misgivings to Mr. Higgins?" asked Holmes.

"Couldn't. On account of the wager."

Pickering then recounted the wager he and Higgins had entered into when Miss Doolittle was first admitted to the establishment. "Higgins had bragged that he could teach her to speak so well he could pass her off as a duchess at last month's embassy party. I offered to underwrite the lessons and all the expenses if he could pull it off. Plus five pounds to seal the bargain. It was by way of being a friendly wager, but it was a wager, after all."

"So you believe that the girl may have been bundled off, or even done away with, and a second girl brought in to replace her, all to win this wager?"

"I know it sounds absurd. But Higgins doesn't like to lose. And she won it for him going away."

"By your own admission, you were recovering from a protracted illness which at times affected your perceptions."

"You mean I shouldn't trust my judgment? Perhaps you're right . . . but I *do* trust my judgment, and so must you, if you're to take this case. Perhaps you'd rather not?" said Pickering doubtfully.

Holmes sank back even further in his chair, until he was almost swallowed by the cushions. He cast a curious glance at me, as if sharing some secret joke. Then he steepled his hands upon his breast.

"On the contrary. I find several points of interest. First, there is the remarkable coincidence of your initial meeting with Higgins and the girl. Second, the fact that you and the girl became ill at the same time, and were treated by the same physician. Then there is your own inability to pinpoint Miss Doolittle's physical defect. Lastly, the fact that the wager is won, yet the girl remains beneath Professor Higgins's roof. This seems a particularly thorny problem. With your permission, I will make further inquiry."

Pickering jumped up and shook Holmes's hand again, nearly dragging him out of his chair. "Absolutely capital. I'm convinced there's no man better suited to plumb the depths of Henry Higgins's mind. Every time you open your mouth, it's as if I hear him speaking."

Holmes grimaced, and I winced. He never liked being compared to other men, at least not in terms of equality.

Chapter Three

It was a glorious September morning the day the American millionaire came to Wimpole Street. The sky was blue as a Dutch platter. There was little traffic that morning in the well-ordered lane, most of it the horse-drawn kind rather than the bright, fierce chariots of the modern age. The gleaming red bonnet of the millionaire's Moreau-Lepton seemed a brazen challenge to the august facades lining the street. Any loafer would have turned to watch as the car lurched to a stop in front of Professor Higgins's establishment. The driver got out, an older fellow with a steel wool moustache, a bit shaky in the legs. He opened the door for his charge.

The millionaire emerged, tall, thin as a whippet, with grey hair standing up like iron filings from his scalp, an aquiline nose, and a pencil-thin moustache smudging his lip. He entered the house like a summer storm, unexpected and unsettling. Mrs. Pearce had been given no warning of his advent, and would have turned him away on the basis of his barbaric language alone. Professor Higgins was not at home, sir. His assistant, Miss Doolittle, was not at home. The two men—the driver was also a secretary, it seemed, a stocky Englishman brought along no doubt to serve as interpreter—pushed right past her into the hall and thence to the professor's laboratory, settling themselves unerringly into the two most comfortable chairs. She would have summoned the police, had not Colonel Pickering intervened.

"What's all this, then, Mrs. Pearce?" he asked, dropping in to the middle of the argument.

Mrs. Pearce was a woman of erect carriage and dignified demeanor. Her starched grey uniform put one in mind of the prow of a battleship. "I'm sorry, Colonel," she said. "I tried to tell them they should wait in the front hall."

The American pulled a thin cigar from his lapel pocket and lit it. The aroma was pungent. "G.B. Morello at your service, pal. You the butler? We could do with some drinks."

Pickering drew himself up. "I am Colonel Pickering."

"A colonel? We got a boatload of colonels back home. I was shooting for a duke, at least."

Mrs. Pearce was aghast, but the colonel seemed unperturbed. "It's all right, Mrs. Pearce. These gentlemen are expected. Leave them in my hands. I'll keep an eye on them."

The housekeeper gave the interlopers a last baleful glare.

"Run off to the kitchen and count the silverware," sneered the American.

"Come, come, Mr. Morello, she's only doing her duty. Thank you, Mrs. Pearce." The housekeeper turned on her heel and went out, huffing to herself.

Morello, that was his name. G.B. Morello. It was the name on the tags on the luggage in the boot of the automobile out front. Mrs. Pearce was not unaware that there was an American millionaire of the same name. Since she was Mrs. Pearce, and no one's fool, she was also acquainted with the rumors of the illicit means by which he had acquired his millions. Well, if this were the same fellow, the robber barons of America were no more civilized than the rabble, she told the kitchen maid. Then she forbade her to repeat it.

In the laboratory, Pickering was pouring sherry for Mr. G.B.

Morello and his secretary—that is to say, for Sherlock Holmes and myself. (I use the word "laboratory" with reservation. The room we were in combined drawing room, library, and music room all in one. It was a scholar's room, with a fine layer of dust over every piece of furniture but the piano, which was polished to a sheen. I was reminded of Holmes's injunctions against Mrs. Hudson dusting his rooms at Baker Street. The peculiar equipment devoted to the discipline of phonetics was confined to one crowded corner of the room. But Henry Higgins always referred to the room as his laboratory, so everyone else followed suit.)

"Your timing is fortunate, gentlemen." Pickering barely spoke above a whisper. "I'd wanted you to meet Eliza without Higgins being present. She's always more constrained in his presence."

I had expected Sherlock Holmes to transform himself into an American gangster with some elaborate costume and makeup, but the spiky hair, the American cut of his suit, and the moustache he had grown in the week since our meeting were more than enough to seal his new character. I had even feared I'd be required to wear some kind of disguise myself. But Holmes had vetoed the notion. "Even the most elaborate disguise holds up for only a short amount of time, Watson," he had said. "We shall rely on the latter-day obscurity of Sherlock Holmes and Dr. Watson to mask our identities." My costume consisted of rather sulky tweeds, worn at the elbows and grimed at the cuffs.

Now Mr. Morello stood in the middle of the room, drinking in every detail. I knew from experience that a few minutes' patient observation of the surroundings would tell him more about his subject than most men would learn after months of intimacy. I wondered what he would make of the Piranesi engravings on the wall, or the score of *Our Miss Gibbs* on the piano. Some fascinating sidelights would follow shortly, or so I hoped.

"Tell me about Miss Doolittle when she first came to you," he directed Pickering. "Before her transformation. What was she?"

Pickering stared hard at the sherry decanter. "'Guttersnipe.' Is that harsh? 'Slattern.' That's not much better, is it? 'Trollop?' No."

"No better than she ought to be?" I suggested.

"Really, Watson!" I had somehow managed to cross a line Pickering's sense of chivalry would not allow.

"I don't mean to blacken her name," he explained. "I felt a sympathy toward her from the very first. But she was a creature of the streets, a bit of rough and tumble, as we used to say in the regiment."

"Can you offer any reason why the professor would wish to foist such an elaborate deceit upon you as you propose?" asked Holmes.

The colonel shook his head. "Higgins is straight as they come."

"Yet you said he tried to pass the girl off as a duchess?"

"He succeeded, too. But that was merely sport. Part of the wager."

"So, by your own account, he's a deceiver and a gambler."

"And has a tongue on him like a sailor. But . . ."

"He is a gentleman," Holmes said acidly.

"An English gentleman!" said Pickering. "Not some French powder puff or Oriental doormat."

"Of course not." Holmes seemed amused by Pickering's staunch defense of the man he was asking us to investigate. "Let's return to the girl, then, and this singular transformation Higgins is supposed to have effected upon her."

"Everyone said it was because she'd been ill. But what kind of illness puts color in the cheeks and light in the eyes?"

On that cue, Miss Eliza Doolittle burst into the room like the ingénue in a Covent Garden comedy. She was a petite thing, barely twenty years of age, but sturdy and full of bounce. She was dressed in the latest mode, all tall-necked and cinched waist, with a jacket like a sailor's, and a gay straw hat with cherries on it perched rakishly upon her head.

"Colonel Pickering? Do you have money for a cab? Oh, I didn't realize you had company!" Her eyes flashed a challenge at us.

"Eliza, this is Mr. Morello from New York. He's here to enlist Professor Higgins's professional services," said Pickering. "Mr. Morello, Miss Eliza Doolittle."

"My sympathies, Mr. Morello. And—?" Her eye rested on me.

"My jack-of-all-trades, Barton," said Holmes, again slipping into his American accent.

I bowed obsequiously. "Secretary, mum. Pleasetomeetyou, mum," I mumbled.

I don't know what I had expected, but it wasn't this. Eliza Doolittle had a way of looking at one that was direct and almost daring, not precisely offering a fight, but totting up your strengths and weaknesses in case she were to get into the ring with you somewhere further down the line. There was not merely light in the eyes but a quick intelligence; not only color in her cheeks but also a firmness of purpose in her line. It was a pleasure to look upon her.

"Welcome, Mr. Barton. Colonel, I'm off to Mrs. Higgins's at-home. And I'm desperately late."

"Want to borrow my heap, Miss Doolittle?" Holmes asked. "Barton can get you anywhere you need to go in a New York minute. I'd take you myself, but all your streets go the wrong way and I just about break my neck every time I get behind the wheel."

"No, thank you. I don't care for autos. I shall take a cab."

I said a silent prayer of thanks. I had nearly cursed out loud at Holmes's suggestion. We had dropped off our hired chauffeur a few streets away and I had managed to bring the vehicle to a white-knuckle stop in front of Higgins's door as part of our deception. It was my maiden voyage as a motorist, and I had no desire to tempt fate further. As for Holmes, he could no more drive than he could fly. The car would shortly be removed to a nearby garage and forgotten. But I thought it boded well that the girl preferred a hansom to a motorcar. Too many young persons in these decadent days are enraptured by the spell of roaring motors and exhaust.

Pickering pressed a pound note into her hand. "You're a dear," she said to him. She kissed him on the cheek. He beamed.

"You going alone?" said Holmes. "Girl like you? City like this?"

"I'm perfectly capable of managing, thank you, Mr. Morello," she answered with some asperity. "London is not New York. We are civilized here." She turned to Pickering, dismissing the newcomer. "I may not be home till late, Colonel. There's to be a speaker on temperance, or child labor, or the housing question. Or perhaps it's all three. But it's bound to be thrilling." She made us an insolent little half-curtsey and was out the door, almost running.

"So that is the transformation you spoke of?" said Holmes. He extinguished the cigar and took pipe and tobacco from his pocket.

"A charming young lady," I offered diplomatically. There was nothing in her bearing that marked her as a girl of the streets.

Holmes frowned. "A sharp-tongued minx."

"The younger generation are more direct," I ventured.

"No question, no question," said Pickering, looking flustered. "But she's also a brass-faced liar."

"Why do you say that?" asked Holmes.

"Because I happen to know that Mrs. Higgins is in Cornwall."

"Watson!"

After years with Holmes, a word and a nod was enough. I snatched up my hat and stick and made for the door.

"Don't let her see you. Don't let anyone see that you are following her!"

As if I needed to be told.

Chapter Four

I sprang down the steps of 27A. Miss Doolittle was already settling herself in the seat of a hansom. There was not another cab in sight in the quiet lane, and I had no time to whistle one up. Determined in my mission, I sprang up on the step next to the driver's seat at the rear of the cab. He gaped at me in astonishment. I doffed my hat. He doffed his. As he leaned toward me I tore the hat from his hand and gave him a shove, sending him tumbling into the street. I jumped into the seat, pushed his hat upon my head, took up the reins and gave them a shake. The horse broke into what it must have imagined was a gallop, leaving the driver sputtering and shaking his fist in the dust of the road. I silently vowed to seek him out later and make restitution. My first responsibility, though, was the girl. "What was that address again, miss?" I called out.

Miss Doolittle called back the address. "You do know it?" she asked. "Please hurry!"

Did I know it! I knew it as one of the most dangerous streets in all of London. It was that very same part of Swandam Lane where Holmes and I had investigated the strange disappearance of Mr. Neville St.

Clair in a lascar's opium den years before. I was loath to carry any young lady to such an evil place, but what choice had I? I gave the reins another jog and we rattled along through the dusty streets of London, plunging into the strangle of midday traffic.

It required all my skill to avoid a mishap. Half the traffic these days seemed to be motor cars, and the horse evidently cared for their roaring and their fumes no more than I. They harried the slower traffic of hansoms and growlers, landaus and cabriolets and omnibuses like collies nipping at the laggards of the herd, worrying at traps and dogcarts and donkey carts and coal wagons and brewer's drays, bicyclists with their knees up churning, costers plodding along with their barrows, a cats'-meat man with his cart and a half-dozen mongrel dogs leaping about in his aromatic wake, ragged children weaving among all in an eternal game of tag without a thought for life or limb. Even once untrammeled lanes seemed choked with vehicles of every kind. Here is a fellow walking in the middle of the street, reading his paper and smoking his pipe, oblivious to the railway van creaking at his heels. There goes a funeral procession all in black, at a stately pace, or a group with placards marching for home rule for Ireland or votes for women. Over there men have torn up the paving stones to work on a gas main. So it was some time before I noticed we were being followed—by a man on foot! My first idea was that the hansom driver, fueled by outrage at my piracy, had managed to dog our trail, armed with a knowledge of the streets even more encyclopedic than mine. But the driver had been as old as myself, and our pursuer was a young gentleman—and when I say gentleman, I mean dressed so, from patent boots to top hat, though his shoes were white with dust and his wardrobe showed an unfashionable amount of wear. Where he had picked us up I could not imagine, but I felt sure he would not be able to keep pace with us. Several times I was sure we had lost him in the turbid stream of humanity. Yet whenever traffic forced us to a crawl, there he was, puffing away behind us, indefatigable as Pheidippides. And at every halt Miss Doolittle begged me to make haste.

Finally we left the crowds behind and were bumping through

the winding, rutted roads, which pock the riverside. There the high streets are knotted into dark alleys and dead ends meant to trap the unwary traveler in their coils. Only my years scouring those alleys with Holmes, sniffing out the black tar of moral turpitude, rendered them sensible to me. We had almost reached our destination when a singular event occurred. We were passing through a muddy strait so close upon the river that I could smell the oil and the brine. It was populated by a set of rather desperate-looking shops whose roofs on either side leaned toward each other as if to crowd out the spying sky. Suddenly a figure emerged from under a low awning and stepped into the street full in our path. It was a man small and stooped in stature, but broad-shouldered and barrel-chested, with the arms of a Borneo ape. His eyes were concealed behind brown-tinted spectacles. I strained with every sinew to drag the horse to a halt. It was sure the man would be trampled to his death. I cried a warning. Still he stood his ground. The horse reared snorting above him. Then it seemed to me that that he reached up and dealt a hammer blow upon the side of the poor brute's skull. The horse shied and staggered. I heard a scream as the cab slued round, broadsiding a shop window, smashing the shutters to flinders. I was hurled from my seat into the street, striking my head upon the stones.

I must have blacked out. Yet I remember as in a dream staring up at the sky, blue as hyacinth, then an eddy of shadows, which resolved into a face demonic in outline. There was a prognathous jaw, with high, sunken cheekbones, and a beetling brow; the eyes peering over his spectacles were yellow as a cat's. Gruesome as those features were, there was yet something beyond the merely physical, unseen and unseeable, an aura that was almost an odor, and absolutely loathsome. The entire vision was but the tick of the clock, and then the world slid away.

When I came to my senses, the horse was standing in the street, head down, listless. The cab was leaning against the wall of a crockery shop on the corner. The young man in the top hat was there, peering inside the ruin of the cab. He swore and kicked the footboard. "Gone!" he cried in anguish. He glowered at me. "You bloody fool!" He threw his hat to the ground and kicked it, but almost immediately retrieved it, dusted it off, and set it back on his head.

He stared round in a daze, stepping one way and then another in indecision, almost tripping over his own feet. From here the street forked into two snaggletooth alleys, impassable save on foot. Miss Doolittle and her abductor—or was he her escort?—could have escaped down either of them. Sherlock Holmes might have said which, but the muddled young fellow in front of me could hardly even guess. He looked back at me and cried shrilly, "You should have your license revoked!" Then he set off down one of the alleys, chosen willy-nilly, and was soon swallowed by the shadows. By the time I picked myself up and brushed the dust from my clothes, the street was silent. The shopkeeper stood in his window scowling at me, but he seemed disinclined to bring his quarrel into the street. Up and down the street there were eyes staring from blank windows, chinks, and crevices, like wolves shadowing a campfire, but no one stepped forth with aid or challenge. The horn of a steam packet lowed upon the air.

What must I do? Leave the horse and strike down one of the alleys? Or find a constable and cry up a search party? Miss Doolittle might be in the direst of circumstances, but again she might not. I remembered the horrid face from my vision, but had there been a second face? The features of Eliza Doolittle, etched with concern? Had I been party to an abduction, or a meeting of confederates? Any police involvement would inevitably lead to my real identity being discovered, as well as that of "Mr. Morello." I deemed that the best I could do was get back to Holmes as quick as I might and let him decide our course.

I settled the horse and inspected the cab. Its hurts seemed superficial enough, remediable by paint and wax. I took my place on the box once more and, taking the reins, returned to Wimpole Street with all haste, full of misdoubt.

Chapter Five

The first thing I saw when I returned to Professor Higgins's abode was the hansom driver, sitting on the front step, eating a pork pie, with a pewter tankard ready to hand. I expected hard words from the fellow, if not outright violence. He offered neither. He inspected the cab, the horse, and his hat, and pronounced them "none the worse for a bit of hijinks." I stuttered some kind of apology. He bid me good day, urging me to "take your drops, guv'nor." I learned afterward that Pickering had paid the man three days' hire, explaining to him that I was a wealthy patient of "Dr. Higgins" who sometimes went barking mad and stole hansom cabs for amusement.

I hurried into the house and broke in upon Holmes and Pickering having tea in the laboratory. "Holmes! The most extraordinary thing—!"

They were not alone.

"Barton! Home is right. About time you made it back, you dog! Stop off for a little tipple?" cried Holmes, talking over me. "Henry Higgins, this is my brand-spankin'-new English secretary, Mr. Hill

Barton. Talks just like the upper crust. Everything's extraordinary or stupendous. I like to split a rib just listening to him."

Henry Higgins was in his early forties, tall and angular, with an intellectual brow and a pugnacious jaw. He was dressed expensively but with a carelessness so extreme that it could only be deliberate. I might have taken him for a racetrack tout or a newspaper editor, but never a man of science. He sat on a low bookcase, studying me over a cup of tea, kicking his heels against a set of *Plutarch's Lives*.

"Private secretary is usually the province of a younger man," he said sharply. I was to find that Higgins spoke almost exclusively in sharps. Every remark was meant to cut.

"He came vouched for by a lord and two dukes. I guess he could be a grifter out to fleece me, for all that. But he's so damn distinguished-looking."

"We'll board him with the lad who blacks the boots. Not much gets past him."

I little appreciated this badinage, especially after the trials of the morning, but I put on my best hail-fellow-well-met and let it pass. I was desperate to tell Holmes about the girl's disappearance, but durst not raise the suspicions of our host.

Higgins set down his cup. "What did you find that was so extraordinary, Mr. Barton?" he asked.

"Oh!" I was at a complete loss. "Er, fellow down the road. With a . . . chicken. A chicken that does sums." I cursed myself. Could I have thought of anything more idiotic? My only excuse was that on my way home a market van had overturned at Oxford Circus, and the crash had freed half a dozen strutting cocks from their cages, to add to the normal hazards of traffic.

But Holmes picked up the thread admirably. "I'm a big fan of animal tricks, Henry. Dancing bears, singing dogs, poker-playing rabbits, you name it. I told Barton to be on the lookout for anything along those lines."

Higgins was noticeably unenthusiastic. "If that is the case, you shall certainly not lack for entertainment in London, Mr. Morello. And at a very nice price, I would imagine."

"Maybe we could bring the fella up here after supper?" Holmes suggested.

"I'm afraid my housekeeper Mrs. Pearce is not an admirer of poultry unless it's been plucked."

"How is she with monkeys?"

"Unyielding. If your goal is to throw my household into disarray, Mr. Morello, you've already achieved it. You were not expected until after tea at the earliest. I hope you're not trying to impress me with your eagerness to begin work. I cannot abide an apple-polisher."

"I was planning to spend the morning taking in the sights," said Holmes. "I got a look at Big Ben and the digs the king lives in, had lunch, and it was just on noon. So I come here direct."

"Do you do everything direct?" Higgins asked archly.

"I don't know why a body would go around anything he could go through instead."

This response delighted Higgins. "Pickering, our American friend is a veritable philosopher!"

"Indeed!" said Pickering, who seemed for a moment to forget that Mr. Morello was not, in fact, Mr. Morello. He was busy fussing over the tea things in front of him. "Tea, Mr. Burton?" he asked.

I nodded gratefully. I did not think to correct him on my name; it had slipped my own mind. He poured a cup and handed it to me.

"Tea not to your liking, Mr. Morello?" Higgins asked. Holmes's cup was still nearly full.

"I'm partial to coffee," was the laconic reply.

Higgins left his perch and came to stand in front of Holmes. He laid a finger to the side of his nose. "But you were not born in America, I think."

"You're on to me, bud." Holmes sat back in his chair, entirely at ease.

"Please refer to me as Professor Higgins. You were born in Sussex, I think."

"Sicily. Dot on the map called Corleone."

"You emigrated as a young child."

"I was nine. Just a bambino."

"To Sussex."

"New York. U.S. of A."

"Schooled at Eton."

"P.S. 34. Brooklyn. Graduated sixth grade."

"And you relocated to England?"

"Three days ago."

Higgins was visibly frustrated. "But surely this is not your first visit to Great Britain, Mr. Morello!"

Holmes shrugged, as if unwilling to contradict his host on such a minor point.

"Well, we'll put that question aside for now. You are yet determined to shed your barbaric yawp and speak the king's English?"

"I wanna sound so damn English even the king won't know better."

"You needn't fret yourself about the king. You won't be dining at his digs."

"You learn me to talk proper and let me worry about the dinner invites."

Higgins rubbed the bridge of his nose, weary of verbal fencing. He turned to the colonel. "Speaking of dinner invites, Pick, would you let Mrs. Pearce know that Dr. Guest will be joining us this evening?"

"Dr. Guest?" Color flooded Pickering's features. "I feel fit as a fiddle. Do I seem otherwise?"

"No, of course not. But I would like him to have a look at Eliza. Her temper seems a bit off lately, don't you think?

"I hadn't noticed."

"Well, it's merely a precaution. I'm certain Eliza will be pleased to see him."

"You're certain Eliza will be pleased to see who?" We heard her voice from the hall, and then the young lady splashed into the room. "Oh, tea! Thank heaven. I'm ravenous."

I nearly sobbed with relief. My fears for Miss Doolittle's safety had been preying upon my mind all that time. Now here she was, miraculously, safe and sound.

"Pleased to see whom, not who, Eliza." Higgins's habitual attitude of superiority became especially spiky whenever he addressed Miss Doolittle.

She surveyed the tea tray and stuffed a napoleon into her mouth greedily.

"Where have you been all afternoon?" Higgins asked her. "You look as though you've been marching about with those suffragettes again."

"I have not been marching about with anyone." Her face was somewhat flushed, and the hem of her dress bedraggled, but she looked remarkably hale considering the circumstances.

"Did you find my notes on Norris and the Assyrian lions?" he asked.

I should note here that while Higgins's laboratory was nowhere near the blizzard of notepapers, news clippings, and scrapbooks that our sitting room in Baker Street had once been, there were yet enough untidy stacks of manuscript strewn across tables and stuffed into bookshelves for lions to hide among. In one small nook stood a Pembroke table with a typewriter and a neat stack of typed pages squared up next to it. This and the piano were Miss Doolittle's province.

"I did not," she gave back. "I don't give a fig for your lions. Great hairy beasts. I've been out all day trying to find you a new dressing gown."

"They're not actual lions, you silly girl. And I was unaware there was anything wrong with my present dressing gown."

"I don't give an actual fig. And your dressing gown's a disgrace, that's what's wrong with it. It looks like it was passed down to you from an early ancestor, possibly an Assyrian. Pleased to see whom?" She popped another napoleon in her mouth.

"Pickering, you see what a devil she's become? That's all those chocolates you feed her."

Pickering demurred. "She's right about the dressing gown."

"Pleased to see whom?" An edge had crept in the girl's voice.

"Dr. Guest is coming to dinner." He said it in an offhand manner, but he was watching her face keenly.

Eliza's countenance went dark. "I'll take my dinner in my room."

"You shall do no such thing."

"The fellow is odious."

"Odious? Where did you learn that word, you cat?"

"Probably at your mother's," said Pickering.

"My mother is in Cornwall. And Dr. Guest saved your life, Eliza. Never forget that."

"How could I, when he expects eternal fawning gratitude?" she cried. "And a level of familiarity which—"

"Familiarity? Good God, Eliza, you sound like Mrs. Eynsford-Hill."

"Now there's an idea! I shall invite Freddy to dinner."

"Freddy? Not at my table."

"Separate tables will suit admirably. Freddy and I can take our meal in the kitchen."

"You got a spirited filly there, Henry," said Holmes.

Somewhere in this exchange, Professor Higgins had crescendoed from good-natured banter to angry bluster. Now he marched to the door and thrust it open. "Gentlemen, I'm sure you'll want to get settled before dinner. Mrs. Pearce will assist you in any way you require." He was dismissing us from the room, and from the row that was brewing.

"Appreciate the hospitality, Henry. We've got dinner spoken for at the hotel," said Holmes.

"Mr. Morello, we shall be working at times from morning till midnight. Separate lodgings will not be practical. You will stay here, at least during the first part of your training. Mrs. Pearce will see to everything." As Holmes made to protest, he raised a peremptory hand. "I won't hear any objections, sir. You will not achieve your goal without constant application." He gave the bellpull a vigorous tug.

"Run while you can, Mr. American. You'll be reciting tongue

twisters at two in the morning. Too true. Toodle-oo," Eliza said as she made to leave.

"Eliza. Remain," said Higgins. He spoke quietly, but there was steel in his voice. "Pickering, perhaps you could assist Mr. Morello and his man."

Pickering seemed discomfited at the proposition that he should be asked to assist anyone, as if he were household staff. But he could see that he was not wanted in the laboratory, and was grateful for the excuse to remove himself. We all withdrew into the hall, leaving the professor with his pupil. Their voices rose as we shut the door behind us.

"Watson, the keyhole!" Holmes whispered urgently. I bent to peer through the keyhole as he put his ear to the door.

"Oh, dear!" said Pickering. He was not accustomed to such an unmannerly mode of spying.

The emotions that had been seething beneath the surface while we were in the laboratory were now boiling over. I could see only Eliza at first, her face lit with fury, fists clenched. Then Higgins was there, his back to me, looming over her. He seized her by the wrists. There was a cry from the girl. I was ready to burst in upon the scene and thrash the blackguard when I heard a voice behind us. "Is this a habit of American gentlemen?"

Pickering squeaked, I nearly jumped, and even Holmes seemed to lose his sangfroid. Mrs. Pearce was standing behind us, arms folded, a look of contempt stealing in behind her bland servant's expression.

"Absolutely appalling," Pickering started. "I was just telling these fellows—"

"Really, Colonel!" It was enough to silence Pickering.

But the shouting behind the door had not ceased. "Somebody don't do something quick, gonna be an English gentleman brought up on a murder beef," Holmes rasped. He set his hand to the doorknob, but before he could act, Mrs. Pearce shoved past us and hammered upon the door.

"Professor Higgins?" she called out. "This won't do, sir!"

And just like that, silence fell inside the room.

Chapter Six

Mrs. Pearce cracked the laboratory door, but paused before going in. "Mr. Morello, this is Robert, the footman." A young lad of twelve or thirteen, heretofore concealed by the housekeeper's skirts, stood squirming on the hall carpet. He was barely tall enough to fit his livery.

"Robert will show you and your man to your rooms. Dinner will be served early tonight. If you require any special accommodations, please address them to me only. The professor is not to be disturbed." Every syllable she spoke was weighted with authority.

Holmes flicked an ash from his cigar onto the carpet. "So is your boss the real goods, honey, or just another hustler with his hand out?"

Mrs. Pearce appeared scandalized by the idea, or perhaps by the cigar ash on her carpet. "Whatever Professor Higgins says he will do, he will do," she answered squarely.

Holmes grinned. "You're English from your gums to your garters, ain't you, Miz Post?"

"Robert?" Mrs. Pearce dismissed us without another word and disappeared into the laboratory, shutting the door firmly behind her.

Left alone, Robert appeared a bit intimidated by his charges, but he braved it out.

"If you'll follow me, gents?" He hitched up the cuffs of his trousers and pushed off toward the staircase, walking on the balls of his feet.

I was still anxious to tell Holmes about the afternoon's adventure, but was again stymied. After showing Holmes to his room on the third floor—"next to Miss Doolittle, sir. She do bang about sometimes at night, it ain't housebreakers"—he directed me to "come on then, old 'un." Perforce I followed him to a small room at the top of the house. It was sparsely furnished, with bare walls, two iron bedsteads, a nightstand between them, and a washstand in the corner. One bed was made up as a sort of burrow of dingy wrinkled sheets. The other had a bare grey mattress on which lay a neat stack of sheets and pillowcases. It looked dismal enough. "Am I to share this room, then?" I asked.

"With me, old 'un!" Robert plopped down on the bed already made, and wrestled off his shoes. He must have noticed the grim look on my face. I hadn't shared a room with anyone since Mary's death, and I hadn't made up my own cot since Afghanistan.

"It ain't the Savoy, but it's a nice kip. There's three housemaids, each one prettier than the other, and my good lady housekeeper ain't so particklar about lockin' up the larder at night as some butlers is." He added an emphatic nod and wink, as between two men of the world.

Apparently my face did not light up at his encomiums. He switched to another tack. "Make your bed for a tanner!"

I confess I felt horribly put upon having to share a room with the footman. It was absolutely beneath my dignity. I imagined Holmes in the comfort of his own room, couched among downy pillows, chuckling in amusement at the thought of my discomfiture. In all our years together, I had rarely been called upon to don a disguise or act the part of anyone save John Watson, M.D. It was always Holmes who capered about in the false beards and broad-brimmed hats, mixing it up with every element. He had never complained when forced to commingle with even the lowest dregs of society. Indeed, he had seemed to relish it. Domestic servants were a wellspring of information on their employers, he had told me often enough. Perhaps if I put aside my prejudices and kept my ears open, I could gather valuable information about Henry Higgins from this rude lad. But the prospect seemed daunting.

Robert set to work making my bed as I unpacked my bags and prepared for dinner. My toilet was in quite some need of repair after the afternoon's expedition, and my mind was unsettled. When I had beseeched Holmes to come out of retirement in this matter, I had no idea that he would ask me to strap on the traces once again as well. But he had insisted that he could not take a single step without "dear old Watson" at his side. Watson was certainly feeling old this evening, decidedly decrepit, and Robert's endless stream of chatter was uninformative and frankly exhausting.

I wondered what Holmes's preternatural powers of observation had made of the professor and his student. I could almost hear him telling Pickering "beyond the obvious fact that he spent time as a missionary in Hong Kong, learned fencing at Heidelberg, and first introduced Charlotte Russe to the kitchens of Great Britain, I can deduce nothing about the man." Robert helped me into my dinner jacket (for the price of yet another tanner), and I hurried downstairs in anticipation.

I was to be disappointed yet again. Holmes and Pickering were alone in the dining room when I arrived, but no revelations were forthcoming. "Still expecting conjuror's tricks after all these years, Watson?" Holmes scolded. "I'm not a calculating chicken. Professor Higgins is exactly as he presents himself, although his self-regard far outruns his talents. The early years in South Africa and his father's untimely demise no doubt influenced his choice of profession, but they have no direct bearing on our present problem. It is the young lady we must train our attention upon. The bruise upon your cheek and the scratches on your knuckles tell a story of far more import than Henry Higgins's battles with neurasthenia."

At his prompting, I plunged into my account of the afternoon's events and their mystifying denouement. Holmes peppered me with questions, but there was little I could tell him beyond what I have already recorded here. He asked Pickering whether he recognized either the young man in the top hat or our hideous assailant.

"The young fellow sounds familiar, somehow, though I can't place him. But the other one sounds more like a Hindoo *yaksha* than a human being," he answered. "I find it hard to believe Eliza could have gone anywhere of her own accord with such a dreadful man. She must have been forced."

"I believe I can settle that question," said Holmes. He pulled a few meager scraps of paper from his pocket, and arranged them on his palm. They were yellow, curled and blackened about the edges as if by fire. There was printed type on a few of them.

Pickering stared. "I haven't the faintest notion what I'm looking at," he concluded.

"Watson?"

"A telegram?" I hazarded.

"A telegram indeed," said Holmes. "I took the liberty of making a quick search of Miss Doolittle's room earlier. I found this in the grate."

"You detective johnnies don't stand on ceremony, do you? What's it say?"

"It says that Miss Doolittle received a wire this morning and went out immediately afterward. But not before making sure to burn the message in the grate. The coals were still warm."

"I'm dashed!" Pickering said.

"Could the man be some relation to Miss Doolittle?" I asked.

"So far as I know, Eliza's only living relative is her father," Pickering answered. "I met him a couple of times, briefly. A common dustman with a penchant for scandalous opinions. He's no beauty, old Alfred P., but he's nothing like the bogeyman you've described. I still can't fathom what Eliza would want with such a fellow."

"There's a father in it? Do you have his address?" Holmes asked eagerly.

"Yes ... well ... I know for a fact that he's not in London at present."

"Whence does this certainty arise?"

"He's up in Scotland right now, on the lecture circuit. He gives lectures on morality or ethics, that sort of thing. Or possibly Wales."

"You said he was a dustman," I reminded him.

"He was, till Higgins got an earful of him. Touted him as the philosopher of the common man. Wangled an American philanthropist into backing him. Thought it was funny. Then he caught on with the cognoscenti."

"It seems a family of chameleons," I said.

Holmes looked as if he was fervently wishing he were back home with his bees. He stared down at the cloth, the gleaming china plate, the regimented lines of silver. "The girl is an enigma," he said. "I see nothing in her attitude or carriage to suggest that she was once a creature of the streets—"

"Then Pickering was right!"

"—but I see nothing in her to suggest anything whatever of her origins. Eliza Doolittle is a cipher. It's as if she were molded out of clay and had the breath of life forced into her lungs by Professor Higgins. Her speech is an echo of his. Her dress—"

"Her dresses were chosen for her, by Mrs. Pearce and the dressmakers," Pickering put in.

Holmes sighted down the table, realigning the wine glasses. I hadn't even noticed they were out of line. "As for her manner, I know not whence it was grafted, but it certainly is not native to the Tottenham Court Road or Drury Lane."

The admission obviously nettled Holmes. When I thought of the dozens of times I had heard him sum up a man's entire biography after what seemed the most cursory observation, I found myself distressed as well. Were his analytical powers failing with age? Or could it be that the mystery of Eliza Doolittle was even stranger than we supposed?

"She seems a perfectly well-bred young lady to me," I said. "I don't understand why Higgins seems so concerned about her health."

"I'm inclined to think there is something in that. I find the professor a man of keen perception," said Holmes.

"You seem to have put it over on him easily enough," I said with a chuckle.

"I doubt it, Watson."

"I'm afraid Mr. Holmes is right there," said Pickering. "Higgins is certain your American 'Mr. Morello' is as English as roast beef and Yorkshire pudding. He told me so this afternoon. He wasn't fooled by your story or your accent."

"By thunder!" I exclaimed. "Then why has he invited us to dinner rather than showing us the door?"

"Curiosity, Watson. Professor Higgins is, after all, a man of science. Indeed, I was counting on it," said Holmes.

"True enough," said Pickering. "Higgins wants to divine who you are, and what your purpose is. He intends to keep you as close as possible, till he discovers your game. He suspects you of being a spy."

"A spy? For whom?" I asked.

"Eliza's appearance at the embassy party gave rise to a mountain of gossip. A beautiful girl of impeccable manner whom no one had ever laid eyes on before? That simply doesn't occur in our circle. There was some rather rash talk that she might secretly be a duchess, or even a princess. A number of eligible young bachelors and their mothers were keenly interested. Higgins thinks the house is being watched. And he thinks you've been hired to find out just what Eliza's provenance may be, if one may use such a word in reference to a young lady."

"Which is not far from the truth. Is Higgins's own interest in the girl . . . proprietary?" asked Holmes.

"Let's call it 'friendly,' and leave it at that, old boy. He asked me to drop hints to you that she's a daughter of the Austrian archduke."

"Which would put her beyond all but the highest station."

"That seems to be his game," Pickering agreed.

At that juncture Robert shuffled in to announce a new arrival. "Dr. Paddy at the door, Colonel, sir," he said.

"Well, don't leave him standing on the mat, boy! And don't call him Paddy. He's Dr. Guest to you." Pickering shooed Robert out of the room. "He picked up that name from Higgins, I'm afraid."

"The young lady seemed decidedly averse to this Dr. Guest," Holmes remarked.

"He's not exactly the fellow for the soothing bedside manner," Pickering replied. "But you'll see for yourself."

Robert returned, alone.

"Where's the doctor, lad?" asked Pickering.

"Still at the door." The boy's face held a peculiar expression, as if he'd been bitten by a favorite dog.

"I told you to bring him in!"

"I tried, sir. But he's too heavy. I can't lift 'im over the doorstep."

At first it sounded like nonsense. Then Holmes bolted for the door, with the rest of us at his heels.

Chapter Seven

The front door was standing open. There was a man lying crumpled in the doorway. We raced to him. He was a long, narrow thing, in an old-fashioned frock coat and high collar. When we turned him on his back, his flesh was so pale I was sure he was dead. Then he moaned softly and his eyes stood open like flung shutters. We helped him struggle to his feet and steered him into the dining room. He collapsed into a chair, and allowed me to loosen his collar and pour a glass of claret down his throat.

"Are you unwell, Guest? Should we call a doctor?" asked Pickering, leaning over him.

The young man held up a hand to stay him. "Please don't trouble yourselves, gentlemen," he said weakly. "The heat of the day . . ." He fumbled in his pocket and came up with a small tin of pastilles. He threw two of them down his throat.

Physician, heal thyself! Dr. Guest looked to be a man in his thirties, thin to the point of emaciation. His strong, almost handsome features and Byronic curls were marred by a sallow complexion and dark circles under his eyes. Were he my patient I would have dosed his liver with Andrews till it sang.

His story came out in bits and pieces. He had been working in the surgery since early morning, without food or drink it seemed, and then decided unwisely to walk to Wimpole Street. "Please don't mention it to Higgins or Miss Doolittle," he begged. I couldn't blame him for being embarrassed. It was warm outside, but hardly fainting weather.

"It's a long slog from Limehouse on a warm day," Holmes said. "Shoulda took a cab."

Guest rose to his feet in a sudden furor. "Who said I came from Limehouse? Who are you?"

"I thought Higgins mentioned some such place. Was I thinking of someone else?"

Pickering cut in with introductions, explaining to the doctor that Mr. Morello was a newcomer to London who didn't know Limehouse from Whitehall. Of course no one had ever mentioned anything to Holmes. He had deduced it from the mud on the doctor's boots, or the soil on his collar, or the nap of the hair on his wrists, or some other "conjuror's trick." It was a slip on his part to mention it, but the explanation seemed to mollify Dr. Guest. "I oversee some charity cases down the East End, but my practice is in Mayfair," he said primly.

"Dr. Guest! Welcome!" Higgins sailed into the room. He touched the new arrival's hand and bade us all be seated. "Don't stand on ceremony, gentlemen. Eliza will join us in good time." Guest fiddled with his tie and collar till he was in no more disarray than Higgins himself.

"Are we expecting Freddy, as well?" Pickering asked.

Higgins snorted mirthlessly. Guest let a crooked smile curl his lip. For a man who seemed at death's door five minutes earlier, he appeared remarkably recovered.

No sooner were we seated than Robert bolted into the room to serve the first course. It took all the agility the company possessed to avoid having our shirtfronts emblazoned with the consommé.

"I don't think I've ever seen so large a company gathered in your dining room, Higgins," said Guest, eying Holmes with naked curiosity.

"Morello here is a new pupil. This other fellow is his fellow.

Pickering is Pickering, and you are you. It's more of an accretion than a gathering."

Guest turned to Holmes. "You couldn't hope for a better teacher than Professor Higgins, Mr. Morello. I can vouch for his abilities myself."

"Guest sounded like a Galway bogcutter when he first came to me," Higgins said, cackling.

A dark cast came into the young doctor's eyes. If he were Irish, Higgins well knew how to get his Irish up. The conversation lapsed into wretched silence.

Miss Doolittle did indeed make her appearance shortly. The gentlemen all rose as she entered, but she refused to acknowledge the courtesy, dropping her eyes to the floor.

"Miss Eliza, you look a vision!" said Dr. Guest, making a stiff little half-bow. He attempted to take her hand, but the hand was not forthcoming. I darted a look at Holmes, and caught a smile playing about the corners of his mouth.

A vision she looked indeed: a spectral one. She was dressed from head to toe in a black frock that might have last been worn at Prince Albert's funeral, lacking only a veil to make her mourning costume complete. She gave a nod to Pickering as he drew her chair out, but as soon as she was seated, her gaze went to her dinner plate and remained fixed there for most of the evening.

"How are you feeling tonight, Miss Doolittle?" Dr. Guest asked innocuously.

Miss Doolittle gave over her whole attention to the turbot, shaving off flakes of flesh as thin as tissue paper.

"Eliza, the doctor asked a question of you." Higgins's admonition was neither sharp nor loud, yet as insistent as a terrier in a rat-hole.

Miss Doolittle swallowed. "Quite well, Doctor," she said to the back of her spoon. Her voice was barely a whisper.

"Not at all feverish?"

"Not at all feverish." The girl's voice mounted. "Not at all phlegmatic. Not at all bilious. Neither scrofulous nor dropsical nor drowsy.

Not anemic. Nor lymphatic nor splenetic. How do *you* feel, dear doctor? You look a bit peaked." By now her voice was fairly ringing.

"Your mastery of medical terminology does you credit," Guest said, trying to arrange a smile upon his face.

"Eliza's a perfect mynah bird. Drop her in the road near Lincoln's Inn and she'll be arguing cases in Chancery within a week," Higgins crowed.

But the doctor had not yet finished probing. "Have you felt any shortness of breath or fluttering in your pulse?"

She smiled daggers at him. "Would you care to palpate me here at the dinner table?"

Pickering attempted to turn the conversation into a safer avenue. "Higgins, have you heard from your mother in Cornwall?"

Miss Doolittle's cheeks splashed with crimson.

"She's miserable, of course, as I predicted," Higgins answered. "I don't know why she goes. I don't know why anyone would ever want to leave London. Is there a happier place on earth?" He looked to Miss Doolittle for affirmation and noticed the color in her face.

"Eliza is no candidate for anemia, Doctor," Higgins said, "but she might well be subject to apoplexy. I declare, her face is bright red!"

So went one of the most miserable dinner parties it has ever been my misfortune to attend. Whether Higgins recognized the implicit rebuke in Miss Doolittle's mourning costume I could never decide. He badgered her mercilessly and merrily, but then he badgered Pickering equally, as well as Dr. Guest, and even had some choice remarks for his new pupil, Mr. Morello. He did not address me at all. I didn't know whether to be relieved or insulted. Pickering kept trying to turn the conversation to less turbulent channels, but his muddle was evident as he repeatedly began remarks addressed to me, then drew himself up short when he remembered that we were meant to be acquaintances of an hour rather than old comrades. After her initial flare-up, Miss Doolittle consigned herself to the silence of the grave.

But worst was Dr. Guest. Except for rather spidery compliments paid to Miss Doolittle at odd moments, each of which she studiously ignored, he refused to join in the ebb and flow of conversation, such as it was. When Higgins attempted to draw him out, he opted to relate gruesome anecdotes related to his medical practice, delivered in low, growlsome tones, laced with anatomical detail so explicit that even I blushed. Higgins seemed to relish these tales from the crypt and twisted them out of the young man like so many noisome corks from a bad vintage. A description of the wounds suffered by a young woman trampled by a team of horses in Saffron Hill seemed to gratify our host particularly—"so drunk she was, she never needed ether—Irish, of course" sent him into peals of laughter. After a gorge full of this entertainment, Miss Doolittle was not the only member of the company picking at her food.

We were all relieved when the last course was served and we had pushed the food around on our plates enough to fool the cook into thinking we had at least sampled it. Eliza rose from the table and excused herself. She evidently felt she had fulfilled her duty as hostess.

"Dr. Guest will see you up," said Higgins.

"I'm promised for the theatre this evening. I can't be late."

"I won't ask more than a few minutes of your time, Miss Eliza," said the doctor silkily.

Eliza's eyes finally met his, and there seemed such a mix of dread and fascination in them as if she had discovered a swamp adder curled upon her pillow. Then her eyes dropped to the floor. She suffered Guest to take her arm and lead her upstairs. Higgins grinned like the Cheshire cat. Pickering sighed.

"You take as much interest in that girl's innards as if you were running her in the Derby," said Holmes.

"I think of her rather as a diamond in the rough, Mr. Morello," Higgins answered. "There's sherry in the laboratory, gentlemen."

As the company filed out of the dining room, a peculiar sight caught my eye. Through the window I spied a man, skulking outdoors in the shadows of the evening. I couldn't make out his face, but he was without a doubt staring up at the windows of the house. I signaled to Holmes as unobtrusively as possible. He caught my gesture, an old signal that had passed between us a hundred times before. He glanced out the window and gave a curt nod. As he followed the others to the laboratory, I lingered in the hall. Then I slipped out through the street door as stealthily as I could manage.

He was standing slap in the middle of the street, blind to the world, his eyes fixed on Miss Doolittle's window. With the light from the window pearling full on his face, I recognized him as the same young man in the battered top hat who had pursued our cab earlier in the day.

He had taken no notice of me. I acted on instinct. I dropped into a crouch and darted across the road so as to come at him from behind. Then I grabbed hold of his arm and twisted it up behind his back. "You're nicked, old son," I hissed in his ear, affecting a police detective's growl.

His reaction amazed me. There was no resistance at all. He collapsed against me, hot tears springing into his eyes. "Don't hurt me!" he pled. "I can't stand pain!"

"Come along quiet, then," I rasped.

"If I could just explain, constable—"

"None o' that!" I took the fellow by the scruff of the neck and propelled him up the stairs into the house. The noise brought one of the housemaids trotting into the entrance hall. She stared at us dumbfounded. "Bring Mr."—what was the blasted alias Holmes had taken?—"Bring the colonel!" I cried. She stood rooted to the spot. "Go, girl!" She picked up her skirts and fled. I pushed the young ruffian before me into the front parlor, and had him face down upon a table when Holmes appeared with the colonel.

Pickering's eyes went wide at the scene before him. "What's all this, then?" he asked.

"This is the fellow I told you about!" I grunted, my knee planted in the interloper's spine.

"Not the one who punched the horse, I hope." Pickering seemed almost amused.

Higgins came in behind them. He took one look at the villain in my grasp, and said, "Hello, Freddy. You're too late for dinner, I'm afraid."

It was evident I had misjudged the situation. I had my knee in the back of Miss Doolittle's theatre escort.

"Guess you can let the cut-throat go, Barton," said Holmes, grinning.

I released the young man. He turned on me. "You're not a rozzer?" he asked. "What sort of fellow—how dare—and why—?" He went on spluttering till he was out of breath.

Higgins sorted him out. "This is my latest student, Mr. Morello, Freddy. The fellow who assaulted you is his secretary. Who doubles as a bodyguard, apparently." He gave me a new look of appraisal. "Mr. Morello, the Honorable Frederick Eynsford-Hill."

"I found him lurking in the street, spying on Miss Doolittle's window," I said stiffly.

"No surprise there," said Higgins pleasantly. "Day or night, you can find him at his post. Mr. Eynsford-Hill is madly in love with Eliza. Aren't you, Freddy?"

"Freddy, you know you're not supposed to loiter in the street," said Pickering. "The neighbors all think you're some sort of cat burglar."

The young man was disheveled and practically purple in the face. "There's a man in Eliza's room!" he burst out in a frenzy. He surged toward the hall. Pickering laid a hand on his shoulder to restrain him.

"That would be Dr. Guest," said Higgins. "A routine consultation. Eliza's health has been a bit spotty lately."

Freddy—and I will always think of him simply as Freddy, awkward and untoward and entirely vulnerable, the model of every young fellow teetering on the threshold of life—Freddy was in sad need of repair. He tried tucking in here and brushing there, all to little effect. Then he turned upon me once again, for the first time really screwing his eyes upon me. "You!" he yelped. This time he had recognized me from the afternoon's adventure.

"Freddy, you know this fellow?" Higgins asked. His nostrils seemed to quiver with suspicion.

Freddy was still staring at me goggle-eyed. Would he expose me to the professor? Were we to be unmasked so soon? How could I plausibly explain my role in the events in Swandam Lane?

But Freddy backed down. "Yes, I . . . er, that is to say, no . . . For a moment he reminded me of my Uncle Algernon. Just around the ears—the eyes, rather." He turned to Pickering, as if for confirmation. "Don't you think? Oh, you never met Uncle Algie. Well, you never shall. Poor blighter died in a boating accident. Salmon fishing in Scotland. Refused to let go the line and the bally creature pulled him right under." He shivered, as if making a physical effort to tear himself away from this tragic memory. Then he turned to Higgins. "Might I be announced to Miss Doolittle, sir? We're engaged for the theatre this evening, and Eliza puts up a whale of a fuss if she's late for curtain."

It struck me that Freddy might be as anxious to keep the afternoon's events a secret as I was. Perhaps he too would have difficulty explaining his role in those events.

"Here's the little lady now!" said Holmes.

As he spoke, Miss Doolittle was descending the stairs on the arm of Dr. Guest. There was no sign of the fractiousness she'd displayed earlier. Indeed, she seemed radiant and serene.

"Freddy, how are you, dear? We missed you at dinner," she said.

"How does your patient, Doctor?" Higgins asked.

"Sound as a bell!" Guest said jovially. The doctor's mood seemed to have lightened with his patient's. He radiated a manly confidence that had been sadly missing during dinner. He handed the young lady over to the professor as if she were a coat newly mended.

"I feel greatly improved, Professor. Thank you for asking the doctor to visit me," said Eliza.

This sentiment was so at odds with the young lady's behavior at dinner that I almost bit my tongue. Pickering was jabbing his elbow into my ribs, just in case I might have missed her about-face. Even Holmes, whose face is normally a mask of calm, looked nonplussed. Only two people seemed unsurprised: Higgins's face was wreathed in smiles, while Freddy looked as though he were thinking of poor Uncle Algernon again.

Dr. Guest seemed to savor Freddy's discomfort, but evidently felt the wound needed more salt. "We're entrusting this precious parcel to your care for the evening, Mr. Eynsford-Hill. Please return her undamaged," he said.

It was an affront that would have offended any man. Freddy looked as though he would make a withering retort, if only he were capable of one. Alas, though his eyes glistened and his face turned bright vermillion, he spoke not a word. The salmon had pulled him under.

Miss Doolittle attempted to come to his rescue. "Would you get my wrap, Freddy? We'd linger, gentlemen, but it's a detective mystery and we can't miss the first act." She gave the young man her arm and wafted out the front door like a June breeze.

The evening had already taken so many hairpin turns that it was hardly astonishing we spent the next hour in the laboratory, listening to Dr. Guest hold forth with his morbid case histories. He had shed his diffidence entirely and decided it was his solemn duty to entertain us. Whether it was the wine from dinner or a private decoction of his own, the Dutch courage was in him. He had spent some little time as an army doctor in India, it seemed, and proceeded to lecture us on that part of the world as if he were the only member of our company ever to tread the wharves at Colaba. His patients all seem to have been either fever victims or madmen. I took advantage of my lowly status, excusing myself to catch up on Mr. Morello's correspondence. By the time I returned, his recitations had reached a fever pitch. He was in the middle of a story about the Tiger Men of Punjab, who he claimed were not merely savage but striped with orange and black fur like their namesakes. Whether he was telling it as a fairy story or a naturalist's account I could not determine. Holmes's mind seemed far away, and Pickering had frankly fallen asleep in his chair. Higgins, on the other hand, seemed to hang on the doctor's every word.

Eventually the evening shuddered to a close. Holmes and I retired to his room. Jealousy nagged at me again as I took in the cheerful floral wallpaper, the mahogany dresser, and especially the brass bedstead with snowy mattress and turned-down coverlet. Holmes once again set aside the American cigars in favor of his old pipe.

"Watson, would you send a cable to my housekeeper? I'd do it myself, but it might arouse suspicion. Ask her to engage Mr. Tarbell to look after the bees for a day or two. It looks as if we'll have to stay the night." Holmes pulled off his boots and set them aside. "A first check to my theories, eh?"

"I'm afraid I don't follow you," I replied.

"I will mention but two names, and you will understand: Jabez Wilson and Hall Pycroft."

The veil was lifted. The men he had mentioned were former clients who had each been the victim of an elaborate hoax meant to keep them at arm's length from the scene of a criminal endeavor.

"When the colonel mentioned the amazingly fortuitous coincidence of his meeting Higgins and the girl beneath the pillars of St. Paul and their hurried removal to this house, I was certain that some such deception was being played upon him. I expected to have the answer to your mystery by dinnertime." He paused, contemplating. "At this time of life one perhaps begins to depend too much upon past experience," he said ruefully.

Had Holmes been shamming? "But what about the several points of interest?" I protested. "You called it a particularly thorny problem. Particularly!"

"All bosh! You brought an old friend to see me, hoping to impress him with your friend the Great Detective. How could I deny my Watson? A day's jaunt to London, Watson's friend saved from sinister plotters, dinner at Simpson's, home on the last train. But 27A Wimpole is no hollow shell. Eight guest bedrooms are beyond the reach of the most prodigal fraudster. Mrs. Pearce is solid as Gibraltar. And the dust on Higgins's father's medical books is older than Miss Doolittle. So my theory can be wrapped in the newspapers with yesterday's fish."

It appeared that he had taken on the case merely to humor me. "So you think there's nothing in it at all?" I asked, crestfallen.

"I did not say that. Now that we are on the scene, there actually are a few points of interest. How is it that Mr. Eynsford-Hill is always on the watch? Why did the cook ruin the Béarnaise using thyme rather than tarragon? Why does Higgins not employ a butler? And why does our Irish doctor so disdain the Irish?"

They seemed to me fairly trivial points, but I seized upon the last one with gusto. "It seems obvious to me that this man Guest is behind the whole affair!" I said.

"He's not the spirit of bonhomie, I grant you. But what affair is he supposed to be behind? Has a crime been committed, or a hoax perpetrated? We don't have the least idea what we're up against."

"But you saw the difference in Miss Doolittle after she was closeted with the doctor!"

"It is no crime for a doctor to give a fractious female patient a tonic to calm her nerves."

"Tonic indeed. The man has some sinister power over the girl."

"Perhaps. We shall certainly ask Colonel Pickering to consult with his friends in India as to the doctor's antecedents. Lestrade tells me the colonel cultivated quite a set of informants during his time there."

"You had Pickering investigated?" The notion was intolerable.

"Save your indignation, Watson. When a fellow tells you an impossible story, the first thing you must do is make sure the fellow is neither a madman nor a mountebank. Your man passed that test with flying colors. Now we must consider our next move."

For a moment I considered telling him not to bother, that the affair was obviously too trivial for the great man's talents. I had forgotten how casually he could trample one's feelings.

Then I remembered what I had found. "Perhaps you can make something of this." I drew a small glass ampoule from my pocket and handed it to him.

"It appears to be empty. I suppose it is not?"

"A few drops remain, I believe. It must be the tonic Guest gave the girl. Perhaps there's enough for you to analyze?"

He scrutinized the ampoule. "Watson, you've become a veritable sleuth! What need is there of the wreck of Sherlock Holmes?"

I blushed at his praise. "I slipped it out of his bag while he was entertaining you."

There was the sound of footsteps in the hall. Holmes immediately began speaking in a loud stentorian voice, and I whipped out a notebook and pen case to write. This was a stratagem we had agreed upon beforehand. He dictated a letter to Morello's cousin Luigi in New Jersey, rife with details about the dispersal of a thousand tons of canned tomatoes up and down the eastern seaboard of the United States. It was the first of many such letters Holmes would dictate to me over the course of our stay at Wimpole Street, duly sent on through the mail after first being steamed open and read by our host. The address on the envelopes belonged to a retired New York policeman, Mr. Wilson Hargreave, an old friend of Holmes who was privy to our deception.

There was a knock at the door. It was Robert. "Want your boots blacked for the morning, sir?" he asked.

"Thanks, kid, you're all right," said Holmes, once again falling into his gangster persona. He picked up the boots and lofted them, one at a time, to the boy. Robert seemed scandalized by the informality, but he caught each boot as it was flung. He executed a little dip, something between a friendly nod and a formal bow, and went to go.

"Hold up, kid." A glimmer of mischief had come into Holmes's eyes. "Second thought, leave the boots. Go get yourself some shut-eye."

Robert turned back. He looked for a moment as if he might try tossing the boots back to Mr. Morello, but his courage failed him. He set the boots next to the wardrobe.

"Hit me next time," said Holmes. Robert dipped again and left us in peace.

"Hand me those boots, Watson. I think we yet have need of them tonight," Holmes said.

My spirits rose. Perhaps my old friend was not so jaundiced as he had seemed. "You have an excursion to make?" I asked as I handed him the boots.

"*We* have an excursion. The board is laid before us. Time we rolled the dice."

Chapter Eight

I t was coming on midnight when the creak and clatter of a growler broke the stillness of the night on Wimpole. Miss Doolittle and Mr. Eynsford-Hill were returning from their evening out. The cab settled to a stop. Freddy descended and handed Miss Doolittle out. The girl was still in warm spirits. She had thoroughly enjoyed the play, and seemed able to recite every line of it verbatim. Freddy's contributions to the conversation consisted mostly of terse nods and stammered agreements. She took no notice. When they arrived at the door, she rewarded his tender attentions with a soulful kiss on the cheek before darting inside, to leave him forlorn in the porch. He turned back to his cab, the weight of the world upon his narrow shoulders. When he stepped up to get in, however, he was startled to find that someone had taken his place in the cab. He hesitated. A voice came to him from the shadows inside, in a low, confidential tone.

"Mr. Eynsford-Hill, a word."

Freddy was not the type for conversations with mysterious strangers in cabs. He shrank back, only to find another man standing close behind him, with a hand planted firmly in the small of his back.

"Get in the cab, please, Mr. Eynsford-Hill," the second man said in a pleasant way that nevertheless sent a chill up Freddy's spine.

"Do you have to pop out of the shadows like that?" asked Freddy, his own voice unaccountably shrill. "It makes a fellow's knees go wobbly."

"Our apologies. I think you'll agree that discretion is necessary. Please step up," said the man inside the cab. Seeing no choice in the matter, Freddy climbed up, stubbing his toe badly on the step. The second man pushed his way in behind him. Freddy was now squashed between his abductors. He looked from one to the other.

"You again!" he gasped.

The first gentleman called through the window: "Driver!" The cab jangled away down the lane.

"Who the blazes are you fellows?" Freddy asked the second man. He had already recognized them as the American who had been introduced to him as Morello and his bulldog of a secretary, but the one no longer sounded American, and the other constantly behaved in decidedly un-secretary-like ways.

"You've heard of Mr. Sherlock Holmes?" said the secretary.

"The detective chappie? Magnifying glass and deerstalker cap and all that rot?"

"I mean the real Sherlock Holmes."

"He really is real? That's just what Liza said! Don't tell me you're him."

The first gentleman leaned forward out of the shadows. "No, Mr. Eynsford-Hill. His name is John Watson. *I* am Sherlock Holmes."

Freddy looked befuddled. "No. You're that Morello fellow. The American gangster. Eliza told me you garroted one of your rivals with a fishing line."

"A necessary subterfuge. We're concerned for the welfare of Miss Doolittle. I believe you are, as well."

"Well, of course I am. I mean, who wouldn't be?"

"You followed her today."

Freddy blushed.

"You've followed her before?"

"May have done," Freddy mumbled.

"Dr. Watson here described a man who intercepted Miss Doolittle's cab today. A rather ugly customer. She may have gone to meet him expressly, or she may have been waylaid. Did you see him?"

"Today? No. But I fancy I've seen him before. You could trawl the Thames with a butterfly net and not find a more loathsome little monster. But he holds some weird fascination for Eliza. It's not the first time they've put their heads together."

"You've seen them together before?"

"Three. No, four times. No, three."

"Always the same place?"

"No, but always the same kind of place. Greasy little pubs in Soho or Limehouse. Nowhere a lady ought to be."

"What do they talk about?"

"Couldn't get close enough to hear, could I? They talk in little snatches of whispers, always on the move, as if they were planning another Gunpowder Plot. Once, though, I stumbled on him with another girl in one of those pubs he haunts. They were right upon me, almost in my drink. She didn't bother keeping her voice down, not she! Screaming like a banshee, 'What about Betsy! What about Betsy Chubb, you beast?' Beating on his shirtfront like a drum."

"Who in heaven's name is Betsy Chubb?" I asked.

Freddy shrugged. "Not the foggiest idea. The girl was a common drab, with a shiner under one eye. But that was the one time I've seen him look scared."

Holmes laid an arm on Freddy's shoulder. "Do you know the man's name?"

"The woman in the pub called him Ned."

Holmes stared dreamily at the park rolling by in the gaslight. The elms guarding the Serpentine looked ready to surrender their leaves in the first chill rain. "Heed my advice, Mr. Eynsford-Hill. Keep your distance from this man Ned. Don't seek to confront him."

"What if he comes back to Wimpole Street?"

"He's been there?" Holmes's voice clotted with tension.

"Well, not to leave his card. I saw him once. On the roof. Staring into Liza's window. At first I thought it was only a cat on the ledge. It moved like a cat, though it was really far too large to be any kind of a cat, unless a panther got loose from the zoo. But then he turned and looked down at me. I've never seen such a scalding look. Turned my knees to jelly, and before I could move or raise the alarm, he was off across the rooftops faster than—well, faster than a cat."

Holmes asked no more questions, but seemed to relapse into a brown study. At length he roused himself and leaned out the window of the cab. "We'll get out here, driver!" he called. "Mr. Eynsford-Hill, I must ask you on your solemn word of honor not to reveal anything you have learned tonight to Miss Doolittle, or indeed to anyone. Only your silence can ensure her safety."

"Oh, well—solemn word!" Freddy started. The cab lurched to a halt. Holmes gave one last nod to Freddy as if to impress upon him the seriousness of the situation. Then we both stepped down.

"But where are we?" Freddy asked doubtfully, peering out. A fog had risen up off the pavement and got itself tangled in the lower branches of the trees. The gas lamps along the road were islands of light in the mist. The rattle of carriages was extinguished as if they had all been swallowed by a monster of the deep.

"Earl's Court, right? You're halfway home," Holmes replied.

"How did you know—?"

"You've got fresh grave-soil on the bottom of your boots. Go and get some rest. Come, Watson, let us stretch our legs a bit." He signaled to the driver. The horse snorted and stepped off, carrying young Mr. Eynsford-Hill to a night of uneasy sleep.

Some things never change, no matter how the years unfurl. Only Holmes would have deemed a walk through the streets of London in the heart of a midnight fog to be a pleasant outing. We put our best foot forward. Age had taken a step from both of us, but I was no more willing to admit it than he.

"We seem to be piling mystery upon mystery, Holmes," I said as we walked north along the boulevard.

"Indeed. This mention of the woman Betsy Chubb troubles me."

"You know her?"

"My dear Watson, do you no longer follow the crime news? Betsy Chubb was a Whitechapel prostitute. A mere girl of sixteen. Mild as a kitten. Last year she brutally slaughtered two young women in the house they lived in together. Then she smothered her own infant daughter with a pillow."

"Sweet heaven! What did she do it for?"

"At her trial she claimed to have no memory whatever of the act."

"That was all her defense?"

"She's to be hanged at Holloway at the New Year."

The fog wrapped around the lampposts like a winding sheet. The branches of the trees creaked like a gallows at midnight. It should have been the most solemn of moments. Yet all I could think to myself was, *He does read the crime news still!*

We continued home in companionable silence.

Chapter Nine

O ver the next few days a brown fog seemed to settle over our quest to discover the secret of Eliza Doolittle. We were like the little match girl, striking a little light time after time, only to see each one extinguished in a moment. Holmes dragged the hours, watching every move Higgins and the girl made, waiting for one of them to make a false move, to reveal the whereabouts of the real Eliza Doolittle, if indeed she existed. Higgins watched Holmes just as closely, hoping to trip him up, make him reveal his true identity as the secret agent of some comic-opera principality. And all these maneuvers and countermaneuvers went on under the veil of daily speech lessons. Higgins rousted Holmes at seven every morning. Shirking was not tolerated. "I have placed myself under the whip of a cruel taskmaster," Holmes complained to me jokingly.

"Still I don't imagine there's much hope of your English improving, Mr. Morello," said I.

"Not a snowball's chance in hell, *paisan*," he answered drily.

It fell to me, then, to do the legwork, to try to find someone who knew Eliza Doolittle before she came to Wimpole Street. Holmes insisted the girl must have relations, friends, enemies, acquaintances, *someone* who could shed light on the real Eliza. So out into the world I was thrust. It was not a role entirely strange to me, but my past forays in the world of practical sleuthing had not been crowned with success. I envied Holmes his snug little corner in the laboratory and his sham lessons, and I suspected it was the detective work he really was shirking; he still seemed less than wholly committed to our cause. Howbeit, over the course of the next few days I became as familiar with the stalls of Covent Garden and the rookeries of Lisson Grove as a body might aspire to.

The market at Covent Garden is a giant bellows of humanity before dawn ever breaks, so I was out upon the pavement before daylight each morning with little more than a cup of cocoa to warm my insides, making my way among the vans and lorries, the ziggurats of crates and casks and baskets, the mountains of cabbages and turnips, the ankle-deep morass of straw and cabbage leaves and broken haybands, all in the chill morning air before the sun has committed himself. The costermongers whose barrows foam out of the market buy and sell from dark till dark, crying their wares, chattering volubly and endlessly about nothing at all, but become close-mouthed as turtles if they think you're trying to pump them for information—which I most certainly was. In the course of loosening the tongues of these curbside sphinxes I wound up purchasing enough groceries for a week, and enough flowers to furnish a dozen funerals. My housekeeper in Queen Anne Street must have thought me mad when they were all delivered to her.

Pickering had been unable to tell us much about Miss Doolittle's antecedents. She was supposed to have been reared in Lisson Grove, and to have lodged most recently in a place called Angel Court near Drury Lane, an address that proved as difficult to find as the Seven Cities of Gold. When he and Higgins had first come across her, she was selling violets from a basket outside St. Paul's. The theatres had just let out, and the porch was crowded with people trying to get out of the rain. She had seemed familiar with everyone, and everyone with her. So ubiquitous a figure should be remembered by many. I assumed I would have no trouble finding a dozen or so who knew her well enough to describe her looks. I was woefully mistaken. I did stumble upon a knot of flower sellers in Oxford Street who knew the name of Eliza Doolittle, and assured me that she would be along any time with her basket. They seemed unaware that the girl had abandoned her trade months ago, and became quarrelsome when I told them so. There were some former associates of her father, Irish navvies playing thimblerig in an alley behind Toynbee Hall, who were aware of the change in Eliza's fortunes, but they could recall little of her looks, save that she was "about so high, but taller wi' boots on," or "dirtier about 'er face than 'er hands," or even "fairer than she appears," whatever that might mean. Still others would stick out their chins and glower at me, muttering about "peelers" under their breaths. They evidently believed I intended to bring the law down like a lightning-stroke on Eliza if only I could lay hands upon her. A few of the Irish women who sell basketry claimed to know her, too. They called her unlucky, or "cursed by the fairies," which I could make nothing of. On one point these women agreed, and that was the haunting sense of unexpressed deformity with which the girl impressed her beholders. It seemed to me I had heard such talk before, but I could not remember when.

Inevitably it was the cryptic comments that interested Holmes most when I returned that first evening, footsore, to Wimpole Street, in time for the last dregs of tea. In my absence, the house had sorted itself into a picture of surprising domesticity. Higgins and the colonel were huddled on the sofa with their heads together, going over scholarly journals and debating some obscure points in the argot of their field. Eliza hovered over Holmes in the phonics corner, demonstrating the proper use of various apparatus. Of these there were a profusion: among them I recognized a row of tiny organ-pipes, an assortment of tuning forks in varying sizes, a chemical harmonicon, a laryngoscope, a metronome, and a phonograph machine with a supply of wax cylinders for recording sounds. There were more items littered about that I could not put a name to. On a shelf behind the desk was a life-size relief of the human head in plaster of Paris, with the vocal organs depicted in section. There was also a bust of some ancient Greek with an exasperated look whom I did not recognize, but I was informed later that it was Demosthenes the Orator, whom Higgins seemed to regard as the patron saint of phonics.

The phonograph's horn was mute. The sound flowed instead through wires into two cups yoked over the ears. Higgins called these "earphones." Every time I tried to speak, Holmes would raise a finger, remove the cups, and say, "Run that by me one more time, bud."

The apparatus appeared to work, at least to a degree; at random intervals Holmes would burst forth with a stream of vowels that made him sound like a flock of congested geese. Every time he did so, Eliza would turn away in silent laughter, while Higgins, sitting across the room, would shut his eyes and give a shiver of opprobrium. The professor had apparently vowed not to let his new student take his ease until some scant sign of progress was forthcoming. Holmes nursed his tea and chatted with us between flocks of vowels. I had not seen him so animated in many a year.

"Here, have a listen yourself, Guido."

"Hill," I said primly, remembering my alias for once.

"Okay, have a listen, Guido Hill." He seemed a bit carried away with his American affectations. He clamped the cups over my ears. They were far from comfortable. But I heard no honking geese sounds as I had expected. Instead, there was the voice of a girl, attempting to pronounce tongue twisters with the most awful cockney accent I had ever heard. I didn't recognize the girl's voice, though I felt I should. I gave Holmes a questioning look. He let his gaze flicker toward Miss Doolittle for an instant. His meaning was clear. So I was listening to the original, untutored Eliza? Could it really be the same girl, I wondered? If only voices left prints as fingers do, our case would have been solved then and there.

"Barton, you Englishers got the world beat with this afternoon tea racket," Holmes said glibly. "Them little sandwiches would starve a canary, but the sugar biscuits and cream are better than cannoli." He continued in the same vein for the next quarter of an hour, larding his conversation with as many Americanisms as possible—meant, I think, to amuse Eliza and confound Higgins at the same time. He seemed as amused with his own performance as we were. If Higgins could indeed pick out the accents of Sussex squiry, he must have owned the most sensitive ears in all of Christendom. As the *coup de grace*, Holmes treated us to a dozen refrains of "I saw Susie sitting in a shoe shine shop. Where she sits, she shines, and where she shines, she sits," which in Brooklynese sounded like "I sawr Sooz settin' nuh shooshoyne shap."

Higgins threw his papers in the air. "Good God, man, have you no ear whatsoever? Shoe. Shine. Shop. Shoe. Shine. Shop! Do you even know what one is?"

"I spent most of my childhood between the pool hall and the shooshoyne shap. From the scuff of your shoes, I bet you ain't never been inside one in your life, Henry," Holmes answered with a lazy grin. "Should I take another crack at it?" Miss Doolittle turned her back to us, but her shoulders were heaving with laughter. Pickering buried his face in a book.

"No, you shall not take another crack at it, Giorgio! You shall cease this assault upon mine ears. You shall go up to bed and dream not of ships or chips or chaps, but of shops replete with shined shoes! And tomorrow you shall sell seashells by the seashore. Here endeth the lesson!"

"Well, I do have a little business to see to. Barton?" We both rose and bade goodnight to the company. We retreated to Holmes's room to discuss the situation as it stood. Holmes ranged full length upon the bed, kicking off his boots, while I took the wicker chair in the corner. I took out the notebook and pen, in case we might be disturbed by the household staff. We lit our pipes and smoked in silence for a while.

"This system of the professor's is truly admirable," Holmes said at length. "I can place a man by a confluence of clues: the weather of his complexion, the wear of his hands, the state of his dress, or the tobacco he smokes. But these are outward signs, which may be shed or disguised by a truly clever man. Higgins knows him by his voice, which he cannot alter."

"But you *have* altered your voice," I pointed out.

"And well he knows it. It's only a matter of time till he sees through me entirely."

"Then our object is folly."

"Folly? Within a week, I should be speechifying like William Gillette, were that my object. In a fortnight I shall have learned the entirety of the Higgins method."

"But what about the attic of the mind and not filling it up with extraneous lumber?" I was referring to a metaphor Holmes had used early in our acquaintance to justify his peculiarly specialized knowledge of the world.

"That was when I was young and crime was my only passion. Ah, Watson, am I too old to go upon the stage?" He gazed dreamily into the middle distance.

"You're in a curious mood."

"By which you mean you are curious about my mood."

"Well, I don't want to pry—"

"Which is your downfall as a detective. Pry, Watson, pry like a nickel-plated jemmy!"

"Well, then—"

"Well, then, why am I so lighthearted? I cannot say precisely. But I have been sitting at that cramped little table in the laboratory all day long, practicing pronouncing perfectly poorly, watching Higgins and the girl from the splendid isolation of my earphones, and I have concluded thus much: they are keeping secrets!"

This was his discovery? "I had thought we were agreed on that from the outset," I ventured.

"Yes, yes we were, Watson, yes we were," he said, his enthusiasm dampened not one whit. "But they are *not* keeping secrets in common."

"Oh," I said, still unmoved, then, "Oh!" as it struck me.

"You see? You see? They are not confederates. They are not of one mind. They work at cross-purposes."

"What did they say that led you to conclude this?"

"Not a word. Not one word. At least not one that I heard. The earphones made it impossible for me to hear. Which in turn made it easier for me to concentrate upon their facial expressions and gestures. The way they spy on one another, their hesitations and their distances."

"Could those not have been expressions of an unvoiced affection between the two?" I had harbored suspicions of such an affection almost from the start.

Holmes laughed. "Not a chance. Of course there is a strong animal magnetism between them which neither will acknowledge even to themselves, but there is no sympathy of heart or mind."

"So this simplifies our problem?"

"On the contrary. It becomes more complex. Which makes it far more interesting!" He giggled girlishly. He seemed absolutely exhilarated. Too much so, it occurred to me. It was unnatural.

"Holmes, I hate to ask this, but you haven't been indulging in any of the old habits?" There had been a time when Holmes had habitually turned to narcotics to combat the ennui occasioned when he had no cases to work upon.

"O ye of little faith! It's been years since I've resorted to the pharmacopeia. Can a man not glory in the intricacies of human iniquity without being accused of eating lotus petals?"

I believed him, but only just. I brought a candle before his face. "Your pupils are dilated," I said, "and your behavior erratic. Would you allow me to check your pulse?"

Instead of agreeing, he put his own finger on his radial artery and held it there. "It's fast," he said abstractedly, as if considering a problem wholly unrelated to himself. "Why is it fast, do you suppose?"

It was a puzzle. If it wasn't cocaine or heroin, what had affected him so? Then a possibility more dire suggested itself. "What about the tonic Miss Doolittle took? Were you able to make anything of that?"

"No, no, no. Not enough for a proper workup. No."

"You took it yourself." I tried not to make it sound like an accusation.

"Just after breakfast. Barely enough to paint the gums."

"And the effect?"

"Only a temporary numbness and a mild euphoria. Lasting about an hour."

"As a doctor, I think I must disagree with you, Holmes. I think the effect of the tonic was so powerful that you are still under its influence, without your even realizing it."

Holmes opened his mouth, and then shut it. He seemed to look inside himself, as if he were examining his own nervous system, neuron by neuron. "Not possible!" he said. Then: "You really think so? Well, well, well. Perhaps you are right. But if that's the case . . ."

He sank back on the bed, staring up at the ceiling, waving his arms to an imaginary orchestra.

"Yes?"

"If that is the case, imagine the effect of a full dose!"

Chapter Ten

I set out again the next morning with an expanded brief. Holmes had urged me to canvass the public houses in the area, and gave me the names of several landlords he knew personally. I viewed the prospect with trepidation. Holmes had always nurtured a connection to the lower classes that I could understand no more than I could duplicate. Charity is one thing; familiarity quite another. The press of unwashed humanity in the open streets was bad enough; the fetor oozing from the walls and floorboards of the pubs was an assault upon the senses. Raw onion met with moldy cheese and sour beer blended with the navvies' sweat. The barmen answered all my interrogations with blank, vulpine faces. Their clientele—rough workingmen and idlers, thieves and villains—eyed me with suspicion or open hostility. I returned to Wimpole Street at twilight with my tail between my legs. I had not stopped for tea. I had purchased a meat pie from one of the street vendors, and thrown it away after one bite told me it was more like to be cat meat than the promised veal. My stomach rumbled, and my feet ached. I had always admired my friend's ability to sift what seemed like random information into a coherent explanation of a

crime, but I had not quite fathomed the exhausting difficulty of collecting that information in the first place. I was discouraged enough
to give up my inquiry altogether, but that Holmes was so obviously
counting on me. I expected him to carve me up with sharp questions
when we sat down together again in confidence, but his manner was
subdued instead, almost gentle. He had Robert smuggle up a cold joint
and some rolls to his room from the larder, and insisted I down half a
pot of tea before we even began. What changes had the years wrought
upon him? In the old days, when he was on the scent, Holmes had been
like a hound straining at the leash, snapping at everyone about him.

"A simple case of dyspepsia," Holmes explained. "The cook put
half a cup of pepper in the tournedos béarnaise. A talented woman, but
blind as a bat. The pipes have been shaking in the house all evening."

I chuckled. The simple repast Robert had provided had gone a long
way toward improving my disposition.

"I'm sure you realize what that means," Holmes said.

Of course I had no idea what it meant. "We should dine out from
now on?" I ventured.

He raised an eyebrow in reproof. "The cook would be unaware of
any change in Miss Doolittle's appearance."

As usual with Holmes's deductions, it seemed obvious once he'd
said it. I had forgotten that line of inquiry entirely. "But there are still
the three housemaids," I returned. "And the footman. His eyes are
sharp enough."

"All of them hired in the wake of Miss Doolittle's illness."

"That can't be right! Pickering said they were the same servants
before and after his attack."

"I don't want to cast aspersions on your friend, but I don't think the
colonel would notice the difference between one servant and another,
as long as they wore the same uniform. But I spoke with Molly, the
upstairs maid. She came into an empty house, except for the cook and
Mrs. Pearce."

"But the former servants? What happened to them?"

"One married, one let go for drink, one emigrated to Australia:

at least that was the rumor. Which was which, she couldn't say. So the only servant who could have witnessed the substitution was Mrs. Pearce. Loyal Mrs. Pearce."

Closemouthed Mrs. Pearce.

"But shouldn't the fact that they were all sacked tell us something?"

"According to the cook, Professor Higgins has a reputation for going through staff like a postboy goes through horses."

"But if we could find them, they would certainly be inclined to tell us something."

"I have begun inquiries in that direction. But it may be hard to track them down if they have left service—or left the country."

Another thought struck me. "But if she's not Eliza Doolittle—who is she?"

"Ah, you've come to that point, have you? From the outset, Watson, there were two possibilities: either the girl had been put away or murdered, as Pickering suspected, and another girl put in her place, or she had undergone a transformation so dramatic that Pickering could not recognize her. The latter supposition indicated the abuse of some powerful narcotic. I know something about the transformations induced by narcotics. Her liaison with the brutal underworld figure called Ned pointed strongly to the latter theory, but we could not rule out the former. But what reason could there be for that? Had Higgins had a prior relationship with the girl? Did she know some secret of his? Could she even be pregnant with his child?"

"Holmes! Whatever else he may be, Higgins is a gentleman."

"The workhouses are full of the by-blows of gentlemen. But we can set that possibility aside for the moment. Well, then, might she be more than the child of the streets she seemed? Who were her people? Alternatively, it might not be about the flower girl, but about the young lady we had actually met. Perhaps she was no garden party duchess, but a real one, perhaps from one of the Hapsburg states that have seen such turmoil recently."

"But isn't that just what Higgins has been trying to convince us of?"

"He may be playing a double bluff. Perhaps she had sought shelter from her enemies with Higgins, and the first girl had been brought into his home as pretext for the second, then sent away with a proper reward, or put out of the way to ensure her silence."

"Our little Eliza might really be a duchess! Perhaps even a princess!" I said. My mind whirled with possibilities.

Holmes smiled at my enthusiasm. "First we must eliminate the flower girl from our calculus," he said.

It was on my third day of sleuthing that I had a turn of luck. I was in a foul hole down off Carting Lane called the Cormorant, which Holmes had recommended to me as a hotbed of underworld activity. It was indeed the vilest place I had set foot in since that long-ago day I walked into the Bar of Gold looking for Isa Whitney. It might have been midday when I stepped in off the street, but it seemed black midnight inside that house, the gloom relieved only by a couple of smoking lamps, the stench of decay oozing from the walls as from a corpse. The room stretched off into obscurity as if into nothingness. I asked for the proprietor, a Mr. Breckinridge, but the name only drew laughter from the moonfaced barman and five or six rapacious-looking fellows slouching round the bar.

"You won't find Teddy Brock in these parts, old geezer," volunteered one of them, a tosher by his coat and lantern.

I bridled at the word "geezer," but let it pass. "Mr. Breckinridge is no longer proprietor of this establishment?"

"He's no longer the owner of his own precious neck, that's what," snickered another fellow. His nose was hooked like a grape knife and his eyes looked in different directions.

"Strung up at Wandsworth last December," explained a third man, whose cheek was corrugated with scars, "after he took a bung-starter to the old woman."

"Strung up?"

"'Anged by the neck until dead," said the barman in a funereal tone.

"And a few hours more, for good measure!" cried Grape-knife, to the delight of the others.

"Ah. Well, thank you for your time." I started for the door. They were all staring at me, at least half a dozen of them now. Realizing I had their attention, I decided to take advantage of the opportunity. Raising my voice, I asked, "Would any of you be acquainted with a Miss Eliza Doolittle? She used to sell flowers in the streets round here. Daughter of one Alfred Doolittle."

It was a mistake. I could see it in their eyes. Idle curiosity had been replaced by active suspicion. I should have ended it there. Instead I stumbled further into the morass.

"Angel Court? Could anyone direct me there?"

"If you're looking for a girl, old flint, there's four on every corner. They all know the same tricks." This from a broken-nosed navvy who tittered at his own joke.

"I am *not* looking for a girl," I said, drawing my dignity round me.

A red-faced fellow with a filthy kerchief and the shoulders of a coal heaver slammed his glass down on the bar and turned around to look at me. He had seemed oblivious of my presence until that moment. "What you lookin' for, then, eh? Oo are you marchin' in here askin' all these questions, upsettin' folk? A copper, maybe?"

"I'm a friend of Miss Doolittle's," I said, a trifle primly.

"If you're a friend, why not bloody ask 'er oo she knows, eh? We don't want toffs swaggerin' in here disturbin' the peace and shovin' their toffee noses where they don't belong."

"I assure you I meant no harm, my good fellow." I was amazed at how quickly misunderstandings multiplied among these men. They seemed absolutely determined to misconstrue my every intention in the worst possible way.

"'Arm? It's 'arm you want, you come to the right shop, Mr. Toffee Nose." The coal heaver stepped toward me, lowering his head like a bull, and his friends closed in around us. It was no good arguing with these men. Reflexively, I raised my stick to ward him off. It was an unfortunate gesture. He grabbed hold of the shaft and wrenched it from me as if I were a wayward child. Then he raised it above his head. Animal rage smoldered in his eyes. The career of

John Watson, M.D., was about to come to an abrupt and inglorious end.

Then a voice rang out from the heavens:

"Doctor Watson?"

Of course it was not really the heavens speaking, although the impression was hard to shake. The voice echoed from the other end of the room, wreathed in smoky obscurity.

"It's Doctor John Watson, isn't it?"

It struck me that anyone who recognized me in such a place would likely be one of the dozens of villains Holmes and I had sent to prison in the old days. My nightmare was spinning down into darkness.

Then a young man emerged from the gloom. Early thirties perhaps— too young to be an old foe. Tall and narrow. A lupine face with calculating eyes, yet there was a smile waiting to break forth on those liverish lips. "Don't say you don't know me, Doctor Watson!" he begged.

Suddenly twenty years dropped away. A line of ragged boys standing in the street, waiting for instructions from Sherlock Holmes. "Wiggins! It's Wiggins, isn't it?" I could have wrapped the fellow in my arms and kissed him.

"Right you are, Doctor!" he shouted, taking my hand.

Wiggins had been the eldest, and the de facto leader of that ragtag band of boys dubbed by Holmes the Baker Street Irregulars, who had helped us in any number of investigations. They could go anywhere, follow anyone, listen at doors, spy at windows, melt into crowds, and were absolutely fearless. Mortal danger was a great game to them, encouraged by Holmes's own reckless example. Now here was their chief, a grown man, with muttonchops and thinning ginger hair. He wore a rusty fustian jacket that reminded me of myself twenty years ago, and a courier bag slung across his shoulder.

"Look here, lads," he cried, "this is Doctor John Watson, friend and partner of the great Sherlock Holmes! If he says he's a friend of someone, he's a friend!"

Silence fell among the men. You could feel them wavering in their hostility.

"And he wants to stand the next round!"

The storm clouds broke. The men surged round me, all trace of hostility wiped away. They tipped their caps and shook my hand. The taps were opened and fellowship poured out. The tosher thanked me personally for my supposed assistance in some dire mystery that would have sent his wife's uncle to the gallows back in '93. Sherlock Holmes had solved the case as the work of an afternoon. These men forcefully reminded me that Holmes's efforts had cleared the innocent as often as they had condemned the guilty. The coalheaver returned my stick to me as if it were a gift he'd made special and offered to stand me the next round. I took it from Wiggins's wink that it would be a bad idea to refuse.

We talked of the old days. Even at that I was clumsy. I asked after his family, only to be reminded that Wiggins was an orphan; nor, he assured me, had he ever married. "What's good enough for Sherlock Holmes, that's good enough for me!" he said, laughing it off. I asked if he still saw any of the Irregulars. "Well, course you know about Teddy," he said.

"Teddy? Little curly-headed fellow, always wiping his nose on his sleeve?"

"Aye, that were Teddy Brock," he said with glistening eyes.

Then I realized that runny-nose Teddy and Teddy Breckinridge, former landlord of the Cormorant, since executed for murder, were one and the same. There was a reason, after all, why the Irregulars were irregular.

"The Cormorant were a bit of haven for the old Irregulars back in the day," said Wiggins. "But times change, eh?" He told me about the other boys, jostling my memory with long-forgotten names and faces. None of the rest of them had come up against the law, at least not seriously. Two had emigrated to Australia, one to Canada, and one was a cowboy in the Argentine: such immense vistas for boys who had once "traveled extensively" in London, as Mr. Thoreau might put it. In return I did my best to recount for him the little mundane doings of two old men who had once been his idols. It made for slow storytelling, and I could see impatience building in his face.

* * *

"So who's this doxie you're looking for, Doctor? You on a case?"

I admitted the fact.

"Holmes and Watson, the game is afoot!" Wiggins laughed good-naturedly. "I knew you had something up your sleeve, Doctor. What's the play?"

"We're not looking for the girl, Wiggins—we've got her safe in our pocket. We need to find someone who knew her before she came to us."

"Ah, the old former friends and associates. A tidy business, that one."

"'Ev another pint, Doctor Wilson!" Grape-knife slammed another tankard in front of me. Wiggins nodded, and I took a drink.

"Wiggy, you should get a picture of us with the doctor, eh?" said the coalheaver, and the others joined in the chorus.

"A picture? You're a photographer?" I asked.

"I'm a detective is what I am," said Wiggins proudly. "But the kind of detectin' I do, Mrs. Brown is as valuable to me as Mr. Holmes' magnifying glass were to him." He opened up his bag and produced a small leather case, which held a Brownie camera. It was the first time I'd seen a camera so small, barely bigger than a cottage loaf. The photographer merely need turn the spool, focus the lens, and press the shutter to capture an image. My new friends crowded round me, all eager to be memorialized in the picture.

"Here, Doctor, you don't mind me saying, what you need is a snapshot of this girl. Flash it around and people can tell right off do they know her."

"I agree, Wiggins. Unfortunately, no such photo exists. And we can hardly ask her to sit for a portrait without arousing her suspicions."

"I could take one, easy as pissing the bed."

"But could you take it without the girl knowing?"

Wiggins grinned. "That's my specialty, mate."

Chapter Eleven

I t was a grey evening when I returned to Wimpole Street. I was about to enter the laboratory when Mrs. Pearce came bustling into the hall to waylay me. "He's with someone, I'm afraid. Not to be disturbed on any account were his directions. I'm sure you understand, Mr. Barton."

"Of course, Mrs. Pearce. Is my employer with them?"

"Mr. Morello is out." She hesitated for a moment. "You look all in, Mr. Barton. Why don't you take some tea in the parlor?"

I nodded gratefully. Soon I was comfortably seated before a cheerful fire, with a cup of tea to my lips and the evening papers on my lap. Mrs. Pearce had brought it to me herself, rather than sending it in with one of the girls. Once I was settled, she made to go, but then turned back to face me.

"Your Mr. Morello seems a bit of a slave driver, if you don't mind my saying so. Have you been with him long?"

"Less than a month," I replied.

"Oh! Are you a Londoner?"

I was a bit taken aback to find Mrs. Pearce ladling her personal attentions upon me. I had thought her rather obvious disdain for Mr. Morello extended to me as well. Was she pumping me for information on behalf of her master? She hardly seemed the type for idle gossip.

"I was with Baron Hastings in Northumberland until he passed away." Holmes and I had rehearsed the answers for just such an occasion. My reply naturally led to a conversation about our past years "in service." I dodged specifics with astounding awkwardness, but she seemed not to doubt me. She herself had joined the Higgins household when Professor Higgins was a mere boy, rising from the position of second housemaid to her present lofty estate. She had married the butler, Pearce, when she was young and he was old. He was struck down by apoplexy in the same week the queen died: proof of his loyalty to the Crown.

Then she hesitated, and sought my eyes, as if wanting to draw me into her confidence. "You seem a nice man, Mr. Barton. Do you know the stories about your Mr. Morello?" She paused as if expecting a protest, and then hurried on. "He is not at all a nice man." Her tone was that of a reproving aunt. I would have passed it off, but that look in her eyes forced me to honesty.

"I might say the same thing about Professor Higgins."

She did not flinch, but gave my words due consideration. "He was a willful child, and his mother encouraged his willfulness. Mr. Pearce promised his father on his deathbed that he'd look after him. I promised Mr. Pearce the same thing." She meant that as an ironclad excuse, and so it was.

We heard the laboratory doors open, and men talking. Higgins saying, "I shall wait upon your results." And the other man, "Good day, then, Professor."

They paused for a moment in the hall where I could see them. The stranger was tall and lanky, almost skeletal, with a face pale as custard. He wore a tweed ulster, which seemed a bit close for so fair a day, with a fore-and-aft cap as though he had just come from a country hunting party. A meerschaum pipe was clenched between his lips. I only had a moment's glimpse, but I was aware of a penetrating gaze, and I could not shake the feeling that I had seen him before.

"Mrs. Pearce, will you see the gentleman to the door?" said Higgins. She gave a little curtsey and followed the stranger out. Higgins returned to the laboratory without ever noticing me.

Mrs. Pearce, I had begun to realize, was an exceptional woman of great strength and poise, with an unusually rigorous mind for one of her sex. She had the fine, noble features of a Roman matron. Her fealty to the Higgins family could not be counted against her. When she passed by the door again, I stopped her. "Mrs. Pearce, I think I've met that gentleman before. What's his name?"

"I never caught his name, sir. He's one of those private detectives."

"Ah. Is the professor worried about housebreakers?"

"Oh, no, sir. I think the gentleman has been hired to investigate your Mr. Morello," she answered pointedly. With that, she went in to see to her master.

I was utterly thrown over. Our investigation was ended before it had properly begun! Even the meanest detective would have no difficulty in unmasking G.B. Morello and Hill Barton as Sherlock Holmes and John Watson, and that in short order. I laid the papers aside, despondent.

That was how they found me when they returned, all three together, Pickering, Holmes, and Eliza. Pickering seemed in fine fettle, and the girl was glowing. They had taken Mr. Morello sightseeing. Now he could boast of seeing more than the lions at Trafalgar and the changing of the guard, said Eliza. "He insisted on seeing Covent Garden, till I convinced him there were no gardens there. We went to Kensington Garden instead."

"You won't see folks in Brooklyn going gaga over a statue of a boy," Holmes grumbled.

"The boys in Brooklyn cannot fly," Eliza shot back.

They were talking about the statue of Peter Pan in Kensington Garden. Mr. Barrie had erected it there in secret in the middle of the night some months ago. There were those who called it a wonder and those who called it a disgrace. For myself, I have never approved of writers promoting their own wares as if they were selling buns two a penny. But I will confess a certain affection for the Lost Boys, particularly Tootles.

"You wanna fly away to Neverland, Miss Doolittle?" asked Holmes.

"Mr. Morello—" she unpinned her hat and let her hair fall down around her shoulders—"where do you think we are now?"

As soon as Pickering and the girl had retreated to their rooms to prepare for dinner, the mask fell from Holmes's face. "I had hoped to get her to Covent Garden, where someone might recognize her, but she was too clever for me. Your blockhead friend Pickering was no help, either. It was he who had the blasted impudence to suggest Kensington Gardens."

"And what *did* you think of the Peter Pan statue?" I asked, chuckling.

"As a grave marker, it's in singularly bad taste."

"Grave marker? What on earth can you mean?"

"Why would a man erect a statute in the dead of night unless he's buried someone beneath?"

This was one of the pitfalls of being the world's foremost detective. The most innocent circumstance was always grounds for suspicion, and murder ever on his mind.

"You suspect Mr. Barrie of doing away with someone? Any hint as to who the victim might be?"

"They still haven't found Loraine Allison, have they?" he asked peevishly.

Loraine Allison was a two-year old girl who had been among the passengers on the *Titanic*. Her body had never been found. "Surely you're not serious," I chided.

"Of course not. The statue alone is crime enough for the hangman's noose."

He was obviously out of sorts. News of my fortuitous run-in with young Wiggins helped lift his mood enormously. "Our investigation progresses, Watson," he said, clapping his hands. "Good to have young Wiggins in our stable. Of course one mourns the death of young Breckinridge, however well deserved. But Wiggins was always the brightest of the lot." Even my last bit of news, that of Higgins having hired a detective, could not sour his mood, though I did my best to impress the gravity of the situation upon him.

He chose to view Mrs. Pearce's revelation in a different light.

"Old Watson the romantic! As soon as my back is turned, he is tête-à-tête with my lady housekeeper," he said, teasing. "A handsome woman, Doctor, but guard yourself. Her first loyalty is to Higgins. Anything you let slip to her by moonlight will be communicated to him before daybreak."

I waved his insinuation aside, though not without a blush, I fear. "Guard yourself!" I rejoined. "It's not me that Higgins has set the hounds upon."

"Cheer up, Watson," he said lightly. "Not every detective is Sherlock Holmes." In vain I pointed out that not every detective need be.

"Don't think of it," he said, brushing it aside. "Anything good in the papers? What scandal is the good old *Gazette* selling these days?" I went to hand him the paper, but he refused it. "No, I swore off the scandal sheets long ago. But here, what's this?" A headline had caught his eye. It was an article I had glanced at earlier.

"Another prostitute murdered, I think," I answered. "Tragic." Truth be told, this kind of penny-dreadful tragedy barely touched me these days. As the world had grown colder, so had my heart.

Holmes took the paper from me. "More than merely tragic," he commented while reading. "Quite sensational. But you've got the story backward, Watson. It was a prostitute that committed the murders. The two victims were, it says here, 'family men the best our age has to offer.' A solicitor and a broker. Almost certainly the girl's clients, though the *Gazette* is too discrete to mention. Stabbed them both to death with a kitchen knife."

My sympathy remained at low ebb. I do not approve of prostitution, and especially of its patrons. I said so plainly.

"Yes, yes," said Holmes. "But that is not the crux of the matter. Look at the girl's name!"

I read the name. It meant nothing to me. My frown told him so.

"I forgot, you have not read about the Betsy Chubb trial. The girl's name is Nancy Kelly. I remember it well. She was a witness in the trial against Miss Chubb. Murky waters ahead, I fear, Watson!"

What this new circumstance might portend, he refrained from saying. He went away, leaving me as always to stagger about in the fog of my own suppositions until such time as he would be ready to reveal the entire chain of events as a fait accompli. The dinner hour fast approaching, I made my weary way up to my garret room to change. I came upon Miss Doolittle, standing in her own doorway, as if expecting someone. She beckoned to me, laying a finger to her lips for silence. When I joined her, she drew me inside her room and shut the door. I didn't know what to expect from this clandestine meeting.

For a lady's boudoir, Miss Doolittle's room held a rather Spartan aspect, with scant trace of the feminine touch. There were some framed prints in the pre-Raphaelite style, which I suspect had hung there long before she took up abode. The dressing table boasted only a few tubes of cosmetics and a small atomizer. There was an ancient concertina lying on the bed, and a lory sulking in a battered cage in the corner. Miss Doolittle stood with her back to me, attempting to stroke the bird's head through the bars, but the lory kept shifting its stance minutely in that maddening way birds have.

"Your Mr. Morelli is the first American I've met, Barton. I don't know quite what to make of him," she said carelessly.

Was this what she had summoned me for in such secrecy? "I'm not sure Mr. Morelli is a typical American," I answered cautiously. "He spent his early years in Italy, I believe."

She turned on me and burst forth with it: "Who is he, Mr. Barton? Who is he really?" Her expression was so earnest and so vexed that I nearly felt moved to tell her all.

"One might ask that of anyone, I suppose. Who are you, really, Miss Doolittle?"

She smiled. "Haven't you guessed? I'm Princess Flavia of Ruritania! Is your employer Count Rupert? Are you Krafstein?" Eliza was evidently a fan of Mr. Hope's novel.

"Miss Doolittle, I don't know what I might tell you. I'm only a secretary, barely a month in service with the gentleman. I'm certainly not in his confidence."

"You're not a secretary."

I believe I harrumphed—it could not have been very convincing.

"I've read the correspondence Mr. Morelli dictates to you. No, don't look so scandalized. Professor Higgins has every one of those letters steamed open. He makes me copy them out, then sends my copy on to your friend in New York. Who, he says, is forwarding them to whoever Mr. Morello really works for. The professor says they're written in code, but he hasn't the least idea what it might be. All that talk about tons of tomatoes and gallons of olive oil, I'm inclined to agree with him. But your handwriting is atrocious. Not a secretary's hand. Nearly as bad as a doctor's."

"It's legible enough to satisfy my employer."

"And he's not your employer, he's your friend. He treats you as an equal. Like an old comrade, I judge."

"Americans have unorthodox notions of how to treat servants. All that brotherhood and democracy, no doubt," I ventured.

"The professor's wrong," she continued. "He's no spy. I've known copper's narks before. They're always obsequious little toads with ink-stained fingers and ragged coughs from standing in the weather peering in windows while their marks are inside, warming their toes at the fender and drinking negus. I don't suppose international spies are very much different. Mr. Morelli *is* different. Mr. Morelli's known danger. I fancy you have, too. Are you part of his ring?"

"What ring is that, Miss?"

"Smuggling ring. Murder ring. I don't know. Have you done any garroting of your own?"

"I don't think Mr. Morelli means you any harm, Miss."

Eliza laughed. "And what if he did? Dangerous men don't frighten me, Mr. Barton. I've lived among them all my life. I find a certain fascination in them."

Was she speaking the truth, or putting on a show for me? We were both groping in the dark, tugging at each other's masks. I remembered the mysterious Ned. Did she find him fascinating, too?

She gazed at me with liquid eyes, but I kept my guard up. She must have sensed that she would get nothing from me. She brushed my cheek with her lips and put a hand to my back. Before the spell was lifted I found myself steered into the hall, standing alone, staring at her door. It occurred to me that Eliza Doolittle, whoever she was, might be considered dangerous herself.

Chapter Twelve

Sherlock Holmes had engaged a neighbor to look after his beloved bees while he was away from home. I could not shirk my own practice indefinitely. Having handed over the detective duties to Wiggins, I felt it incumbent upon myself to put in a day at the surgery. My patients at that time ranged from infants with the croup to expectant mothers to rheumatic old pensioners. They all seemed to share a secret knowledge of my comings and goings. Somehow the news got out that Dr. Watson was in, and I was kept busy from early morning to late afternoon. But I could not banish the Doolittle case from my mind for more than two minutes together. With all the distractions it posed, it was a wonder I didn't kill half my patients that day. We were no closer to discovering whether Eliza Doolittle was a flower girl or an adventuress or Marie of Roumania. We could not divine the link between her and the mysterious troglodytic Ned, who seemed in turn connected to not one but two murderous prostitutes. And now there was a detective on our tracks. Had I been followed to work that day? Might I be followed back to Higgins's? Our every step was shadowed. Our case seemed hopeless.

I must here interpose an incident that at the time seemed of no consequence to our investigation but in time rippled outward to some significance. I had just returned to Wimpole Street after seeing my last patient. Dusk was gathering in the street. As I hung my hat on the peg, I heard voices coming from the front parlor.

"There's no recovering the wreck?" I heard Miss Doolittle say.

"Lost! Did I not say so? The fools! Utterly lost." Her interlocutor was Dr. Guest, at his most growlsome.

"I mourn for the departed. And the terrible loss to their families," Miss Doolittle said gently.

"Their loss? What about my loss? Did I not tell you what they carried?" His voice was choked with bitterness.

I should mention that it had been a scant few months since one of the greatest maritime disasters of modern times had occurred, when the fabulous ocean liner *Titanic* sank, along with fifteen hundred souls. It had been the talk of all London for weeks, and would continue so for months. Now here was Guest plunging his hand in the wound: the incompetence of the crew, the cowardice of the captain, the hubris of those who attempt to face the perils of the sea without proper precautions. From his talk I gathered he had lost friends or relatives in the accident, and I felt an upwelling of sympathy on hearing him bemoan his loss. I wanted to extend my sympathies to him, but I was certain that neither he nor the girl would take kindly to my eavesdropping. I moved on quietly past their door and into the laboratory.

I entered to find Holmes, Higgins, and Pickering, all dressed in evening wear. They had abandoned the tedium of lessons and were leaning hard on the sherry decanter.

"Barton!" cried Holmes. "Hurry upstairs and put on the monkey suit. We're dressing for dinner tonight. Chop-chop!"

"We're entertaining," Pickering added mildly. "White tie, old fellow."

I was tired and irritable. "Another dinner with Dr. Guest?" I asked plaintively.

"Guest isn't coming. Where would you get such an idea?" asked Higgins.

"I just heard him in the parlor with Miss Doolittle. Rehashing the *Titanic* tragedy." I hadn't meant to mention it, but it came tumbling out.

"Tragedy? You mean debacle," rejoined Higgins.

"Oh, for heaven's sake, Higgins, let's not start on that again."

"Really, Pick? Still defending the venal and corrupt? Were it not for the captain and Mr. Ismay, not a single life would have been lost."

"Were it not for the captain, every life would have been lost," said Pickering, indignant.

"Hear, hear!" I said. I should not have.

Higgins rounded on me. "Hear, hear? And what are you doing listening at people's doors anyway?"

"It was unavoidable. They were quite loud."

"Can you help standing there wafting all the dust of London upon Mrs. Pearce's carpet? Get you gone, fellow. My mother will be upon us at any moment."

I skulked away, humiliated as the meanest servant. Behind me I heard Higgins and Pickering resume their argument. "Thank Providence for the courage of captain and crew!" Pickering's voice rang through.

I hurried into my dinner clothes with Robert at my elbow. The boy told me that Professor Higgins's mother had returned from the wilds of Cornwall and wanted to see Eliza. "Watches her like the poor cat in the attic, she does."

I asked why the old woman took such an interest in her son's amanuensis.

"Dunno. Bette says she's worried Liza will try to trick the guvnor into marrying her. Moll says she's worried she won't."

I met Mrs. Pearce on the landing. She stopped to give me a sour look.

"If you'll excuse my saying it, sir, your tie is a fright. If you'll allow me the liberty?"

Having no glass in my room, I had depended on Robert's sartorial eye to complete my dress. He had nearly strangled me before pronouncing my appearance as "top 'ole, old 'un."

Her touch was cool, her fingers quick and sure. It was a moment's work untying and reknotting my tie and setting my collar to rights. I couldn't see the results, but had that inexpressible sense that the world had been set right. She leaned in and spoke confidentially.

"Watch yourself, sir. She's a shrewd woman. She doesn't ordinarily notice staff, but if you earn her attention, she'll winkle all your secrets out of you in no time."

She patted my shirtfront as if to test my solidity, and then continued up the stairs, leaving me to wonder if she suspected me of having secrets, or had already winkled them out herself.

I flew down the stairs as the gong sounded. Higgins was leading his mother into the dining room as I came into the hall. He and Pickering were still trading barbs on the subject of *Titanic*.

"Witness heroic Captain Smith, who blew his brains out rather than go down with the ship," Higgins sang, drawing out his mother's chair.

"That is simply not true!" Pickering sputtered.

"Of course they hushed it up afterward."

"If the two of you would hush, we might have our soup hot for a change," said Mrs. Higgins smartly, commandeering for herself the head of the table. The kitchen-maid was indeed standing by the door with the tureen, ready to serve. "No, Eliza, come sit next to me. Mr. Morello—you are Mr. Morello, I presume?"—she cast a baleful eye on Holmes—"you will sit on my other hand. Henry, you there." Pickering and I were left to find our own seats.

"Now let us have as little discussion of ideas and events of consequence as possible, please," Mrs. Higgins said as the soup was served. "Eliza, have you taken up drawing, as I suggested?"

Eliza nodded brightly. "I've found the most wonderful teacher. Monsieur Vernet."

"A Frenchman? Henry must loathe him. Good for you."

"I do not loathe the French, Mother. I simply pity them," said Higgins. "Should I ask Cook to whip us up a platter of gastropods?"

Mrs. Higgins was in her sixties, a small woman who cast a long shadow. A soft, heart-shaped face was set off by a cleft chin and fierce blue eyes. She wore a pearl-grey velvet gown with a peacock turban and shawl. It was evident that she was even more domineering than her son, without his continual need to fling his personality about the room. As I watched her direct the flow of conversation and the timing of the service, I had the uncanny feeling that I had met her before.

Higgins and Pickering kept returning to the subject of the *Titanic* tragedy throughout dinner, unable to let it be. Higgins thrived on stirring up hornets' nests. Pickering argued for the heroism of captain and crew, and those who faced their deaths with the stoicism of old Romans. Higgins was quick to point out the venality and ineptitude of certain of the ship's officers, including the captain and Mr. Ismay. He took the owners and investors of the White Star line to task for their lack of preparation in the matter of the lifeboats. Pickering became quite red in the face as he tried to defend them.

Mrs. Higgins scolded Higgins repeatedly, but he took it like a saucy schoolboy. At one point he turned to Miss Doolittle and asked, "What did Dr. Guest have to say about the shipwreck?"

A sudden flood of panic came into her eyes. "What do you mean?" she stammered.

"What's the doctor's opinion of the *Titanic*'s captain and crew?"

She seemed to recover herself. "I have no idea. He has never mentioned it to me."

"Did you not discuss it with him this very evening?"

"Of course not. I haven't spoken to the doctor in a week."

"I had no idea I had surprised a secret tryst," Higgins said bantering. "Come, girl, what did you and our friend Guest talk about this evening?"

"Tryst? Have you taken leave of your senses, Professor?" Her face was hot with anger.

Mrs. Higgins rallied to her. "Come now, Henry, there's no need to browbeat the girl."

But Higgins had taken the matter too far to drop it now. The parlor-maid was clearing dishes from the table. He caught her by the wrist. "Was Dr. Guest here this evening?" Higgins asked her.

"I'm sure I couldn't say, sir." The girl blushed and tried to pull away.

"I'm sure you could say, but your loyalties are obviously with Miss Doolittle rather than your master." He tightened his grip on her wrist.

"Oh, for heaven's sake, Henry, leave it!" Eliza snapped. Higgins released the maid and she ran from the room, almost in tears. "Dr. Guest stopped in, yes, but only for a moment. He brought me a tincture for my headaches. He wasn't here two minutes. He certainly did not bend my ear talking about *Titanic*."

It was that use of Higgins's Christian name that suddenly brought it home to me. Mrs. Higgins had seemed familiar because all her speech and manners were mirrored in Eliza. Higgins had called the girl a mynah bird. Here one could see the original stamped upon the copy.

The force of Mrs. Higgins's personality was underlined at the end of dinner. It was the normal custom for the gentlemen to remain at table after the ladies removed themselves, fortifying themselves with port and cigars. But as soon as Mrs. Higgins had gone with Eliza to the parlor (Mrs. Higgins always held court in the parlor, apparently: she considered the laboratory to be the proper domain of hirsute savages only), Higgins rose and said, "Gentlemen, please make yourself comfortable. As for myself, I shall join the ladies." He departed with happy alacrity.

"A most formidable woman," said Holmes after he had gone.

"Quite fond of Eliza," Pickering chimed in.

"Like a daughter," I said.

"More indulgent. More like a granddaughter," said Holmes. I caught the edge of speculation in his voice.

"Good God, Mr. Holmes," cried Pickering, "you're not suggesting that Eliza is Higgins's daughter?"

"I merely postulate, Colonel. At this point we cannot dismiss any avenue of inquiry."

"You still haven't formed a theory, then?" I asked.

"Bricks without clay," Holmes muttered irritably. "Bricks without clay." It had always been Holmes's favorite aphorism when faced with too few data points to form a proper theory.

Chapter Thirteen

After a decent interval, we too repaired to the parlor. But Mrs. Higgins was already saying her goodbyes, and Eliza her goodnights. We retreated therefore to the laboratory to close out the evening. There was still a bit of strain between Higgins and Pickering after their tiff, so each was inclined to choose a new companion. Pickering sat down with me at the piano, and we were soon busy plinking out some of the old regimental songs. Holmes entertained Higgins with some card tricks he claimed to have learned in New Orleans. His skills at legerdemain soon had the professor clapping like a nine-year-old. It seemed at first marvelous that the two could forget their acrimony in such innocent amusement. I had to remind myself that, despite Holmes's disguise, they were both—indeed, we were all four—English gentlemen who had come of age in the lap of Victoria Regina, an empire the like of which the world had never seen, and a city of wonders such as only old Rome could match. It was a world perhaps fading away, but it had seemed eternal to us. The house on Wimpole Street was a well-heeled vessel carrying us against the storm.

Then the peace was broken: a call from the street, and a rock smashed through the window, raining glass across the floor. I don't recall who was first out the door. I only remember that we all spilled into the street. There was Freddy standing in the middle of the street, like David against Goliath, shying bricks and shouting up at the windows of the house. There was Pickering, grabbing the housemaid, ordering her to fetch a bobby. There was Higgins, berating Freddy for throwing rocks at his windows. And there on the narrow balustrade outside Eliza's dormer window was the shadow of a man. He stepped this way and that in seeming indecision, seeking safe footing maybe, or a way down that did not involve joining the growing crowd in the street. There were footmen and housemaids with lanterns, and by this time one or two constables with whistles shrilly admonishing the intruder to descend, and Higgins taking down their language and sniggering at their accents, and me turning to ask Holmes if I should fetch my revolver and finding no Holmes there. Then suddenly Freddy launched himself at the side of the building and proceeded to scrabble his way up the brickwork toward the third floor, and people were shouting at him to get down before he'd break his bloody neck, and then Eliza was at her window staring down in blank amazement at the carnival in the street below, and the intruder disappearing like a puff of smoke, and Freddy all the way to the second floor before he indeed fell and had to be carried inside. Colonel Pickering on the hall phone berating Scotland Yard for not already having a flying squad on site. Mrs. Pearce scolding the housemaids for their shamelessness. Higgins swearing like a sailor. Eliza clattering down the stairs to come to Freddy's rescue. Then Holmes was at my side, drawing me away to whisper in my ear.

"All this excitement is unwarranted, Watson. They won't find the intruder."

"Did you see? He vanished like a ghost! Is he a man or a devil?"

"He had assistance, be sure of that." Holmes led me away from the confusion to the quiet of his own room. He opened the door and ushered me inside.

"This is your devil, Watson." He produced a purloined bottle of brandy from his coat pocket and tossed it to the fellow sitting on the bed. "He may have a few cuts and bruises that require your attention."

The devil on the bed saluted me and took a swig of brandy. "Got those shots you wanted, Dr. Watson," he said. "Didn't think I'd raise the household."

The devil on the bed was not the depraved, debauched, double-damned homunculus whose shadow loomed over Eliza Doolittle. It was Wiggins, examining his trusty Brownie to make certain it had suffered no damage.

"Fortunate for you that my window is adjacent to Miss Doolittle's, my lad," said Holmes cheerfully.

"Might have warned a bloke you had a watchdog posted, Doctor," said Wiggins.

"My apologies. It's not you he's on the watch for," I said. I touched a purple cut on his cheek. He flinched.

"I'm afraid I don't have my bag, as I'm traveling incognito. We'll have to make do with some of that brandy and one of Mr. Holmes' pocket handkerchiefs."

Wiggins laughed. "It's as we used to say back in the old days. 'No worries, Mr. Holmes has your back.' Doctor, I can have these pictures ready for you in two, three days. But why not let me manage the rest? I'll pass them round in the proper circles and let you know what hares we start, eh?"

I was doubly grateful to Wiggins now. I had little appetite for continuing my tour of London's wretched underbelly.

None of Wiggins's hurts turned out to be serious. I bandaged another cut on his hand and asked if I could bring him anything.

"We'll have to keep you here till the household has gone to bed, Wiggins. No more rooftop promenades for you this evening," said Holmes.

"I am a bit peckish," said Wiggins. "Would there be any kidney pie lyin' about? And a pint of bitter?"

When we came downstairs, Eliza was preparing Freddy for mummification, or so it appeared from the wealth of bandages she was applying. Freddy bore up under her tender ministrations with a look of dreamy delight. One of the maids was sweeping up the broken glass from the window, while Pickering tried to fit a bit of tile over the empty square. Higgins marched up and down the room, looking on fretfully.

"Stop coddling him, Eliza. He'll think he's done something heroic," he said with asperity.

"So he has done," she answered. "And very foolish it was, too," she said to Freddy sternly.

"Ah, the American contingent," said Higgins as we entered. "Where did you disappear to? I would have thought you'd be in the middle of all the excitement."

"I'm too old to climb walls, Perfesser," Holmes answered. "I was looking for this." So saying, he drew from his jacket a large, long-barreled revolver "You want to pick crows off a wire, a hogleg like this is what you need." I was as shocked as the rest of the company. In the old days Holmes had rarely carried anything more lethal than a sword-stick. He had left the firearms to me.

"I say, that's the ticket!" said Freddie, admiring the gun. "Where can a chap get hold of one of those?"

"When Freddie blows his brains out, it'll be your fault, Mr. Morello," Higgins chided.

"What I don't understand is what the fellow was doing skulking about the rooftops to begin with. Don't burglars these days have the patience to wait till everyone's abed?" said Pickering.

"Another admirer of Eliza's, no doubt," said Higgins. "Soon we'll have them crawling the walls like black beetles."

"None o' your mouth, 'Enry 'Iggins," said Eliza in a music-hall cockney accent, but her cheeks went red with pleasure.

"Perhaps we should call Dr. Guest to come look at you, Freddie," said Higgins.

Pickering vetoed that idea. "You bring that death's-head here tonight, Higgins, and I'll be forced to ask Mr. Morello for the loan of his firearm."

For his part Freddy seemed blissfully deaf to all voices but Eliza's.

She alternated soft words of praise for his courage with scorn for his foolishness. It seemed a good night for those who'd put their stake on Freddy, and a bad night for Dr. Guest's stock. The young man might have taken more advantage of it, but first he yawned, and then he snored. He was laid out on the settee and covered with a blanket. The electric lights were extinguished shortly after, and everyone went quietly to bed.

When the house was well asleep, I led Wiggins down the back stairs to the tradesman's door, I in my stocking feet and he in rubber-soled plimsols that made no sound. The door boasted more locks than a bank vault, but Wiggins produced an electric torch from his pocket, which helped make short work of them. The door creaked open and the night air spilled inside. Wiggins and I exchanged a comradely handshake and he slipped away.

Just like that, he slipped back in, his mouth against my ear. "Crusher!" he hissed. I peered out beyond him into the darkness of the mews. There was someone there, the shadow of a man walking up and down the alley, a familiar silhouette. It was not a constable's helmet on his head, however, but a battered top hat. Freddy! Did the fellow never sleep? I communicated as much to Wiggins. He gave a wry smile. He picked out a lump of coal from the coal scuttle and hefted it. Then he flung it down the alley, as hard and as far as he might. The coal hit a dustbin with a clang. A cat screamed. Freddy jumped, and ran toward the sound. Wiggins shot off in the opposite direction.

I locked the door, yawned mightily, and headed upstairs to my attic kip.

Chapter Fourteen

I had planned to sleep in the next morning, but woke restless in the early grey light, my body already habituated to my morning odysseys. I staggered down to the dining room only to find Holmes already astir, eating breakfast from the sideboard.

"A house full of sluggards. You and I are the first up." Holmes had been a famous sluggard himself in our Baker Street days, but life in the country seemed to have changed him.

I looked over the sideboard, trying to summon an appetite.

"The kippers are excellent," said Holmes. "Avoid the eggs at all cost."

"Oversalted again?"

"I believe they were cooked in castor oil."

I made my selections carefully and joined Holmes at the table.

"Wiggins get off all right?" he asked.

"Once he got past Argus-eyed Freddy."

Holmes seemed puzzled. "Freddy in the mews? You're sure?"

"I don't know when he sleeps. I wish I had half his energy."

"You do look haggard, Watson. Have I kept your nose to the grindstone too long?"

"I'm afraid I didn't sleep well last night. My roommate had an awful bout of indigestion and kept me up with his moaning and groaning. If I could have laid my hands on some of that castor oil, I'd have made short work of him."

"Nothing too serious, then."

"He took advantage of the excitement last night to liberate a plate of strawberry tarts from the pantry."

"Indeed? He didn't join the mob in the street?"

The kitchen maid entered with a pot of coffee. Holmes held out his cup and she refilled it. "Would you like tea, Mr. Barton?" she asked.

"No need, I'll have some of that coffee," I answered. She poured a cup for me.

"Bette?" Holmes stopped her as she was going out. "Have you seen the boy this morning?"

"Robert? Yes, sir, he's folding linen for Mrs. Pearce."

"Ask him to step in, please."

"Yes, sir."

I cast a questioning look at Holmes.

"Watson, do you remember the curious incident of the dog in the night?"

I did indeed. It was an important clue in one of our cases from the nineties. But before I could answer, Robert entered. He seemed no worse in the morning after his night of discomfort.

"Robert, Mr. Barton and I are going out this morning. Need you to brush off my dark suit and give a lick of polish to my black shoes."

"Yes, sir."

"And Mr. Barton's shoes, too. They're looking pretty sour."

"Yes, sir."

"Feeling alright, son? You look a little green around the gills."

"Quite well, sir."

"That plate of tarts didn't go down so well, though, eh?"

Robert cast his eyes to the floor, though I fancy he stole a sidelong glance at me.

"Don't worry, I won't snitch. A man's got to look out for himself. Shame you missed all the hubbub, though."

"I suppose so, sir."

"Weren't you curious?"

"No, sir," the boy mumbled.

"Burglars crawling around rooftops not your shine?"

The boy mumbled again.

"Especially when you're used to them, eh?"

Robert hung his head. Holmes had tumbled him somehow. "It's only business, sir. He's paid to keep his eye on her, he says."

"And he pays you to keep an eye on her, too?"

"Sometimes. Like wot I said, only business."

"Who pays him? Speak up and don't be scared."

"Shirley Combs of Scotland Yard. A famous detective, so he says, sir. Miss Eliza's a secret princess or some such, so he says, sir, wot needs watching."

I chuckled at the name "Shirley Combs." Fame does not merely fade away; first it must be pierced with a thousand darts of mortification. Robert shot me a hot look, as if I had questioned his veracity.

"He's not the only one, is he?" Holmes persisted.

"I seen some others about. Hard-eyed men. But they doesn't talk to me."

"What's this fellow look like, then?"

The boy described a man who could only be the attacker from Swandam Lane. "His looks makes my blood run cold, sir, but he gives good coin, does old Ned Hyde."

"Hyde?" Holmes rasped.

"Sir?"

"Edward Hyde?" Holmes's face went ashen.

"That's the chap, sir."

"Leave us. Hurry with the boots."

"Yes, sir. Sir?"

Holmes had already plunged into the deeps of thought, but he dragged himself back to the surface to give attention to the boy.

"Did you really strangle Gino Donati wif a piano wire, sir?"

"Mum's the word," answered Holmes, winking. The boy scampered away happily.

Holmes sat staring into space while I pushed my food about my plate. "Are we still going out, then?" I asked, when I could hold my tongue no longer.

Holmes slammed his palm upon the table and the cups jumped. "We are indeed, Watson. A most formal visit. Make sure you look your best. But first I must send a wire."

There was a new urgency in his voice, and a deep well of light behind his eyes. The gloom which had hung about him so long, like a December fog, had been swept away, as if the lumber room of his mind held no more cobwebs, no more scraps of warped or knotted wood, but only true, straight-stacked planks, planed to an exactness. Whatever sluggishness had attended his mental exercises before had vanished and would not return. And all, I guessed, because of the potency of that one name: Edward Hyde.

Holmes bounded upstairs. As I made to follow, Mrs. Pearce entered from the kitchen. Her eyes fell upon our half-eaten breakfasts.

"No appetite this morning, Mr. Barton?" she asked.

"Oh . . . I suppose not." I didn't want to lay charges against the cook.

"I'll ask Cook to make up a special batch just for you, sir." She gave me a conspiratorial wink, which seemed most unlike Mrs. Pearce.

My confusion must have been evident. "I heard you moving about last night," she said teasingly. "The strawberry tarts were my husband's favorite, too."

Enlightenment struck. Mrs. Pearce had apparently discovered the theft of the tarts, and laid blame for the crime upon my shoulders. I had not the heart to disabuse her of the notion. Besides, what favors could I not purchase from Robert with those tarts as my currency? I attempted to return her wink, though I may have only managed to blink.

The house was barely stirring when Holmes and I made our

departure. The streets were already busy with traffic, and we soon found a cab.

"Where to, sir?" the driver asked.

"Necropolis Station."

It didn't take a detective to guess who we were making our visit to, but my heart welled up when I heard those words. A fine cold mist lanced against our faces as we huddled into the cab.

Necropolis Station was as I remembered it. There were all the sights and sounds of any London railway station, yet the sounds were muffled and the hues muted. The latter no doubt was engendered by the fact that nearly all the passengers were dressed in mourning, even the golfers out for a cut-rate trip to Woking. There was silence in the chapel, and the quiet conversations were absorbed into the heavy padded furniture and thick carpets. Holmes and I sat silent in one of the waiting rooms, drinking chocolate until boarding time, each buried in our own thoughts.

It wasn't till we were on the train and our journey underway that I leaned toward Holmes to ask the question burning in my mind. "This fellow Hyde. It seemed you were familiar with the name."

Holmes looked at me as if considering how much to share with me. At last he asked, "Do you recall the Carew murder case?"

"Sir Danvers Carew? The M.P.? I remember it vaguely. Wasn't he robbed in the street? They never caught his killer. Must be over twenty years ago now."

"That was the story Scotland Yard fed to the papers, to stave off a panic. It was a ghastly affair. Bludgeoned to death with the head of a walking stick. We knew from the first who the murderer was. He had killed before, but this was the first time we had a witness to the attack. It was the whereabouts of the man that was the puzzle. The Yard should have had him in its net from the start. I found a dozen strong leads, which all turned inexplicably into blind alleys. He vanished into thin air."

"Slipped off to the continent, no doubt."

Holmes gave me a look full of disparagement. "If he'd fled to

Holland or France or Scotland or the Isle of Capri, we'd have known. We might not have been able to touch him, but we'd have known. I tell you the man vanished into thin air. He was well known in certain quarters, detested and feared by all who knew him. He had no friends to turn to and no ready money to make a run with. Yet we could not get a whisper of him. That man's name was Edward Hyde."

"Holmes! You're saying this is the same man? After all these years?" It seemed an outlandish proposition.

"I'm saying it is a name of ill omen, and a face from a nightmare. I've taken the liberty of calling in an old acquaintance to consult on the matter. But now our train is about to pull into the Necropolis, and we have our respects to pay."

Chapter Fifteen

The mystery of Miss Doolittle had driven it from my mind, but that day was the anniversary of a sad occasion, the death of our long-time, long-suffering landlady, Mrs. Hudson. She may have been the only soul on earth that Sherlock Holmes ever displayed simple genuine affection for, but he had been unable to attend her funeral, being detained in Montpellier on family business. When he had removed himself from his Baker Street rooms to the Sussex countryside, he had begged me to look after her, and I had done my best to honor my promise. I had urged her to sell the Baker Street house and come live with me, but she insisted on her independence, though she did hire a maid to see after chores she could no longer do herself. I caught a glimpse once of Mrs. Hudson's new tenants after Holmes had left: a young couple with one child toddling behind them and the other crying in a pram. They were entirely happy with the rooms, Mrs. Hudson told me, except for the occasional disturbances from visitors who insisted on seeing Mr. Sherlock Holmes, always on a matter of life and death. The couple assumed that Mr. Holmes had been a doctor, she said, and that he had passed away. She did not attempt to correct them on either count.

This was the first chance Holmes had to visit her grave. Brook-wood Cemetery, or the London Necropolis, as it had styled itself when its gates first opened fifty years ago, was meant to be frozen in a sort of eternal spring, so by design most of the trees planted there were evergreens. The main avenues of the cemetery were lined with tall stands of American redwood and sequoia like cathedral columns. There was a dark clump of magnolias close at hand, the rain beading off their waxen leaves. We stood together before a cold marble angel, hats in hand. The angel's finger pointed not heavenward but straight ahead, as if in accusation. Our cheeks were wet with the mist and the cold settled in our shoulders. There was a sough of wind through the wet grass.

"How did she make her end, Watson?"

We had both witnessed our share of sudden, violent death. We were less inured to death as it comes to the mass of humanity, like a thief in the night that first robs us of sight and hearing, and strength, and at last hope. "Her maid said that she had gone to bed early the night before, claiming tiredness. The next morning she was dead."

"Ah, that is something I have wanted for myself."

"An easy death?"

"To be tired."

We gave ourselves over to reminiscing about that good lady who had shared a part in so many of our adventures. As young men we had taken her good will and solicitude for granted, though we were perhaps the queerest lodgers any landlady ever admitted under her roof. But as the years went by, affection grew between us, and we took on something roughly in the shape of a family. I would never have got through the death of my dear Mary without her kindness.

I cannot say when I knew we were being spied upon. The green-sward about us sloped upward to the tree line. A man stood crouching among the low branches of a magnolia, watching us. He wore a dark frock coat and his face was shadowed by the foliage. There was a glint of light along the barrel of the revolver in his hand.

Holmes, whose back was to the stranger, had been recalling the unique talent Mrs. Hudson had revealed in the case of the Salisbury hunchback. Now he broke off, alive to the warning in my eyes. "What is it, Watson?"

"A man in the trees. Watching," I answered tersely.

"Ah, yes. He's been stalking us since Wimpole Street. And now we have lured him to this desolate spot, it's time we beard the lion." He started toward the trees, but I threw him to the ground as a shot rang out.

I found myself lying on top of Sherlock Holmes in the grass. "I should have said 'a man in the trees *with a gun* watching.'" He grunted in agreement as I rolled off him. We both dove behind Mrs. Hudson's angel as another shot whistled over our heads.

"Mrs. Hudson would undoubtedly disapprove of this untidy state of affairs," said Holmes.

I stared at him in amazement. Either he had the coolest nerve of any man I ever met or else he had descended into senility. Another shot exploded; the bullet ricocheted off the angel's wingtip. "You wouldn't happen to have your service revolver about you?" Holmes asked. I was panting too hard to answer, but I threw up my hands helplessly.

"Then we must wait," he said. He did not say what we must wait upon.

"Who is it?" I asked.

"I believe I can reduce the number of possible instigators to a round dozen, but further intelligence must wait upon our rescue."

Another shot rang out. We huddled closer together behind our granite redoubt.

"What if I try to work my way around behind him?" I said.

"You will be shot. Patience, Watson."

At that moment along the path behind the magnolias appeared a stocky, white-haired, rubicund old duffer dressed as a country gentleman in a Norfolk jacket and gaiters, a shillelagh in hand and a pipe in his mouth. He looked as if he had wandered in from the nearby golf course, looking for a misplayed ball. As another shot was fired, he leaned nonchalantly against a gravestone, knocked the dottle from his pipe, and drew a pistol from his coat pocket as casually as if it were the *Sunday Times*. Then the mask of suburban complacence fell away.

"Scotland Yard!" he barked. "Drop your weapon!"

The man in the trees twisted swift as an adder and shot. But his shot was hurried and went wide. The old fellow returned his fire, and the assassin tumbled from the tree with a cry. He hit the ground, rose jerkily, and aimed. Then he seemed to crumble like a sand castle: trigger finger first, then in waves from his wrists to his shoulders, the torso cascading into his knees, till there was only the surprised look on his face; then, that too dissolved.

The old man lowered his gun and started toward the assassin. Holmes and I got to our feet and collected ourselves. My knees creaked as I straightened up.

Holmes signaled a thumbs-up to our rescuer.

"Holmes! You know him?" The conjurer at work again.

"I invited him." Holmes chuckled. We joined the old fellow, who was crouching over the wounded man, holding his wrist. The man's lips were working, endeavoring to speak, but a pink froth bubbled from his lips and his eyes stared into eternity.

"Damn damn damn damn. I fear I've killed him, Mr. Holmes." He dropped the man's limp hand.

"He spoke to you," said Holmes eagerly.

"Wasn't any of it English," the man from Scotland Yard answered. "There was only one word I understood: 'Vendetta.' He said it more than once."

"Is there any hope, Watson?"

I opened the man's coat and peeled back his blood-soaked shirt-front. I probed for the wound. I shook my head. When I found the hole I winced. "Turn him over," I said. "Gently. He's drowning in his own blood." The other two turned the man on his side as I worked to stop the bleeding.

But my efforts to stanch the wound were in vain, as I knew they must be. The inspector's shot had perforated a lung. The man stiffened suddenly, and then slumped over in Holmes's arms. We laid him down to face the sky. I wiped the mess from my hands on the wet grass.

"I'm sorry," said the old man. "I don't like to kill a man, especially a young man."

"He gave you no choice. Watson, you remember George Newcomen?"

Indeed I remembered Inspector Newcomen. He had been among that small cadre of young Scotland Yard detectives who were not ashamed to throw up their hands and seek assistance from Sherlock Holmes when they got in over their heads. Whether I truly recognized the young, zealous inspector in this blear-eyed, grizzled old man with hunched shoulders, or simply recognized in him the dour attitude of a career police officer, I am not certain. He shook my hand eagerly enough, the admiration in his eyes reminding me that I had once myself been celebrated in certain circles.

"If the man can't talk, perhaps the body will," the inspector commented philosophically. He started going through the man's pockets, searching for clues. "Did you know him, Mr. Holmes?"

"Not I," Holmes answered. "Hello? What's this?"

The inspector had pulled a blood-spattered paper from the man's coat pocket. He peered at the writing. "It's Greek to me," he said. He handed the paper to Holmes.

"Italian, I would say," Holmes corrected.

I peered over his shoulder at the letter. There were only a couple of paragraphs, partially obscured by blood. I couldn't recall whether Holmes knew Italian. "Can you make anything of it?" I asked.

"Enough to know it's of little use to us. It's a letter from a girl named Susanna to a man named Piero. That must be this fellow. She pleads with him to come home soon. And she warns him to look out for someone named Carlo. Probably a rival." He handed the letter to the inspector.

"That word 'vendetta.' It don't take a scholar to parse that one, Mr. Holmes."

"Indeed, Inspector. He was almost certainly a member of one of our Italian crime societies."

"On a mission of revenge. Against you?"

"I rather fancy someone else."

"Always something knotty with Mr. Holmes. Is this why you invited me to Brookwood on a Saturday morning?"

"No, but I'm grateful you came along just when you did."

Newcomen flashed his gun again, alert. A young man in work clothes came crashing through the trees. He stopped like a stone a few yards above us, seeing the gun leveled at him. His face was pale under dark curls, and a vein beat on his forehead. "I hear the—the gunshots," he said falteringly.

"This is a police matter. Who might you be? Friend of this chap?"

"I'm assistant . . . caretaker here. Is—is he dead?" He crouched over the body in morbid fascination, unable to tear his eyes away.

"You should have seen enough corpses to know," said Holmes.

"I'm not used to 'em this fresh, sir, am I?" the young man answered with a sob in his throat.

Newcomen strode over to the young man and clamped a hand on his shoulder. "What's your name?"

"Charlie, sir."

"Charlie, is there a telephone nearby?"

"There's one in the chapel of the souls. Not so far." He made a vague gesture up the path.

"Charlie, I need you to get to that phone quick as ever you can, and call the metropolitan police. Can you manage that?'

The young man rose and mopped his face with his kerchief. "Right you are, sir. I go."

"Good lad."

Charlie bounded off among the tombs, leaving us alone.

"Well, gentlemen, it looks like we're in for a bit of a wait. Now we can talk, Mr. Holmes. There's shelter beneath the trees."

"I'm afraid not, Inspector. I deem it essential that we depart from this spot with all due expedition," said Holmes.

"We can't leave the scene of a shooting. And we still need to learn this boy-o's identity."

"We can learn all we need to know by simple observation. Watson, let me direct your attention in particular to the young man's wardrobe. But this is of more immediate concern." He reached into the corpse's shirtfront and lifted out a medallion hung round his neck. I had noticed it before, but did not assign it any importance. "Santa Rusulia, patron saint of Palermo, in Sicily."

"We knew he was Italian," Newcomen reminded him.

"Yes, but did you not observe that your young grave-digger wore the same medallion? It was hanging from his neck while he leaned over the body. When Charlie—or I should say Carlo—returns, he will neither be alone nor with the police. We are not equipped to deal with a gang of these men. I only hope we are not being watched now."

Chapter Sixteen

—◦◦◦—

Further debate was moot. "If we make for the tree line to the west, we'll come upon the railway," said Newcomen. We began to move.

"I would suggest we remove our shoes," said Holmes. "Make it harder for our foes to track us."

Were there any more watchers in the trees, the sight of three old men in their stocking feet snaking their way single file through the wet grass among the graves must have moved them to laughter. We were fortunate enough to face no further opposition. Holmes and I were soon drying our toes in the station bar, sealed inside from the rain. The sign above the bar proclaimed "Spirits served here" in tongue-in-cheek fashion, but we contented ourselves with tea and toast. After the inspector made a couple of phone calls, he joined us. "I've called the Yard to recover the body," he said.

"They will not find it," Holmes answered. He stirred his tea absently.

"Always darkest with Mr. Holmes," chuckled the inspector. "Is this what you wanted to meet about? Your telegram only mentioned a case from the past."

"I wired you because you're the Yard's foremost authority on Edward Hyde."

The inspector blanched. "Why blacken the day with that name?"

"Because I fear he has returned."

A curious look came into Newcomen's eye. He drummed his fingers on the tabletop. Then it seemed he arrived at some resolution. "I can set your fears to rest on that score," he said. "Edward Hyde is dead."

"Dead?" It hit Holmes like a hammer blow. "Whence comes this news?"

"I saw him myself in the cabinet of Dr. Henry Jekyll, lying on his back, with his limbs curled up grotesquely above him, as if he were some sort of insect. He had taken—or been given—a massive dose of poison. It was August . . . the fifth, I think. Eighteen-eighty-five."

The news obviously caught Sherlock Holmes unawares, a position as repugnant to him as it was unaccustomed. His pride had always been rooted in superior knowledge. He drew back stiffly in his chair. "I was never informed," he said. It was meant as censure.

"No . . . er, the public weren't supposed to know," Newcomen answered uncomfortably. "Sir Edmund forbade us from telling anyone. Anyone at all. We hoped then that we could lure Henry Jekyll out of hiding, if he were still alive. But it's twenty-five years ago now. Jekyll never reappeared, Sir Edmund is in his grave, and we are in our dotage."

"You're certain it was Hyde?" Holmes asked sharply. The revelation had sorely wounded his amour propre.

"The body was identified by the lawyer Mr. Utterson and Jekyll's butler. Both men had had dealings with Hyde when alive."

"So we know Hyde is dead," I concluded.

Holmes gave me a look of pure vinegar. "We know a man *identified* as Hyde is dead."

"You think Utterson and the butler lied?" asked Newcomen, incredulous. "To protect Edward Hyde?"

"They may have lied to protect Jekyll. Who by all accounts did have some reason to protect Hyde."

"Who is—or who was—Jekyll?" I asked.

Holmes clapped his hands together. "A question for the ages, Watson. Dr. Henry Jekyll. Paragon of respectability. Pillar of the community. Friend of the great. But he was also somehow a patron of Edward Hyde. It was my theory Hyde was in the way of acquiring certain pharmaceutical substances for the good doctor's rather outré researches."

"It was Mr. Holmes who first put us on to Jekyll," said Newcomen, by way of apology. "We kept a sharp eye on him. We were sure Hyde would try to contact him sooner or later. Then the strangest thing of all occurred. The day Hyde reappeared—dead—was the same day Henry Jekyll vanished from the earth."

"Another piece of the puzzle I was not vouchsafed!" said Holmes, his bitterness renewed.

"Well, now you know as much as I do," said the inspector, trying to salve my friend's feelings. "But what's all this about, Mr. Holmes? Is it something the Yard needs to fret over?"

Holmes told him then all we knew about the emergence of the man named Ned Hyde, so like his namesake in every frightening aspect. At his urging, I added my own brief impression of the man.

"Quite a story, gentlemen," said Newcomen when we concluded, "and I wouldn't give it much credit if it didn't come from Holmes and Watson. Sounds like our man from the eighties has an admirer."

"Which would not explain the physical resemblance Dr. Watson reported," Holmes countered.

Newcomen looked uncomfortable.

"Perhaps . . . perhaps it's his son," I ventured.

"There now!" cried Newcomen. "Dr. Watson has sussed it out! Most logical, too. Hyde the Younger."

Holmes said nothing, but I could see that he was reluctant to accept such a singular proposition. The idea of Hyde as a paterfamilias embracing his domestic duties was hard to square with what we knew of the man. Yet even scorpions breed.

"Well, son or nephew or cousin, the fellow hasn't popped up in any police reports so far as I know, certainly not under that blighted name," Newcomen concluded. "Any known associates?"

"One," said Holmes. "The murderess Betsy Chubb."

The inspector whistled through his teeth. "I'm glad you retired, Mr. Holmes," he said. "My heart couldn't take the excitement of working with you every day. Dr. Watson, my hat's off to you."

Holmes set the comment aside. "What can you tell me about the girl Nancy Kelly, who has followed in the footsteps of Miss Chubb?"

"A bad business, that. The Home Office is threatening the commissioner's job if this spree continues."

"What defense has she offered?"

"No blasted memory of any of it, same as the other two."

"Two?" Holmes seized on the word like a hawk.

"Ah! You're unaware of the case of Susan Wallace?" asked Newcomen, glad to have news to share. "We've just laid our hands on her. Murdered four men in a pub down by the docks, she did. Middle of the afternoon."

"And remembers nothing of it?"

"Even worse than that, she had no connection with the murdered men whatever. They were Norwegian sailors off a coal tender. First time in jolly old England. It's got them spooked along the waterfront, I can tell you."

"Was she acquainted with the other girls?"

"Says not. But Chubb and Kelly once shared rooms in Angel Court with a third girl. Wallace, it turns out, was the landlord's daughter." He looked at Holmes searchingly. "Does that shine any light on the business?"

"On the contrary, I confess it throws a new layer of obscurity on the problem. But then it is always darkest before the dawn."

The name of Angel Court had a familiar ring. Though I could not place it then and there, it clawed at the back of my mind for days.

"Right, then. Now it's my innings. Why are underground assassins on the trail of Sherlock Holmes, who retired from the world a decade ago?"

"A case of mistaken identity, I believe. Their quarrel is not with me, but a man named Morello."

"And who's Mr. Morello when he's at home?" Newcomen asked.

"When at home, he is head of one of the most powerful crime families in New York City. But at present the New York police are holding him incognito in the Tombs, and have put out the story that he's been kidnapped by a rival gang. They expect great things from this stratagem."

"Which you suggested to them?" Newcomen's eyes twinkled.

"Inspector! You know I'm retired. I merely took advantage of Mr. Morello's enforced sabbatical to clothe myself in his gaudy raiment."

"Sounds a risky play. Always thought those disguises might land you in hot water someday."

Holmes made a wry face. "In hindsight, I am forced to agree."

There was no more information to be got out of Newcomen except news of his wife and family, which seemed to include an indecent number of grandchildren. He bade us farewell at the station, returning in the fly to his own home in nearby Woking.

We were soon steaming through the fields on our way back to London. I was bursting with questions for Holmes, but as soon as we were settled in our car, he drew his hat down over his eyes and fell fast asleep. It may seem absurd, but the truth is that I had never laid eyes on Holmes asleep before in all my life. There was something uncanny about it, as if the locomotive had stopped in midstroke, or the tide had ceased its restless rocking.

I had only my own thoughts to fall back on, and they were bleak enough. I thought about Newcomen, his children and grandchildren, and found that I was jealous. I thought about Edward Hyde—father and son? Sherlock Holmes would not pass his genius on to the next generation. Nor would Higgins or Pickering bequeath their amazing talents to posterity. Even humble Dr. John Watson would die childless. We were a society of bachelors, with tepid water in our veins. The new century would be peopled by a generation of Hydes, with only slow-witted policemen and their issue to stem the flood of savagery.

When we pulled into the station, Holmes sat up and tipped his hat back to reveal a gaze so steady and alert that I wondered if he had ever been asleep. The gears of deduction were once again fully engaged.

The rain had lifted, though it left the air raw. Holmes suggested we walk. We were crossing the Hungerford Bridge, huddled in our coats, and Big Ben chiming the noon hour when my mind flew back to the assassin in the graveyard.

"What did you mean about the young man's clothes?" I asked.

Holmes halted upon the bridge. "Ah, yes, the clothes. I wondered when we'd come back to that. What did you observe, Watson?"

"Nothing." My eyes smarted as the wind whipped against my face. I wanted to keep moving, but Holmes was rooted in place.

"Come now. Apply my methods. Describe him."

I tried to summon up the image. "He was dressed as a young man about town. Grey lounge jacket, spongebag trousers, toothpick shoes, gloves—nothing out of the ordinary."

"Nothing out of the ordinary if he is a young man about town. But hardly the uniform of a clandestine assassin."

"I grant you that." It seemed a ridiculous thing to fuss over. There was no uniform for assassins. "Can we go on now?" I meant it literally, and matched the act to the word.

But Holmes remained behind, calling to me: "Here is the question you ought to ask. Who told these fellows that G.B. Morello was in London? It's not as if it were announced in the *Times*."

I swirled about to face him for a moment. "Hyde could have told them!" I flung at him, continuing my march.

Holmes caught up with me in long strides. "You know better than that. This Hyde is a solitary creature. He has no confederates. Nor would the *fratelli* be likely to trust him."

I studied the sharp contours of his face, the eyes that seemed to see beyond the horizon. "Then there is yet another agent of destruction at work upon our ruin?" I asked.

"We shall be fortunate if there be only one."

We stepped off the bridge onto the Embankment. After our brush with death in the peaceful atmosphere of Surrey, I had felt relieved to get back to the bustling familiarity of London. I had not considered that danger might now crowd in from every corner.

"What must we do now?"

We walked on in silence for a bit. I imagined Holmes painting one scenario after another upon the canvas of his mind. He stopped and seemed to sniff the air.

"Lunch, I think."

Lunch we did.

Chapter Seventeen

ate afternoon saw us back at Wimpole Street. As we turned the corner and gained sight of 27A, Holmes took hold of my arm and stopped me. He spoke quietly: "Now, Watson, quickly. Tell me what you see."

"The Higgins residence," I answered in staccato report. "The door is shut. Nothing stirs the curtains in the windows. Wisps of smoke from the chimney pots."

"And in the street?"

"A tinker passing with his pack. A hackney cab moving down the street at a slow clop. A pair of schoolboys arguing yesterday's cricket match. And yes"—as he prodded me—"I do see Freddy at his post."

"Do you not find it remarkable that he can be found there day or night, rain or shine?"

I remembered Freddy's midnight patrol in the mews the night I had thought him asleep on the settee. "Love breeds fortitude in young men," I offered half-heartedly.

"A sterling platitude. But are you certain it's Freddy? Observe the wardrobe."

There was nothing remarkable in Freddy's clothing. It was the uniform of the flaneur—lounge jacket, spongebag trousers, toothpick shoes, gloves—my knees nearly buckled. "Holmes! The assassin! He wore the same outfit."

Holmes nodded, grinning. "One of the hard-eyed men young Robert mentioned. And unless I miss my guess, this is another of his ilk. It was obvious from the beginning the house was under watch, and by someone far more clever than Freddy. Our expedition this morning was meant to draw them out. I was not expecting quite the level of success that we experienced."

"How shall we take him?"

"Ever the bulldog. No, Watson, he is but a little fish. If his master has not yet been apprised of this morning's failure, this one will scud off to tell him the news. Our secret adversary will soon become desperate, and then we shall have him in our grasp."

Holmes strode forward, pulling me along. "Freddy" must have recognized us as we neared, for he swung away on his heel and retreated down the road, twirling his stick and whistling a music hall tune. It was so admirable a performance that Holmes laughed as we mounted the steps and went in.

"Where the devil have you two been all day?" Higgins was upon us in a moment, like a schoolmaster eager to give his charges a caning. "I woke up this morning and there was nary a soul in the house!" By this of course, he meant that he had fallen out of bed at noon to find only the half-dozen usual servants, all of whom presumably owned souls. "Where's Eliza?"

We looked at him dumbfounded. "I haven't got her in my pocket," Holmes drawled.

"No, but I dare say you'd like to," Higgins said sneeringly.

Holmes stopped cold in the act of lighting a cigar, the vesta burning in his fingers. His eyes flashed fire. "You want to elaborate on that?" he said quietly.

I shudder to think what might have happened had I not been there. Holmes has the world's longest fuse, but his powder is black.

"Perhaps the colonel and Miss Doolittle went out to take the morning air," I said fatuously.

"Morning air!" sniffed Higgins. "It's killed more people than the cholera. Mr. Morello, you shall take the afternoon air, and the evening air, and I hazard to say the midnight air tonight in this laboratory. You will make progress today, sir, this I vow."

Holmes lit his cigar and barked a laugh. He still spoke not a word, but I could see that his dangerous mood had passed. I took this as a signal my services would not be needed that afternoon, and attempted to slip quietly from the room. But Higgins turned on me imperiously: "As for you, you blackguard," he said, "find Pickering!"

With nothing else on my plate, and no wish to be subjected to further tirades from the professor, I decided to go look for Pickering after all. Knowing Pixie's habits, I inquired of Mrs. Pearce where the closest two or three bookstalls were to be found. This led to a chin-wag on the state of modern literature. Mrs. Pearce thought novels the worst habit of idle young ladies, but she was an avid reader of poetry, and could recite "Dover Beach" by heart. We both preferred Ruskin to Hazlitt. At length she wrote down some directions for me, and I jour-neyed forth to find the colonel. I had done better by far to stay indoors and treat Mrs. Pearce to my dramatic rendition of "My Last Duchess."

I had already tried the first shop and come up empty-handed and was approaching the second when I thought I spied Freddy coming down the street toward me in the company of another man. I should have been on my guard. As I raised my hand to greet him, I was snatched by the collar and slung like a grain sack into the shadows of the alley behind the shop. I was slammed against a brick wall and felt the breath whistle out of me.

At first there seemed a dozen of them, moving everywhere at once in a clickety marionette cadence, like spiders securing the corners of a web, but as my sight cleared, I counted four: all Freddies. There was a Freddy pinning my left arm, and one on my right, a Freddy standing lookout, and the another with a knife pressed against my Adam's apple, and all of them were Freddies. I mean to say they were all young men identically dressed in the kind of clothes Freddy might wear, even to the dented top hat. Their faces were all nearly identical as well, but not at all like Freddy: olive-complected, with dark angry eyes and cruel mouths. These were the "hard-eyed men" Robert had described. I was utterly at their mercy.

Looming before me was the man undoubtedly their chief, though he resembled them no more than the hawk does the crow. His countenance was pale, with thin bloodless lips beneath a hussar's moustache. His grey hair was cropped close under a bowler hat. His eyes were a calm grey sea beneath the welkin of heavy brows. He was carapaced like a turtle in a caped astrakhan greatcoat with blinding brass buttons. He paced back and forth in front of me, a malacca laid casually across his shoulder. He was watching me, waiting for me to come to my senses. Then he began:

"Attention, please!" he rasped, in a thick German accent. "I have a message for your master."

Sherlock Holmes or Henry Higgins could have placed the accent within any of a score of petty principalities, and perhaps to the very village and street he had been born in. But they had not the disadvantage of six inches of cold Sheffield steel at their throats to distract them.

"I have no master but the king of England, sir. Please remove your hands from my person." I meant to show defiance, but my voice quavered like a dove's.

Quick as thought, the malacca whipped around and cracked against my temple. Fireworks exploded before my eyes. Were it not for the Freddies holding my wrists, I would have dropped to the pavement in a dead faint. "Attention, please! I speak of your employer, the Italian Morello, who attempts to seduce the fraulein Eliza Doolittle."

"My employer is not seducing any fraulein." I was dazed, but I was certain of that much.

"I have studied the courtship rituals of the English. I have seen him with the fraulein. They take the walks together, the afternoon rides in the park. They share the tender looks."

The idea of Holmes in a romantic engagement with any young

lady was risible. In less dire circumstances I would have laughed. "You have confused him with the young gentleman. Mr. Eynsford-Hill."

"You think I do not know Herr Freddy?" He said something in Italian to his four accomplices. They all laughed. "They speak no English," he said as an aside. "The young gentleman Herr Freddy is inept and entirely unworthy, but he is a gentleman. I have challenged him to a duel."

"Freddie? In a duel?"

"*Ach*. I know, the outcome is inevitable. But we must observe the proprieties." He said it as calmly as if he were a broker touting shares. The man was stark raving mad.

"Who *are* you?" I asked, incredulous.

I swear he winked at me. "I am the great detective Sherlock Holmes."

"You are not!" I cried shrilly. The sheer inanity of his answer infuriated me.

But he meant to torment me. "*Ach*. Of this you are certain? You have met Herr Holmes? You are intimate friends?"

"Sherlock Holmes is English!"

"A common mistake. Because I speak English like the native."

"And who are these ruffians then? Baker Street Irregulars?"

"Alas, no. I make do. These young men are in fact partisans of Don Salvatore Maranzano. Perhaps you have never heard of this man, but your employer knows and fears him. They are sworn to Signor Morello's death. And now you have murdered their brother, Piero. Unfortunate."

"He shot at us!"

The German shrugged. "In his eagerness, he exceeded his orders, *ja*. These Italians are more accustomed to the knife than the gun. His brothers have forgiven his sin, but they cry out for the blood of his killers."

"Then kill me," I said, but it was a feeble retort.

"*Ach, nein*. If I kill you, I should have no one to deliver my message. These partisans still obey me. But their instincts are for anarchy. That is the nature of their race. I cannot restrain them much further. But murder is undiplomatic. It draws too much official attention. I prefer that your Mr. Morello should live. Tell him therefore he must flee for his life. Time is of the essence. You can remember that, *ja*? You will tell him? Now: do you know the German word which translates as 'pig-dog'?"

I was utterly mystified, but I nodded.

"These men also know that word. It is the entirety of their German vocabulary. It is not my wish to turn you over to them, but they are expecting it. Your one hope of survival is to call me 'pig-dog' as loud as you might."

"Pig-dog?" I repeated in disbelief.

"In German. Now, if—you—please!"

"*Schweinhund*!" I cried.

The effect was immediate. The malacca whistled round again. But it was not my face it struck. The stick cracked against the knife-man's hand. He shrieked and dropped the blade. In their momentary shock, the other two Freddies lost their grip on my wrists. I flung myself to the ground. They went for me, but I went for the knife and came up first, slicing at the air. They fell back and I ran. The lookout tried to stop me, but I barreled past him. I believe I may have left the knife in his shoulder.

I lurched down the street with two of them at my heels. My head felt light, but my legs were like lead. I heard footsteps drumming behind me, but could not turn to look. At some point I came up against a shop window and stopped, beating on the transom in a frenzy. I remember the shopman's frozen face, then—wonder of wonders!—Pickering and Eliza staring out at me in blank disbelief. There were hands laid upon me and I felt myself drowning. From somewhere came a high piercing whistle, and shouting. A flash of lightning forked across my sight, and then I knew no more.

Chapter Eighteen

There were voices rolling about in my head, clacking together like a monk's beads. My head throbbed in time with them. The first voice, a tenor tripping across the staff, that was Pickering, then the other, a soubrette, light and airy—and yet a third voice intruding, and from its gravelly steadiness, I marked it as a police constable's—the second voice returning, lips and then eyes full of tender concern, and that was Eliza.

I was in the bookshop, dusty yellow shelves suspended above me. There was a bandage wrapped round my forehead, threatening to slip down over my eye. Pickering leaned over me from one side, Eliza from the other, till their heads almost touched. Between them stood a police constable sawing at his notebook with a pencil. The bookseller hovered at his table off in the distance, shuffling papers like Jove's thunderbolts.

"Here he is come round, constable. I told you he was a tough old bird," said Pickering.

"Sir, can you hear me?" asked the constable, waving a hand in front of my eyes like a flock of pigeons.

I was sunk deep in a horsehide armchair whose springs had long ago collapsed. I tried to rouse up. The pain hit me like a shot.

"Do you know who it was attacked you, sir?"

Who had he been? Not one of those comic-opera courtiers wearing monocles, with scarlet sashes across their fronts, or generals with gold braids and barrel-organ chests that I had imagined when Pickering first mentioned foreign spies. No one had posed the possibility of a quietly efficient killer in an astrakhan and bowler hat.

"German." The single word exhausted me.

"Yes, sir. Couple of your foreign cutpurses, then?" The constable sounded bored.

"They were dressed as gentleman, I thought," said Eliza.

I nodded vigorously, working my lips.

"Calm down, old thing," said Pickering. "You'll have a stroke."

My mind was a chaos. How could I say anything in front of Miss Doolittle that would not expose our entire enterprise to her? I couldn't even give the constable my proper name.

Pickering must have fathomed my predicament. He beckoned to the constable and led him outside to talk. The bookseller followed, full of imagined importance.

Eliza put her hand in mine, soft and warm. In that moment I realized that whatever the threat she faced, she would have my absolute protection, whether she proved a duchess or a bawd.

"Poor Mr. Barton. How do you feel?"

I smiled feebly. I may have spoken, but my words were less than a whisper. I touched my cheek where the wound still stung.

"You'll have some bruises. Mr. Barton, I don't know how you ever got tangled up with that Mr. Morello. You're like Colonel Pickering. Innocent of the world."

Innocent, thought I! I could tell her stories of London's criminal underworld that would curdle her blood. And any man who has been with the army in India and Afghanistan has seen enough mayhem to last a lifetime.

I found my voice at last. "I know what danger is, Miss."

"I don't question your courage. But you walk down every street as if it were your own garden walk, and you greet every stranger as if he were your neighbor. You have to be a woman alone in the streets to know what a devil a man may be."

"You've nothing to fear from a gentleman."

"Few gentlemen are gentle."

"There are brutes in the world, I know." Indeed I had seen them, countless numbers of them, wives and sweethearts in the wards of the Women's Hospital of a Saturday night, bruised and bleeding from the loving ministrations of their helpmates. I thought of Eliza and her trysts with Hyde. "But some women let themselves be brutalized. Even invite it."

Eliza colored. "The brute fears every shadow in the dark, every whisper in the night, like a wild thing that scents the hunter. It's the fear in their eyes that draws us to them."

"You have protectors now, Miss."

She looked at me searchingly. "Perhaps I do." She withdrew her hand from mine and straightened up. I felt faint again and shut my eyes.

"Tell the colonel I had a little errand to run," I heard her say.

"Wobbs?"

I opened my eyes. Eliza had vanished. Pickering stood in her place. I saw the misgiving in his face. "I fear I may have put you and your friend in a bad spot."

The German's threats flooded back upon me. "I've got to get back. Warn Holmes." I struggled to my feet, but the world still heeled and yawed away from me.

"Here, take my arm, there's a good fellow. Where's Eliza?"

It was but a short distance to Wimpole Street, but in light of my weakness, Pickering elected to hire a cab. He had purchased several books, and he held them on his lap, stroking their spines fondly.

"Look what I found at Trelawny's. A monograph here written by your friend cataloguing two hundred and forty-three different types of tobacco ash. Can't wait to dive into that one."

When we arrived at Wimpole Street, Mrs. Pearce took one look at me before she hustled me into the kitchen for repeated applications of vinegar and brown paper to my bruises. The cool efficiency of her ministrations drew the pain from me. She seemed an indispensable sort of woman, a ministering angel.

Higgins caught Pickering in the hall. "Where's Eliza?" we heard him snarl.

"Running errands. Shopping. Swimming the Channel. What do you need Eliza for?" he asked cheerfully.

"I do not need Eliza. I don't need anyone. I am entirely self-sufficient. But after last night, I'm beginning to think Eliza needs looking after. What if that second-story man is lurking about, ready to knock her down in the street and snatch her jewels?"

Holmes's voice joined in: "I never seen that girl wearing jewels."

"Mr. Morello, get back in the laboratory and resume the exercise!"

His anxiety soon reached a fever pitch. He called Robert and the housemaids on the carpet. They bore his abuse in silence. He came barging into the kitchen to berate Mrs. Pearce over the matter. What he made of my head wrapped up in brown paper like Ramses's mummy I have no idea. Mrs. Pearce was having none of it, and scolded him like a schoolboy. He held his tongue under her instruction, but his face turned purple with indignation.

Then Miss Doolittle walked into the kitchen, unpinning her hat. "Are you better, Mr. Barton?" she asked pleasantly. Her face was red and her hat askew. The hem of her dress was heavy with dust.

"Where have you been?" thundered Higgins.

"Don't bully me!" she cried, and ran from the room. We heard her on the stair, her door slamming, then silence. The air seemed to have been sucked out of the room. Pickering and Holmes stuck their heads in the door. Higgins looked about him at the crowd he had gathered.

"Did she seem upset?" he asked innocently.

Chapter Nineteen

We did not see Eliza again until dinnertime. She entered quietly, greeting us with a nod and a murmur, and took her place. Her face was pale, her eyes dull, but she seemed to be trying to put a brave face on whatever was troubling her. She thanked the servants when they brought her anything, and answered any questions that were set to her. But her answers were short and spiritless, discouraging any conversation. When left to herself, she lapsed into silence.

For his part, Higgins went to work trying to trip up Holmes. He had played this game before, mentioning different obscure parts of London, or restaurants or shops, and asking Mr. Morello's opinion of them. Holmes was voluble on the subjects of Buckingham Palace and Big Ben, but shrugged mulishly whenever Higgins mentioned any but the most famous landmarks of the city. Then he bragged about the wonders of Brooklyn, New York, waxing poetic on the Soldier's Arch and the Brooklyn Firehouse.

After Mrs. Pearce had mended my hurts, which Pickering put about were the result of a run-in with a foreign strong-arm, she had ordered me up to my room for bedrest and complete isolation. Holmes had been able to sneak in for only the briefest exchange before the upstairs maid ran him off. It was not until after dinner that I could fill him in on the details. He listened intently to the story of my attack.

"Watson, you're dealing with a muddleheaded fool!"

"He seemed exceptionally clearheaded to me," I answered drily.

"Oh, not our friend the German, but this old fool of a detective. I misjudged the swiftness of his retaliation. It nearly led to your death, and that is my fault entirely."

I shrugged off that aspect of the matter. Courage grows as peril recedes. There was something else that bothered me.

"He accused you of—he said that you and Miss Doolittle had been . . . well, he said you had been wooing her."

"Of course I have."

His answer took me aback. "Well . . . do you think it seemly?"

"My dear Watson, there are only two women in this house who can tell me anything at all about Miss Doolittle's past, real or imagined—Mrs. Pearce and Miss Doolittle herself. Miss Doolittle likes older men and is especially attracted to the criminal type, perhaps as a result of her upbringing. She admires brutality. She believes I am 'on the lam,' as they say in American gangster parlance, a notion which she finds particularly romantic. Mrs. Pearce, on the other hand, is convinced I mean to murder the household in their beds. I have been hoping you might throw your lackadaisical courtship of the woman into high gear. We must acquire data by any means possible."

I erupted in anger. "One does not bandy with a lady's affections!"

"Watson! How many housemaids and governesses and widows have I courted over the years, even betrothed myself to, merely to place myself in the confidences of these women, to learn the secrets which could aid me in my work? And all of them eager to give themselves up to Holmes the constable, or Holmes the navvy, Holmes the sailor or candlestick maker for the mere hope of attention from a man who exists almost entirely in their imaginations? Show me a woman with both feet on the ground, with heart and mind devoted to hearth and home, never listening for the knock at the door that presages her abduction by a gypsy prince or a shepherd out of Arcady! And you wonder at my contempt for the fair sex."

"Then tell me what you've learned by wooing Eliza Doolittle?"

"That she is not a lady! She may be a princess, for princesses do not abide by the suffocating rules of middle-class ladies. She may be a Covent Garden flower girl or an actress, or a scarlet woman, but she is no lady. Ladies do not flirt and they do not take carriage rides with Americans of doubtful reputation. Ladies do not do anything but simper or bleat like sheep. And because Eliza is not a lady and therefore is unafraid to speak her mind and exert her will, we have hope of learning what she is."

I retreated into a stubborn silence. I did not want to believe that Holmes was doing wrong. But I did believe it. Had I indeed entertained the idea of courting Mrs. Pearce? It was ludicrous. Two people in the twilight of life, disporting themselves like fond youngsters. And yet, looking back, I confess to the impulse, though I had buried it before it even became a full-fledged notion. But Holmes's blistering diatribe was beyond the pale.

"Forgive me, Watson. I know you for a man of tender feeling, who has always been careful where he disposes his affections. But I have seen women in the madhouse with all the manner of a bishop's wife or a princess of the blood, who would cut your throat with a paring knife if once you turned your back on them. Indeed, I—"

But here he fell silent, no doubt realizing that further argument could only harm his case with me. He let it stew for a bit. "Did you learn anything else from the German?" he asked at last.

I shook my head sulkily, reluctant to revisit the memory. Then it came to me, sharp and piercing. "He's challenged Freddy to a duel."

"Freddy?" Holmes looked at me, incredulous.

"Yes. The fellow is intent on murdering any man Eliza might look favorably upon. Freddy gets a duel because he is a gentleman. You get a dagger between the shoulder blades because you're a *schweinhund* of an American."

Holmes cackled. "But this is excellent news!"

"Are you mad? This is one of those German *paukanten* who revel in blood. How will Freddy being murdered help solve our case?"

"Of course, one hopes that nothing will happen to young Freddy. But a gentleman doesn't issue a challenge to a duel under an assumed name. Freddy will be able to tell us the German's true identity."

Miss Doolittle did not appear at breakfast the next day, nor lunch, nor tea. Higgins swore at the servants. He swore at the glazier, who had come to repair the window. He swore at the tea, and spilled it in his lap. When she didn't come down for tea, he threatened to break her door down, or even worse, send for Dr. Guest. Pickering steered him away from these thoughts calmly and assiduously. He asked Mrs. Pearce—Mrs. Pearce herself, not any of the maids—to take a tray up to Eliza. Eliza thanked her through the door, but did not let her in. Mrs. Pearce left the tray outside.

After dinner, with Higgins still stewing and Pickering still clucking, Holmes tapped me on the shoulder, pointing toward the door. We threw on our coats and hats and sought the tonic of the night air.

"Are we stretching our legs again?" I asked.

"Not this time, Watson. We don't want to be late for our appointment with Wiggins." He showed me a note that had been delivered by hand that afternoon. "Snaps ready—W." The address mentioned was a place called Castor's, a pub in Berwick Street. We flagged down a cab as soon as we could, and proceeded toward that address.

When we arrived, however, we were immediately faced with a conundrum. Castor's was not one pub but two, side by side; two of the same name, sharing the same building.

"Wiggins might have mentioned this," I said. "Shall we each try one door?"

"That won't be necessary, Watson. Wiggins will of course be waiting in the establishment on the right."

"How can you be certain?"

"The Castor on the left has only two windows. The Castor on the right has three. Given a choice, a detective will always choose more windows."

Sherlock Holmes's logic was unassailable. I followed him into the right Castor. It was a long narrow room with a long narrow bar, and casks of beer and porter and sherry piled against the opposite wall. The space between was so narrow, and so crowded, that we almost had to walk upon the casks. A slim figure detached itself from the shadows by the door and interposed itself between us.

"Good evening, Mr. Wiggins. I pray we have not made you wait."

Wiggins screwed his eyes up at Sherlock Holmes in mild astonishment. "You came as yourself!"

"Who else should I come as?"

"I thought you'd be a one-eyed lascar, or a preacher with a limp, or an Irish infantry sergeant. You was always in disguise in the old days."

"I no longer have need of disguises. No one remembers me."

"Bollocks they don't," said Wiggins under his breath.

"What did you think I'd come as?" I asked.

"Never thought you'd come at all, Doctor. Come, there's more room in the snuggery."

He led us back through the room, dodging table-corners and chair-legs as they attempted to snatch at us. The snuggery was no roomier than the front room, but it was less crowded, possibly due to the half-hearted scrapings of a fiddler in the corner of the room. We took a table by the fire. I could not help but stare at the fireplace.

At once there was a presence leaning over me, hot upon my neck like dragon's breath, and soft against my shoulder in a way that was most embarrassing. It was the waitress of the Castor Pub, and she was neither long nor narrow, leaning over the table with her bosom lodged upon my shoulder like a bindle.

"What's it to be, gents? We've a nice kind of a peppery stew with potatoes and mutton tonight." Then she spied Wiggins. "Tommy Wiggins! Looks like you're comin' up in the world, old son."

"Cheers, Maud. A pint of your best bitter all round."

"Right you are. Put your troubles in old Tommy's hands, have you gents? You couldn't do better if you had the flying squad at your elbow." Her bosom swished away and the side of my neck went quite cool as she turned to go. But by now my curiosity had got the better of me.

"Maud?"

"Yes, dearie, something else?"

"The fireplace." It was not a proper fireplace at all, unless fireplaces came in halves, like pints of beer. There was a perfectly good half a fireplace, with half a mantel, half a grate, half a screen, and half a fire. Only the poker and the firedogs were whole.

"First time here, eh?" The bosom lodged itself once more upon my clavicle. "The Castorini brothers. Fought over a girl. Came to blows, they did. Nearly came to knives. So they went their separate ways instead of murderin' each other. 'Cept they both owned the pub, and neither one didn't want to give it up. So they built a wall right down the middle of the place, right up to the hearthstone. They agreed to share the fireplace and the chimney."

Having enlightened her audience, the bosom rocked away again.

"You have the photos, Wiggins?"

"Indeed I do, Mr. Holmes, and I must say I think they're some very fine work, given the adverse lighting conditions." Wiggins opened his camera case and produced the very fine work, three photographs of Eliza taken through her bedroom window. I cannot vouch for their artistic quality, but they looked enough like Eliza to serve our purpose.

"I'll take these round to Covent Garden in the morning. We'll try Drury Lane, and Lisson Grove, and Tottenham Court, and by Jupiter we'll find someone who knows the girl as well as Dr. Watson knows you," Wiggins said.

"An admirable plan, Wiggins. Deduction is no substitute for legwork. There's one other place I would wish you to make inquiries. Colney Hatch."

Wiggins whistled. "Colney Hatch! You think she's a nutter?"

"Her behavior is certainly erratic enough to qualify. I've already had her name circulated at all the lunatic asylums, to no avail. But there's no reason to believe that Eliza Doolittle is her real name, is there?"

I had to object. "Miss Doolittle may be subject to wide vacilla-
tions of mood, but I would hardly call her a candidate for the asylum,
Holmes."

"I value your medical opinion, Doctor, but you have not the experience with the female lunatic that I have. They are fiercely cunning.
Mild as a lamb one moment, poisonous as an adder the next. No mere
man is so dangerous."

I felt Holmes was overstating his case, but there was no gainsaying
him. He continued: "And Doctor, if you will, there's someone I would
like you to show this photograph, as well."

I sighed like a truant schoolboy. I had thought myself excused
from canvassing the taverns. "Where must I go?" I asked.

"Edinburgh."

"Edinburgh? Scotland?" I was incredulous. "Surely the girl's never
been further north than Golder's Green."

"I'm sure you're right, Watson, but tomorrow evening at eight
o'clock, the Edinburgh Fabian Society will be hosting the celebrated
moralist and lecturer Mr. Alfred P. Doolittle. Surely his opinion of
those photos will be useful to us."

Eliza's father! I had forgot his existence entirely. The illiterate
dustman magically transformed into a man of letters by Higgins's
sorcery. I should have realized Holmes would track him down, whether
among the braes and firths, or halfway around the globe.

"Now then, gents, three pints, sixpence." Maud slammed our
glasses down on the table, somehow without spilling a drop. Holmes
and Wiggins both looked at me. I fished a shilling from my pocket.
She pinched it from my hand and made it disappear somewhere in the
folds of the bosom. "You're a right sport, you are," she said, and tousled
my hair. I'm afraid I blushed like a schoolboy.

"Who got the girl at last, Maud?" Holmes asked, grinning.

"Oh! A green-grocer from Lambeth."

Chapter Twenty

The next morning found me on the platform at King's Cross before ten, boarding the Flying Scotsman to Edinburgh. In that bright cold morning I could not help but feel like a schoolboy on his first journey to Rugby or Winchester. There is something about a great metropolitan train station that always lifts my spirits beyond themselves and toward the great empyrean. The chuff of the engines rises like a psalm, echo upon echo, to the vault; passengers and porters and well-wishers all moving with a definition of purpose only seen in monks at sacred hours. I am closer to the Creator at King's Cross or Waterloo than at St. Paul's or Westminster.

The Scotsman is one of those rare trains that combine speed and comfort. I settled into my compartment, knowing that we would pull into Waverly in little more than eight hours. Had I been accompanied by Holmes, we would have spent the hours discussing the case, he dispensing just enough clues to leave me entirely befuddled. Any silences would have been the tense lacunae of waiting for more vatic utterance from my friend. On this occasion, I had borrowed a book from Pickering. I was afraid he might offer me something to do with Urdu idioms or Tibetan prayer wheels, but he had surprised me with a new adventure novel, a bit of fluff having to do with a scientific expedition to South America that encounters a mob of prehistoric beasts. First London and then the countryside sped past my window as I delved deep into primeval jungles rife with pterodactyls and iguanodons. I may have nodded for a bit along the way. I woke thinking I should head to the dining car for lunch, but the conductor was already announcing our arrival at Waverly. I gathered up my things and made ready to deboard. I could see Castle Rock swing into view outside my window, with the ancient fortress louring down upon the granite denizens of the city.

I checked into the station hotel and found a pub nearby that served a passable finnan haddie. The lecture was to take place at the university at eight. It crossed my mind that Mr. Alfred P. Doolittle, dustman turned lecturer, had made a transformation as radical as Eliza's. Perhaps the diabolical Henry Higgins had done away with father as well as daughter and sent in substitutes for both. The alternative proposition, that anyone could change their God-given rank and station in life by a simple change of manner or wardrobe, was anathema to Sherlock Holmes's method of order. If souls could change skins with such easy fluidity, then how could one judge a man by his outer habit? The design of society had once seemed unyielding and eternal, but the changes the new century had ushered in had undermined all our expectations. What use was it to recognize the telegrapher's thumb or the coachman's wrist in an age of telephones and automobiles?

Doolittle's speech was in a lecture hall at the Old College. Some fifty or sixty people were in attendance, mostly men, with a handful of ladies, all presumably dyed-in-the-wool Fabians. Most were dressed with the studied loucheness of the academic socialist. So there was one young woman who caught my eye immediately. She was dressed in peacock blue, with a trio of bedraggled feathers in her hat that might have been snatched right from the peacock's tail. Her cheeks were rouged and her mouth was a crimson soup bowl. She spoke to no one and seemed to know no one, but sat breathing hard and watching the podium as if it might weigh anchor and slip away.

A tremulous little fellow with white muttonchops and a tartan shawl took the podium. He cleared his throat portentously several times as the audience found their seats. The speaker he introduced seemed to be a member of every society of honor in Europe and an intimate of every great man of the past century. I began to wonder whether I had found my way to the right venue.

Then Alfred Doolittle himself appeared. No porridge-eater, he. He was a man of about my age, above the average in height, with broad shoulders and the profile of a freighter hoving to port. His garments seemed meant to restrain rather than fit him, especially his waistcoat, which was of gold brocade with a threatening battery of brass buttons. The buttons were like rivets on an overstoked steam engine, ready to fly at any moment. When he commenced speaking, his voice was sonorous and full, as if his boiler had been stoked just prior to his entrance. When his voice reached its highest volume, the rivets trembled.

As for the subject he spoke on, I can offer little report. Some socialist folderol about the needs of the undeserving poor, which I would be ashamed to repeat even if I remembered it. What drew my attention instead was the silent rapport between himself and the young woman in the peacock frock. He would often punctuate his speech with a nod, and the nod was to her, and at times a ribald wink accompanied it. Nor were his attentions unreciprocated, for as often as he would nod, she would nod back, and as often as he would wink, she would return the wink.

Miss Peacock sat unaccompanied in the front row. I had been standing in the back, but I soon moved down to take a seat in the front myself, hoping for a better look at the girl. I stole several glances at her, but each time I chanced a look, she seemed to be stealing a look at me. She was obviously on her guard, which put me on my guard. An idea formed in my mind: a monumental, stupendous idea! Here was Alfred Doolittle, father of Eliza Doolittle, with a young woman in tow, a young woman who admired and respected him. The girl was barely twenty-one, square-shouldered and fleshy with red hands and red face—just as Pickering had once described her. There was no question in my mind that I was sitting three seats down from the real Eliza Doolittle.

Just as the idea hit me, the girl bolted.

She didn't actually run, but she was up and across the room to the door as quickly as propriety would allow. Her hasty exit upset the speaker. For a moment he lost all sense of time or place and merely stared at her dumbfounded. Then she was out the door.

I followed. After all Holmes and I had been through, there was no way I could squander this opportunity and let the girl disappear again. Doolittle once again faltered as I passed by, and there were angry murmurs from the audience. I ignored them and made for the door.

She was rustling down the hall as I came out. She glanced over her shoulder. Seeing me, she continued down the hall, tripping faster now, the peacock feathers dancing. I followed. She broke into a little trot.

"Miss Doolittle!" I called.

She ran. Not like a young lady, but like a scalded cat. I was so taken aback that for a moment I stood as I was, simply watching. Then she turned a corner and disappeared. I hurried after, reluctant somehow to run in the fusty wood-paneled corridors of academe. I turned the corner. She was nowhere in sight. The hall was lined with the doors of lecture rooms on either side, ending in a blank wall with a portrait of John Knox staring down at me censoriously. Eliza Doolittle was concealed behind one of those doors.

I began trying each door one by one. Empty lecture rooms, deep in shadow. Empty. Empty. Empty. Locked. It could be no accident that there was one locked door. *Quod erat demonstrandum.*

I put my shoulder to the door. It was solid oak. I worked the handle back and forth. It would not yield. I knocked on the door. "Miss Doolittle. Please! I need to talk with you! Open the door!" She made no answer. I waited. She would have to come out eventually.

She did not come out. A janitor came down the hall with a dustbin in his hand. He drew a ring of keys from his pocket and opened the door. He set the dustbin inside and took a broom out. He gave me a sidelong look and continued on down the hall. I had miscalculated.

But the game was not lost. Where the father was, there the daughter would be, sooner or later. Back to the lecture hall I sped, to face Mr. Doolittle.

Mercifully, the lecture was ended, and the grim-faced attendees were filing out. Doolittle was sitting in a chair by the podium, counting the evening's receipts. He was obviously no bookkeeper. The counting was a slow process, which required frequent consultation with a bottle of gin, which peeked out of his coat pocket. His waistcoat was unbuttoned. His fires were banked, his superstructure safe for the nonce.

"Mr. Alfred P. Doolittle?"

He barely glanced at me. "If you're here to discuss the witherin' away of the state, mate, I'm all fagged out for tonight. Try me another time."

"No, sir. My name is John Watson. You may have heard of me. I'm an associate of the renowned detective Sherlock Holmes. I demand to speak to your daughter."

The name of Holmes roused him. "Sherlock Holmes? Go on. Sherlock Holmes is dead!"

"I assure you, he's quite well. I spoke to him only this morning."

"Oh, no, I remember it well. Twenty years ago now it must be. We was all devastated to hear. Fell off a mountain in Switzerland, I think it was."

I realized what he was talking about. The Reichenbach Falls. Moriarty. "That was a mistake," I said.

"I certainly hope it weren't done a-purpose."

"I mean the reports of his death were mistaken. He survived the fall."

"Oh. Is that a fact?" he said grudgingly. "Well, I mighta been notified." He consulted with the gin bottle. "What's it to me or you if he's alive or a walkin' specter, anyway?"

"Mr. Doolittle, I demand to see your daughter immediately."

"My daughter? What, Eliza? You're askin' for a hard one, mate. Last I heard tell, Eliza's in London still."

"I saw her here this very night."

"Gorblimey, you're not serious! Why would Eliza drag herself all the way up to Scotland? She's never been further north than Golder's Green. Is she here to put the touch on me? He's finally got rid of her, has he?"

"Who's got rid of her?"

"Henry Higgins!"

"What can you tell me of Professor Higgins?"

"Look, Mr. Whitson, don't you trust that devil. Look what he done to me. I'm on the run, I am. Every bloke I've touched for forty years is tryin' to put the touch on me now."

"Just let me speak to your daughter, and I think we may discover Higgins's intentions."

"I won't stop you. I'm not one to interfere. You take care of Eliza, and I'll take care of old Alfie."

At that moment, Eliza herself flounced in. Without a glance at me, she threw herself into her father's lap, wrapped her arms about him, and kissed him hard upon the lips.

"Oh, Alfie, I've had the most dreadful time!" she cried.

"Don't fret yourself, my dear." His hands moved over her body in a most unpaternal way. I had made another error, this time a colossal one. I remembered that Doolittle had married recently. This young lady was not Miss, but Mrs. Doolittle.

"There was this toff chasin' me about the halls. He was ever so scarifyin'. I had to hide in the loo."

"Smart thinking."

She looked at me for the first time. She gave a little shriek. "That's him, Alfie! That's the fellow assaulted me."

Doolittle looked from her to me.

"My apologies, sir. When I saw your wife, I thought—"

"My wife? Is she here, too? Her and Eliza both? Sounds like conspiracy."

"I apologize again. This is not your wife?"

"My wife? Of course not. My wife's a respectable woman. Why would I want to tramp around Scotland with her? This is Fanny. Good old Fanny." He gave her a pinch upon the bottom that nearly sent her jumping into my arms.

"Miss Pritchard to you." She stood upon her dignity, no matter how narrow that stand might be.

I bowed. I had made an unmitigated ass of myself. But I hoped I could still save the situation.

"Fanny's been out of sorts lately, so I brung her wi' me. Bit of a holiday for her."

"Torquay would ha' been ever so much nicer," the girl lamented.

"Mr. Doolittle, I would like, if I might, to show you some photographs."

"Oh, I don't go that way, mate. Give me real flesh and blood any time."

"No, sir, I apologize again. These are photographs of your daughter, Eliza. Not—not compromising photographs," I added, seeing the look that came into his eyes. "I would merely ask you to confirm that the girl in the photos is in fact your daughter Eliza."

I handed him the photos. He fumbled inside his coat pocket. He handed the gin bottle to Miss Pritchard, who took it as an invitation to partake. He dove in again and came up with a pair of eyeglasses, which he set low on his nose. He moved the photo back and forth in front of him, trying to bring it into focus, something the gin bottle may have impeded.

"This is Eliza?"

"That's what I hoped you could tell me."

"I haven't seen that much of her in the past, well, twenty years, at least not sober. I thought she were twins for several years. We're not what you would call intimate." He almost seemed to be trying to stare the photo down. Then he bethought himself, handing the photo to Miss Pritchard.

"Here, is that Eliza?"

"Lemme look."

"I beg your pardon, Miss, you're acquainted with Miss Doolittle?"

"We grew up together, didn't we? Even if she has moved on to spoonin' her tea with duchesses and such." She studied the photo. "She looks pale. And puny."

"That's the fault of that Higgins I told you about," Doolittle explained. "Feeds her buttermilk instead of gin. Slow poison, that."

I tapped the photo. "But you would say that is Miss Doolittle?"

"Well, if it is, she needs a trip to Scotland to put her right!" She and Doolittle both burst out in laughter. I felt distinctly uncomfortable. I gave a discreet cough. Miss Pritchard perhaps caught the disapprobation in my face; her own turned sour. She handed back the photos.

"No. It might be her, but then again it might not. I han't seen her since first I trod the boards at the Gaiety. Diff'rent circles, don't y'know?"

By this I was given to understand that Miss Pritchard had had a career upon the stage at some point, however brief or ignoble, which vaulted her into a society superior to that of mere flower girls.

"It's a nice frock," she remarked. "Like the cut ever so much. Couldn't you find out from the birthmark?"

"Miss Doolittle has a birthmark?" I asked, excited.

"Dunno. But ain't that how they always find out if it's the true Duchess of Golliwog and not the evil imposter from the neighborin' kingdom?"

Naïve as the remark seemed, there was something in it. Why shouldn't Eliza have a birthmark, or a scar, or some identifying feature? This girl didn't know, nor would the negligent father, but who would? Her doctor!

But that hare would not start. "Doctor? What's Eliza need a doctor for?" said Doolittle when I asked. "She takes after her father. Iron constitution. Never been sick a day in her life."

Thus ended my mission to Edinburgh. It was hardly covered with glory. I did not look forward to being questioned by Holmes. Was there some way I could glide over the fact that I had chased a young woman up and down the halls of the university in the mistaken belief that she was another young woman entirely?

I was lying in bed in my hotel room, about to give myself up to sleep, when it came to me that a woman who had never been sick a day in her life should not need to be under the constant medical supervision of Dr. Guest.

Chapter Twenty-One

Any report I might make to Sherlock Holmes was completely overshadowed by the news I received on my return to Wimpole Street the next evening. Mrs. Pearce met me at the door, her eyes like a spaniel's. "Oh, Mr. Barton, thank heaven you've returned," she said.

"Why, Mrs. Pearce, what's the matter?"

Mrs. Pearce poured it all out. Eliza, the girl who was never sick a day in her life, was ill once again. She had locked herself in her room and would admit no one. Food and drink were left at her door, but barely touched.

How Mrs. Pearce thought I might remedy the situation, I could not think. I found myself patting her awkwardly on the shoulder. The men in this house all had their heads in the clouds, she complained, and Professor Higgins the worst of them, helpless as a baby—was it wrong for a woman to wish for a single person she could rely upon?

Had Dr. Guest not been summoned? Summoned indeed, peremptorily, imperiously, imploringly, desperately. Guest did not come. At first Higgins's messengers had been turned away without a word of explanation. At last came a reply: Guest would not come, could not come, was himself too ill to leave his bed, much less attend upon his patients. There were thousands of doctors in London, Pickering protested. Higgins dug in his heels. He would have none other but Guest, and Guest would not come.

I had seen Higgins storm and rage before, but his tantrums had always had an element of the theatrical in them, as though he relished watching his own performances. Now he paced the halls muttering dark imprecations against the doctor as the hours turned to days. Mrs. Pearce was distraught, moving through the house like a ghost, and the other servants all hid downstairs, whispering to each other.

Worse than Higgins was Freddy. Freddy was gnawing his fingernails off with worry. If he had been Eliza's spaniel before, he was now her Doberman, trotting back and forth before the gate. He'd have worn out the stones in the street had Mrs. Pearce not taken pity on him and invited him into the kitchen for sustenance. Would that he had been a less faithful watchdog!

The atmosphere was suffocating. A brown fog settled in over the city. You could look out the window and not be able to make out the houses across the street. The air crackled with danger. Holmes felt it, too. "Soon, Watson, soon, we shall see a break in this fog about us. Then let us be on our guard," he said.

That night I saw him again. He might have been invisible save that the brass on his jacket was polished to cavalry standard. He stood watching the house, erect as a sentry, solitary as a menhir. I signaled for Freddy to join me at the window.

"Mr. Eynsford-Hill. The man across the road. Have you seen him before?" I asked.

Freddy peered out, squinting. Then a smile came to his face, the last thing I expected. "Ah, yes! Colonel Von Stetten! Has a terrific pash on Eliza. Poor fellow must be chilled to the bone."

"This poor fellow has threatened to murder you in a duel." I thought that would give him pause. It did not.

"It's not murder if it's a duel, that's what the colonel says. Anyway, we already had the duel."

I was dumfounded. "How is it then that you—that both of you yet live?"

"Oh, yes! Rum thing, that. I won the toss and fired first. Of course I missed. I would have missed if he were an elephant, or a herd of them. Then he took aim at me. I expected to die at any moment. He held out that pistol so long he might have been painting my portrait. Then he fired—into the air. He came over to me, shook my hand, and said I was the most courageous fellow he'd ever met. He thought certain that I'd turn tail and run."

"I applaud your courage as well."

"Courage! I was too frightened to move a muscle! I wonder, should I ask the girl to make him some cocoa."

"But you're rivals! Shouldn't you be jealous of him?"

"Jealous? He's out there. I'm in here."

The point was well made.

I found Holmes pacing in his room. He was in the volatile mood that used to call for the violin back in our Baker Street days. Unfortunately, G.B. Morello did not play the violin.

Of course he did require from me a full accounting of my Scottish adventure, and of course he winkled every humiliating detail out of me. Well, then, we had a good laugh about it, or he did, anyway, and we moved on to matters of more import.

"Colonel Von Stetten!" he replied to my overture. "I haven't brought you up to date. Adjutant to Prince Rupprecht of Bavaria, whom you'll remember was recently widowed. Attached to the Bavarian embassy. Apparently as matchmaker plenipotentiary."

"He's a madman! He almost killed Freddy."

"Of course he's mad. Most aristocrats are mad. In the German states it's practically a prerequisite. I was Freddy's second. He was never in any real danger once I doctored the pistol muzzles. Still, there was a glorious Tolstoyan atmosphere to the whole affair. The sun rising bloodred over the Serpentine, the combatants posed in silhouette, bareheaded, lithe of limb, pistols raised—both museum pieces. The cacophony of morning birdsong silenced by the explosion of young Frederick's pistol—"

"To no effect."

Holmes shrugged. "The sun was in his eyes. Von Stetten takes aim—"

"But never fires."

"A magnificent display of noblesse oblige upon the field of honor. It only lacked a gypsy violin. Pity you weren't here to witness. You would have written it up splendidly for one of your vignettes in *The Strand*."

"As I recall, this Von Stetten also vowed to murder you."

"And you as well, old friend."

"Yes, but I was safe in Scotland." Even as I said it I realized, to my chagrin, that the true purpose of Sherlock Holmes in sending me to Scotland had been to keep me out of harm's way while he dealt with the German. I bit my lip and let it pass. Instead I asked, "How then did you scotch the snake?"

"It became necessary to unmask myself to him."

"Holmes! Was that wise?"

"It was, thanks to your spadework. The colonel has read every one of your accounts of our adventures. He despised Morello, but he worships Sherlock Holmes. He has called off his Italian friends, convincing them that I am not the same Morello they are sworn to assassinate. Of course, there is every possibility that one or two of them may not have believed him, so we must still be on our guard."

"Does he still plan to whisk Miss Doolittle off and deliver her to his prince?"

"Only if she is in fact Princess Sophie or Princess Augusta, or some other lady of highest station. He awaits my verdict in the matter."

"He's out there waiting in the fog now."

Holmes looked out through the window, and nodded. "He shares our concern for Eliza in her indisposition."

All right, then. A mortal enemy had been transformed overnight into a jolly good fellow while I was chasing pixies in Scotland. There were other flies in the ointment. "Dr. Guest doesn't seem to share that concern."

"Dr. Guest is himself gravely ill, or so his man informs us."

"It seems a remarkable coincidence."

"Perhaps. By the by, Pickering received a letter from his friend Bentley in Calcutta. He never met Guest in person, he said, but knew him by reputation. Guest was considered a most promising young doctor in Lahore. Took part in Ross's malaria trials at Mian Mir. Spent his free time treating inmates in the lunatic asylum. Very much the *pukka sahib*."

Holmes seemed all too forgiving for my tastes. "Then where is he in Eliza's hour of need?"

"Bentley also mentioned that Guest contracted malaria himself during his tenure in the army. I think it not unlikely that he has suffered a relapse."

I felt a sudden unaccountable dejection. I subsided into a chair before the fire, and stared into the glowing coals. It seemed that I had led my friend on a fool's errand. Every time I thought we were close to an answer, it slipped from our grasp.

"Never fear, Watson. The case is drawing to a close," said Holmes.

I was used to him reading my mind. "What makes you think so?" I asked glumly.

"Autumn is upon us. I have to get home and prepare my bees for winter."

"What, then, should our next step be?"

"I still believe the man who calls himself Hyde holds the key to this mystery. I think we might profit by interviewing the Misses Chubb and Kelly. I've already spoken with Dr. Scott at Holloway Prison and he has agreed to make the arrangements."

Chapter Twenty-Two

———◆◆◇◆◆———

The next morning we set out for Holloway. The weather continuing dismal, we took the Piccadilly line to Holloway Castle. The Underground, with its swift, quiet electric carriages had become a favorite mode of travel for me in recent years, but Holmes seemed dispirited. He drew strength from the noise and crowds of London's surface as Antaeus drew his from the earth.

We left the Underground at Parkhurst Road and emerged into a sea of fog. The frowning towers of Holloway Prison, constructed some half-century ago as some perverse homage to the Dark Ages, reared out of the mists, dampening the soul further.

Then we heard the singing. Women's voices raised, muffled perhaps by the mist, but still strong and stern, almost rousing, singing a march. We looked at each in wonder.

The governor had dispatched a wardress to meet us at the gate. A capable young woman she appeared in her blue holland dress and black bonnet. "It's suffragettes, sir," she said as Holmes nodded toward the courtyard, where the singing seemed to originate. "They send 'em here to break their spirits, it's said. But they seem to leave here as termagant as they come, or more. That's their anthem." She seemed to harbor a rather unprofessional sympathy for their cause.

She led us through the courtyard to the main building. Women's faces, raised in song, shining and potent, appeared and disappeared like ghosts as we moved through the fog.

"Have no fear, sirs," she said as we gained the great hall. "None o' them suffragettes here, only the real hard cases. Miss Chubb, she's come down ill and can't see anyone, but Miss Kelly will talk all day long to anyone about anything."

The singing, indeed all sound save our own footsteps, seemed to die away in the silence of the tomb as we moved into the wing that housed "the hard cases." The wardress sorted through her keys and unlocked a door, opening it just wide enough for us to pass through.

"Knock when you want out," she said, and bolted the door behind us. We were alone in a narrow cell with a murderess.

She hardly looked the part. Nancy Kelly was seated in the only chair in the room, in front of a small deal table, for all the world like a fine lady at her vanity, save that there was no mirror, nor brushes, nor any of the accessories one would find in a lady's boudoir. She was dressed in dark green serge with a blue check apron, the same we'd noticed on the other inmates. She turned to us to reveal a boyish face framed by dark cropped hair, with hollow, probing eyes.

"You're the prison inspectors?" she asked. "There's rats in this place big enough to pull a mail-coach up Holborn Hill."

"I'm a private detective, Miss Kelly. My name is Sherlock Holmes."

"Sherlock Holmes? I heard o' you!"

"You enjoy stories of detection? My associate Dr. Watson is responsible for those." He nodded toward me.

She glanced at me in confusion, mixed perhaps with contempt, and then locked eyes with Holmes. "My mum told me about you. Said you was a right ole billy goat. My mum knew lots of famous men. Knew Disraeli, she did—he wasn't really a Jew, y'know—knew the Prince of Wales, not this one, but two back: Bertie. Said he liked to be whipped with a silk curtain sash."

"I'm sure you have a wealth of anecdotes," Holmes replied, unperturbed. "Perhaps you could tell me about Herbert Jaggers and Norris Shaw." Those were the names of the men she had stabbed to death.

Her eyes narrowed. "Why should I tell you anythin' about anythin'?"

"Why not?" Holmes already had her marked as an inveterate prattler.

"All right, then." She mulled it for a moment, as if they were not printed on her memory. "A pair o' flash coves they were. Shaw was a real cover-me-proper. Jaggers not so spruce, but he had the chinks, and didn't mind to spread 'em."

"How came they to you?"

"Stage door Johnnies. From my days in the Gaiety."

"You were a Gaiety girl? For how long?" Holmes sounded dubious.

"You needn't take that tone with me, Mr. High-and-Mighty. I was a different girl in those days, togged out proper and rouged up like an apple. I danced in the Gaiety a whole season, near-like. Two years ago. Seems a lifetime."

"How'd you land a plum crib like that, Nancy?"

"That was the doctor, y'see. He fixed it all up for me. A few words in the right ear and I was in clover." She reached out, embracing the memory.

"Tell us more about this doctor."

"Oh! Dr. Henry, he was a real gent, through-and-through. An angel from heaven that one was."

"How did you come to meet him?"

"Women's Hospital. He fixed my split lip along of a Saturday night after my husband flogged me once with a firedog."

"Your husband sounds a man of singularly violent disposition."

"He was like that. He'd say, 'here, what're you lookin' at me like that for?' and fetch me a clout on the head. When I wasn't even lookin' at him. Men are like that, though. Brutes, every one."

"Where's your husband now?"

"Australia? Argentina? One of those places they say the gold is layin' out in heaps on the ground right for the takin'. Not a word from him since he lit out." There was bitterness in her voice, though you'd think she'd be glad enough to see the back of the man.

"But you saw the doctor again?"

She perked up again. "He took a real shine to me, right from the start. Said I had a quality. Gimme money of my own. Not sixpence, but pound notes."

"Did he . . . bring you into his home?"

"Not he. Set me up in my own digs, proper as a queen. A bit lonely that, but ever so genteel. Course, he drew the line at gentleman callers. Then when he saw how fearsome lonely I got whenever he was away, he got me the crib at the Gaiety."

"Did Edward Hyde never visit you?"

"Oh, you know Neddie? That was different. He was Dr. Henry's man, or his pal, I was never sure. Thick as thieves. He used to bring me medicines from the doctor. Not that he didn't take no liberties on occasion. What's a girl to do?"

"What sort of medicines?"

"Pick-me-ups. Mother's milk they were, better than gin. Lit you up inside and out. Wish I had one now," she concluded morosely.

"Did Dr. Henry light out on you, too?"

"Dropped me for the landlady's daughter. Conniving little tart!"

Holmes looked deep into her eyes. "Why did you kill Jaggers and Shaw, Nancy?"

Her eyes went opaque, and her mouth set in a rictus. It was as if her spirit had fled, leaving only a wax shell.

"Nancy?" He touched the palm of her hand, where a white welt stood up.

"That wasn't me, copper. That was somebody else." She said it mechanically.

Holmes went on, inexorable. "You were found all three sitting at the kitchen table. The men had each been stabbed five or six times."

"It wasn't me. It was some bad girl." Her whole body shook. "Not me."

"The bloody knife was in your hands."

"Not me. Not me! Not me!" She was shrieking it now. She leapt to her feet, grappling with Holmes, clawing at his face. "Not me!"

The door banged open and the wardress strode in. She caught hold of Nancy's wrists and forced her back on her bed with far more strength than I'd credited her. After a bit of struggle, Nancy gave up and went limp, her eyes rolling back in her head. The wardress laid her across the bed.

"I'd ask you gentlemen to go now. Her nerves are overtaxed, I'm afraid." Her voice was matter-of-fact. Perhaps this was how all interviews with Miss Kelly ended.

Holmes and I put on our hats and went to the door. Then Holmes turned back. "Nancy. What was Dr. Henry's last name?"

Nancy made no response, if indeed she heard him at all. The wardress gave him a pointed look. We tilted our hats to her.

"Jekyll."

It was the wardress who had spoken. She looked as if the name had just come to her. "She talks about him all the time. Dr. Henry Jekyll. But he doesn't visit. No one does."

"Henry Jekyll! Alive, Holmes!" Our footsteps drummed down the long corridor as another wardress led us out. "Should we alert Scotland Yard? Get hold of Inspector Newcomen?"

"Not yet, Watson. Not yet, I think." He seemed preoccupied with some private thought.

"An odious woman!" muttered Holmes, once the wardress had seen us off at the gate.

"Nancy Kelly? You thought so?"

"You found her sympathetic?"

"Far from it. But the woman is mad. She should be in a lunatic asylum, not a prison."

"Half the women in asylums would be better off to put their heads in a hangman's knot and cease upon the midnight with no pain."

"Holmes! Can you really be so unfeeling?" We could still hear a few women singing in the courtyard. High and thin and lonely it sounded now.

"Believe me, Watson, if you could delve the hearts of those women, many of them would welcome death with open arms."

"Have you been spending your retirement years visiting lunatics, then?" I sneered.

"My God, man, why do you think I retired?" he exploded.

His vehemence shook me. I had somehow touched a nerve on a man who was celebrated for having none. We stood staring at each other.

"I asked," I said quietly. "You know I asked over and over, begged you to tell me, and I was always met with the silence of the Sphinx."

He nodded. "It was wrong of me." The dam had broken. "Come, let us walk," he said. We pushed through the fog as though we charged the Valley of Death, my companion holding his fire until he had gathered his thoughts. When he was ready, he began:

"You recall the case of Amelia Ascher?"

I cast my memory back. "The Saffron Hill baby farmer."

"So-called. It was never conclusively proven that she was in possession of her faculties when she committed those crimes. The older woman, Barnett, exercised undue influence upon her judgment."

"She was found guilty but insane." I did not add that she was found so mostly on the evidence provided by one Sherlock Holmes. "That was in 1902, I think."

"She was committed to Colney Hatch Lunatic Asylum. Where, I may add, she was considered a model patient."

"You . . . followed her progress?"

"Oh, no. I consigned her to the files and gave her no more thought. Until the fire."

The image rose to mind. The Colney Hatch fire was notorious in the annals of official disgrace. In 1903, early on a February morning, a fire broke out in the women's annex, a "temporary" shelter built of timber. Fed by gale force winds, the fire swept through the building, taking the lives of over fifty women. Six hundred lunatics escaped and had to be rounded up by the constabulary.

"Was Miss Ascher one of the victims?" I asked.

"The prison authorities were unable to answer that question with any confidence. Many of the bodies were burned beyond hope of recognition. Some few of the escapees were never found. Ascher may have been among those. Certainly she would not have been caught up in the panic in the first few minutes of the blaze."

"How can you be sure of that?"

"Because she set the fire herself. That was the one fact I was able to establish beyond the shadow of a doubt. No one else among the patients had access to the tallow."

"Holmes, surely you don't hold yourself responsible for this woman's actions."

He halted, holding up a hand. The worst was to come. "Wait. Please. I have spoken to you of my mother, have I not?"

"You've told me what you remembered. She died when you were very young, I think."

"I remember her voice. She used to sing about the house."

I nodded, affecting sympathy. I could not fathom this sudden shift to personal reminiscences.

"Mycroft claimed not to remember her voice. Mycroft remembered less than I did, somehow, though he was seven years my elder. My father never spoke of her at all."

"Yes, but what has this got to do with—?"

"There was a list. Of course. A list of the patients who were missing. The list shrunk day by day as the runaways were collected, until it stood at fifty-two. Fifty-two helpless madwomen who had burned to death like moths in a candle flame."

He seemed to lose heart. He gestured helplessly, like a mute. There was something he wanted me to understand, but he could not say it. He wanted me to divine it from the tenor of his silence. The air was full of ghosts. The waiting was unbearable.

"One name on the list was that of a woman named Louise Vernet."

"Vernet?" Tread lightly, John Watson. "Don't you have relations by that name?"

"Louise Vernet was my mother's maiden name. My mother, I had been told, died in 1857. The same year this woman was admitted to the asylum."

It all rushed in upon me. "Oh, but Holmes, you must be mistaken! It's some devilish coincidence!"

He shook his head. "Mycroft admitted it to me when confronted. Without reserve. Indeed, without sentiment. My father had my mother committed to Colney Hatch Lunatic Asylum in the year 1857, after she made an attack upon Mycroft with an oyster knife. She believed he was trying to strangle me in my crib, she said. She continued in that place for forty-six years until Amelia Ascher set fire to a barrel of tallow in the annex pantry. Forgive me, Watson, but I do feel the weight of responsibility belongs upon my shoulders."

"You could not have known—"

"I knew she was alive! I knew it and never let my knowledge come to the surface. Mycroft said he was surprised I hadn't divined it years earlier."

I tried to find the words, words of comfort, words to dispel the horror, words to carry us backward from that awful moment in time. But there were no words adequate to the moment. It was vain to argue that Amelia Ascher and Louise Vernet no more represented their sex than James Moriarty or Tiger Moran represented ours. The point was trivial. Sherlock Holmes had cornered his villain, judged him, and passed sentence.

The moment passed. Though it lasted an eternity, the moment passed. We plodded on through the fog.

The break we had been waiting for came on the fourth night of Eliza's illness. The weather broke, at least, as a cold rain beat down steadily upon the roof and filled the gutters. Freddy had been taken inside by Mrs. Pearce to dry himself by the kitchen fire. Dinner was a mirthless exercise. We could hear Eliza prowling about her room, muttering to herself in low tones that sounded almost like growling. The sound was so pitiful that I prepared a toddy to soothe her throat and brought it to her door of mine own accord. Alas, when I knocked, she growled at me to let her be.

Eventually sleep must have taken her, or exhaustion. No more noise came from her room. Soon enough weariness and heartache took all the rest of us to our beds. Even Freddy snored in a chair in the entrance hall, his head propped upon a cushion.

It was on toward three in the morning when I woke to a tap on the shoulder and the whisper of my name in my ear. Holmes was crouching by my bedside with a lit taper, a finger to his lips. He was fully dressed; perhaps he had never been to bed. I rose swiftly, threw on my own clothes, and retrieved my revolver from my bag. Robert slept on, untroubled. I followed Holmes down to the next floor, where his room stood next to Eliza's. Pressing my ear to the door, I could clearly make out two voices, speaking in furious whispers. I recognized Eliza's voice, though it was hoarsened by illness, but there was also a man's voice, a voice that might have been the bark of a mastiff or the howl of an ape.

Holmes raised his hand to signal action, but as he did so, there came a storm of footsteps on the landing, and Freddy's voice crying, "Liza! Liza! Liza!" Freddy steamed past us full tilt, nearly cracking his skull as he tried to run through a locked door. There was a roar from within and a scream, then the thump of a body hitting the floor. Holmes and I charged the door in unison. It shuddered once, twice, and then the lock gave way. We rushed into the room and saw first the window standing open, the curtains dancing with the night wind, and next the figure of Eliza Doolittle huddled on the floor, dead or unconscious. I knelt at her side and took her wrist to determine which. Freddy entered, fluttering spastically, and joined Holmes, who was gazing out the window.

"It's him, Mr. Holmes," Freddy cried, pointing to the street. "Look! It's Ned!" He would have climbed out the window after the intruder, but Holmes held him back. For my part, I had ascertained that Eliza still lived, though she was unconscious and her breathing was shallow. I caught her up and laid her on the bed. She moaned. Her flesh was grey and a scent rose off her like mildew.

Freddy broke free of Holmes's grasp and threw himself out the hall door, determined to swoop down upon his hated rival.

"Don't go alone, Freddy!" Holmes cried, but his warning fell on deaf ears. Freddy was already thundering down the stairs. Holmes turned up the gaslight by the bed. His eyes swept the room. He stooped to pick something up from the floor.

"How is the girl, Watson?"

"She'll live."

"Then come."

At this point the room began to fill up with housemaids, all wakened by the noise, with Higgins and Pickering and policemen and any neighbor who lived within five streets, so far as I could tell. Mrs. Pearce was among them, shouting orders and chivvying them about. Holmes and I plowed our way through the crowd in the hall and on the stairs and got free of the house. The rain had ended, but the air was wet and chill, and the fog hung about our shoulders. Freddy had disappeared down the street, but we could still hear him yelling like a madman, splashing through the gutters.

"He'll catch him!" I said.

"Pray God he does not!" Holmes rejoined.

We ran toward the sound of Freddy's voice. Up Wimpole, across Queen Anne into Wellbeck, doubling back through a mews, across a courtyard, and out onto Henrietta Street and Cavendish Square, and still we had not caught up with them; indeed, we were losing ground. This was where age caught up with us. We were hardly decrepit old men, but we could not match the pace of Freddy or his indefatigable quarry. Their trail was easy enough to follow, however, even had I not had the world's greatest detective by my side. There were broken hedges and overturned dustbins and yowling cats, aggrieved by the passage of men through their nocturnal haunts. But we could no longer hear any footfalls but our own. We stopped to catch our breath. The air was leaden and silent, foreboding. Then we heard the sound of a police whistle, sharp and piercing, just down the street. We ran toward it.

We debouched into Regent Circus. The first thing we saw was a police constable, doubled over, vomiting in the street. Then we saw the body.

We crouched over it. There was no question that life had quit this ruin. It was as if it had been run over by an omnibus. Every major bone in the body was broken. The skull was shattered like a china teacup. There was the shank of a hazelwood walking stick, snapped off near the top, lying nearby. I picked it up and handed it to Holmes. He examined it closely, and passed it to the constable, who had recovered himself.

"You know this poor wight, sir?" the constable asked Holmes.

How many corpses had Sherlock Holmes and I examined together over the years? I had learned long ago to look upon them as a set of facts, an evidentiary exhibit, rather than the shell from which a living soul had fled. But the sight of this poor foolish child, whose heart had beat for nothing more than love, made my eyes sting.

Holmes stood up, grim-faced. "Send someone to 27A Wimpole Street. Inform the household that Mr. Eynsford-Hill is dead," he told the constable. He looked to me then, pointing to a set of bloody footprints that tracked down the street. "We'll need Toby."

The game was afoot.

Chapter Twenty-Three

Toby, of course, had long since joined his lop-eared dewlapped ancestors in the next life. Rather amazingly, Mr. Sherman, Toby's owner, was still rattling along this mortal coil, still stuffing animals, still manning the shop in Pinchin Lane. We hung on his bell till we heard the window on the second floor being wrenched open above us.

"Stand back, Watson," said Holmes, pulling me aside. Glad I was that he did so; the first thing that came out of the window was a bucket of dirty water, which splashed to the pavement at our feet. The second thing was Sherman's head in a nightcap. "Go away!" he yelled. "I'll have the law on you!"

Holmes stepped forward into the light. "Mr. Sherman! We have need of your aid!"

"What? By heaven, is that Mr. Sherlock Holmes? And Dr. Watson with him, or I'm a beggar!" The window banged shut, and in a very few minutes, the door was opened to us. In the light of a spitting taper there was little visible but a host of eyes—the glass eyes of the birds and beasts Mr. Sherman made his living stuffing, and the glimmering eyes of the menagerie he shared his shop with, dogs and cats and birds and beasts, a molting parrot and a one-eyed badger and a mother weasel with her litter of newborns.

Sherman was delighted to see his old friend Holmes, but he seemed even happier to see me. He pumped my hand till I thought he'd dislocate my shoulder. "Oh, yes, yes, Doctor, I owe it all to you! After you wrote that glowing recommendation of Toby in *The Strand*, my business was made! Everyone wanted to hire out the old fellow, to find everything from lost earrings to lost husbands."

Toby's talents had been featured in my account of the Sholto family and the rajah's treasure. It was the case that had brought me together with my dear Mary. This was what Sherman meant by my "recommendation."

"You'll be wanting Bert, then? Toby went to his reward ten years ago. There was a notice in the *Times*." Toby had been a tracker nonpareil, but Sherman swore that Toby's grandson, a young hound named Prince Albert, "Bert to his friends," was nearly his match. We were introduced to Bert. Toby had been an ugly mix of spaniel and lurcher. Bert had inherited the ugly, along with his grandsire's friendly disposition and, we hoped, his nose. We returned to the scene of the murder with the dog on a lead, urging the hansom driver to put on his best speed.

When we returned, the police had removed the body, but there was still blood in the street and a crowd of gawkers. A callow young detective-inspector was in charge of the scene, a little, sharp, dark, ferret-faced man. He seemed eager to detain us both for questioning, till he was made to understand that the elderly fellow with the mournful-looking mongrel on his leash was the legendary Sherlock Holmes, working under cover. Once Holmes had explained the presence of Bert, whining on the lead, he was an eager enlistee.

"I'll keep your secret, Mr. Holmes," said the inspector, "as long as it doesn't impede my investigation. But who is this fellow anyway?"

"His name, I believe, is Edward Hyde."

The name meant nothing to the young man. "And what was his beef against this Mr. Eynsford-Hill?"

"He was in Hyde's way."

"That's a pretty picture you paint of the man, Mr. Holmes."

A figure swallowed up in an astrakhan coat stepped out of the crowd. "May I join you, Herr Holmes?"

"Colonel Von Stetten!" Holmes greeted him warmly.

I stared in disbelief.

"Herr Eynsford-Hill was a young man of great courage," said the German. "I should have been here to protect him. He shall be avenged. Dr. Watson," he nodded toward me, "this is neither the time nor the place, but I owe you the profoundest apology, sir. I only hope that when you write the story of this affair, you do not cast me as the villain." He reached down and scratched Bert's head. The dog licked his hand.

I still saw madness in those calm grey eyes. But perhaps a madman could help catch a madman.

"Who's this, then?" asked the inspector. "Another amateur sleuth?"

"Colonel Von Stetten is a diplomatic attaché with the Bavarian embassy," Holmes answered.

"Well, all right then," said the inspector, impressed in spite of himself. "The more the merrier, I suppose."

Thus the four of us—five, counting Bert—began our hunt through London town. Our prey had not made it easy. He had criss-crossed a dozen or more streets in his flight, scaled walls and bounded over fences. But we moved steadily south and east from Marylebone to Soho. I remember hearing the sounds of Oxford Circus awakening to a new day, the whinny of horses, the squeaking of costers' barrows, the sleepy cooing of pigeons. We passed through Compton and then Wardour Streets, both still drowned in slumber, beggars and their children stretched out beneath the sodden awnings of the storefronts, till at last we came to a low house of grimy red brick in Greek Street, wedged between a pawnbroker and a laundry. Bert whimpered and scratched at the door, eager to be let in. The inspector followed up with his best copper's knock, loud enough to open windows up and down the street. Still, he had to knock several times before the door finally juddered open to reveal an old woman in a bedraggled dressing gown and kerchief. She looked extremely put out. It struck me that it must be getting on toward daylight.

"Are you the landlady?" the inspector asked. The woman cocked her head quizzically, like a mynah bird.

"Are you the landlady?" the inspector repeated.

"*Non ho capito.*" She tried to shut the door, but the inspector wedged himself into the opening. Persistence was always the best quality of Scotland Yard.

It was quickly established that the old woman was both Italian and half-deaf. She comprehended none of the inspector's questions. She stood with her hands on her hips croaking "*Non ho capito!*" to every question. Holmes became impatient and stepped forward. "This is Inspector McKay of Scotland Yard, Madame! Either direct us to Edward Hyde's rooms or we'll have the whole house out in the street and take names from everyone."

Inspector McKay's name was feared and hated in Soho. The woman's transformation was immediate. "'E ain't here now, I can tell you that. 'E come bangin' up the steps near an hour ago, and banged back down again in good time, as like he were being chased by the devil."

"Where did he go?" asked the inspector.

"Where'd 'e go? Where'd 'e go? You think I ask my lodgers that? Specially not that villain, 'e'd as soon cut your throat as give you time o' day. And don't ask when 'e'll return, neither. I don't see him some-times for weeks on end."

"We'll see his rooms, then," said Holmes. "Which are they?"

At that moment Bert sprang forward, jerking the lead from my hand. He brushed past the woman and vaulted up the steps.

"Never mind," said Holmes, following Bert's lead. We piled in after Holmes, with the landlady bringing up the rear, muttering to herself and fussing over her keys. We ascended to the third floor, where Bert was whining at the door. The landlady made a great show of pushing her way through us and counting over her keys, as though it were the labor of Hercules. The inspector leaned over to Holmes and whispered, "My name is Privet, sir, not McKay." Holmes merely shrugged.

At last she found the key and unlocked the door for us. The rooms were surprisingly well kept, considering the lodger, but there were signs of a hasty retreat. There were a pair of Hepplewhite chairs before the sitting room fireplace; one lay on its side. There were embers still glowing in the grate, and ashes ground into the rug. A rolltop secretary stood in the corner, with all its drawers standing open.

Holmes knelt before the fireplace and raked up the ashes with the poker. "He's been burning papers here."

Inspector Privet stooped over his shoulder. "Anything left?"

Holmes retrieved a scrap of paper. He showed it to the inspector.

"A check?"

"What's left of it," Holmes answered. "Fifty pounds. Drawn from Coutts, I would imagine." The bearer's name was left blank, and the check was torn so that the signature was unreadable: Gabriel was the first name, but only the first initial of the second name was visible at all. It could have been a G or possibly an S.

"Bad luck. Even Sherlock Holmes could never guess that name in a million years," said the inspector.

Holmes smiled thinly.

In the bedroom, Bert was worrying at a bloody bundle of clothes on the floor. Holmes took it from him and laid the clothes out on the bed: shirt, pants, waistcoat, shoes.

"So he's changed clothes, eh? The dog's no more use to us," said the inspector.

"Bert won't be confused by a change of clothes. It's the man he's got the scent of," Holmes replied coolly.

The inspector turned to an old oak wardrobe. It held nothing but a heavy wool ulster and a few handkerchiefs in the drawer. As the inspector went through the pockets of the ulster, Holmes gave the suit of clothes a thorough going-over.

"Here, what's this?" The inspector had discovered something in the pocket of the ulster. He held it up: a small glass ampoule, apparently empty. "Our man was a drug user."

"It seems to be indicated," said Holmes. He took the ampoule to examine it.

"Opium?" asked the inspector.

"Cocaine is more likely, given the man's savage disposition," said Von Stetten.

Holmes pocketed the ampoule without comment.

"Here we are!" The inspector had found something wound up in one of the handkerchiefs. It turned out to be the handle of a walking stick, ivory chased in silver, carved like a boar's head, broken off an inch from the top of the shank, and stained with blood. "This is more to the point. I'll wager this will match the stick we found at the murder scene."

"No doubt," said Holmes, who seemed unimpressed. The inspector felt the sting of it.

"Well, what has the great detective discovered, then?"

"Ask the landlady about the other man who was here."

"What other man?"

"There's a partial footprint in the ashes by the grate. It's not Hyde's. His foot is small and wide. This other fellow is tall, with a narrower foot. And that ulster belongs to a much taller man than the clothes on the bed."

The inspector seized on this clue eagerly, but it led nowhere. The landlady swore up and down there had been no other man, that Hyde never had visitors. Even worse, Bert could find no scent. Hyde had come down the same stairs that he had gone up, the landlady was sure of that, but Bert could not pick up his scent again. Holmes was more dismayed by this turn of events than anything else. The trail had gone cold.

"Change of clothes, that's what it's about," said the inspector. "Well, we'll put men on all the ports and train stations. According to the description you gave, this man should stand out like a sore thumb in any crowd. We'll get him, you can bank on that."

I thought of Hyde's disappearance after the murder of Sir Danvers Carew, and of the futile attempts of the entire force to bring the Ripper to justice. But Holmes seemed satisfied.

The sun was sifting through the chinks and crannies of Soho as we parted with the inspector. Those streets were hardly more inviting by day than by night, but Holmes was sanguine. "Let us return our friend Bert to Mr. Sherman, and find ourselves some breakfast. Then we can take up our business again, renewed."

"Yes, but where in the wide world do we begin to look for Mr. Edward Hyde?"

Holmes showed me the torn check again. "Tell me, Watson, if you were a gambling man, would you say the initial of the last name was a G or an S?"

"A 'G,' I'd guess."

"I agree. After breakfast, then, we shall pay a visit to Dr. Gabriel Guest. Colonel, will you join us?"

Von Stetten demurred. "I am no Sherlock Holmes, but I have my own resources. I shall hunt in my own way, if you don't mind. If I find Hyde, you will know of it, Herr Holmes."

Chapter Twenty-Four

Our interview with Dr. Guest was not to come, not that day. His flat was in Montague Street. His door was answered by his valet, a middle-aged, whey-faced fellow who answered to the name of Mead. He regretted to say that his master was ill and would see no one. Had his master gone out that morning? His master had not left his bed for days. He had suffered a relapse of an illness contracted during his years in India. What was the nature of his illness? That was between Dr. Guest and his own physician. Holmes explained that the situation was dire. Mead was implacable. Was his master aware that Mr. Eynsford-Hill had been murdered that morning by Edward Hyde? He could not say whether his master was acquainted with either gentleman. Holmes offered to converse with the doctor through a door. Mead countered that his master had lost his voice. Holmes offered to pose his questions in writing. Mead allowed that it would be acceptable, but didn't know when a reply would be forthcoming. His master was too weak to read or wield a pen.

Stymied, Holmes requested pen and paper. The valet looked as if he was trying to think of a way to refuse him, but he lacked that much nerve. "Please remain here," he said.

He disappeared into the next room. As soon as he was gone, Holmes legged it down the hall and around the corner. I was so surprised I was speechless. The valet would surely return at any moment. I had no choice but to act. I went into the sitting room, coughing like a man in a house on fire.

The valet appeared. He had pen and paper in hand. "I asked you to remain in the front hall," he said peevishly.

"Something to drink, for the love of God!" I said between coughs.

The valet gave me a sidelong look, but he acceded to my request. He went to the kitchen while I continued coughing myself hoarse.

By the time he brought me a glass of water and watched me drink it, I felt it safe to return to the front hall. Indeed, at that moment, I heard Holmes call, "Hello! Did you forget my pen and paper, my good fellow?"

We returned to the front hall, where the valet grudgingly handed over pen and paper. Holmes appeared ready to write, but then said, "Never mind all this! I'll see your master later," and he handed paper and pen back to the valet. By this point the fellow had seen quite enough of us both, and he ushered us to the door without a word.

We were on the step, and the valet shutting the door, when Holmes thrust his foot in the door and said, "One more thing. Dr. Guest's own physician is Dr. Watson in Queen Anne Street, is that correct?

"No, sir," said the valet, visibly angry. "Dr. Strachey, in Harley Street."

"Ah, yes. That was who I meant."

Once the door was shut, Holmes led me around the side of the house, and pointed up at the top window. "Think you could climb up there, Watson?"

There were no windows or doors beneath, no corbel or projection of any kind, no clinging ivy or kindly shade trees, only sheer stone blocks. "Not even when I was a boy!" I answered.

"Nor could I. But Hyde can. He's in there with Guest. The door was locked, but I heard his growl. Man and master are *in camera*. Though which is man and which is master, I cannot but wonder."

"Hyde hardly seems the kind of fellow to tend an invalid."

"Guest is no invalid. I saw his print upon the runner in the hall. It's the same one I saw on the rug in Greek Street."

"What can two such men have to do with one another? Could they be members of some sinister brotherhood?"

"Brotherhood?" mused Holmes. "There you might have something, Watson. Indeed, there are only two instances I know of when such disparate personalities are so close. When one is blackmailing the other, or when the two are brothers."

By now it was getting on for noon. We decided to return to Wimpole Street to give what aid and comfort we might. There was a constable posted at the door who gave us the once-over reserved for the most egregious miscreants, but we passed muster.

The house we entered was a calamity of confusion. Higgins was in and out of the servants' quarters, giving all sorts of contradictory orders that no one paid the slightest attention to. Mrs. Pearce followed behind him, telling him it wouldn't do, sir, it simply wouldn't do. Freddy's mother, Mrs. Eynsford-Hill, and his sister, Clara, were both there, under the aegis of Mrs. Higgins. It seemed that Pickering had been deputized to break the awful news to Freddy's family, and had enlisted Mrs. Higgins in the cause. Mrs. Eynsford-Hill and her daughter were absolutely overcome, so patently incapable of coming to terms with the news or making any kind of plan for the future that Pickering had brought them back with him and deposited them in the blue parlor. Clara Eynsford-Hill seemed as flighty as her brother, concerned that his violent death would be misconstrued by the better tiers of society, yet her affection and grief for her brother seemed real enough. Her mother sat staring into space, a querulous look on her face. Mrs. Higgins sat next her, holding her hand, and urging her to drink a cup of tea. Inspector Privet was there, sleepy-eyed and morose. He seemed more wrung out by the Eynsford-

Hills than by Hyde, trying to draw out any pertinent information about Freddy. We stood in the hall, watching them, uncertain of our place.

"I warned Freddy over and over about his associates," said Mrs. Eynsford-Hill piteously. "All wastrels and vagabonds!"

"Oh, Mother, do stop talking drivel!" riposted Clara.

"Was Hyde an associate of your son?" the inspector asked.

"Hyde. Hyde . . ." said Mrs. Eynsford-Hill distractedly. "Who is Hyde?"

The inspector folded his notebook and put it away. He saw us standing in the hall. His eyes slid over us as if we were not there.

Then Higgins descended upon us like a driving rain. "What are you still doing here?" he asked the inspector. "Have you arrested the man who broke into my home?"

"We'll get him, sir. Don't trouble your mind on that score."

"Of course not," returned Higgins pettishly. "Because we know Scotland Yard always gets their man. What I want to know is, how can you guarantee our safety here?"

"I don't make guarantees, sir. We'll have a man watching your house round the clock until we've apprehended the suspect."

"You don't make guarantees? My butcher can guarantee the freshness of his beef. My tailor can guarantee the fit of my trousers. I can guarantee my clients the results they want." Here Higgins noticed Mr. Morello in the doorway, his greatest failure in phonetics, but our presence only seemed to fuel his sermon. "Why can Scotland Yard afford me no guarantee? This fellow has made an attempt on Eliza's life. There's no reason to think he won't try it again."

"If he'd made an attempt on her life, she would not still be alive. It took him no time at all to dispatch poor Freddy," said his mother drily. Clara Eynsford-Hill broke out in a sob.

"Now see what you've done," said Mrs. Higgins, chiding her son.

"What *I've* done?" Higgins was vexed by an accusation he considered wholly unwarranted.

"Could I see the young lady now, sir?" asked the inspector.

"Are you out of your senses? The girl is prostrated, practically at death's door!" Higgins fumed.

The rest of us looked to the colonel for a saner opinion.

Pickering steepled his fingers together and blinked like an owl. "Well, the fever has broken, or the spell, or whatever you call it. She's sitting up, and taking some tea and toast, but she's still quite weak, and with the terrible news about Freddy, her nerves are in quite a delicate condition. I don't think she could stand up under a police interrogation. I'm sure she never got a look at this burglar to begin with—Freddy was on the scene so quickly. Can't it wait?"

The inspector agreed to return the next morning to interview Eliza. He made his bows to the ladies, fixed his hat on his head, and beat a hasty retreat from the house. Higgins recalled a few choice words that he had not yet launched, and chased after him.

"Mr. Higgins is always so abrupt," said Clara. "It's like having a cat. You never know which way he will pounce."

"My son has no manners," said Mrs. Higgins summarily.

Holmes and I stepped into the hall. Pickering stole out to join us. I could spy Mrs. Pearce and one of the maids setting out a cold collation in the dining room for lunch. We spoke in confidential tones, though they seemed to pay no attention to us.

"Damned uncomfortable, that!" said Pickering. "I hardly knew what to say to the fellow. One wants to be truthful with the police, but I'm not even sure what the truth is!"

"I think we are coming close to the truth now, Colonel," said Holmes, "though we have purchased it at a terrible price."

"Yes. Who would have thought Freddy had a hero in him?"

"And to help us come closer to the truth, I have a question for you."

"This is my day to be grilled. Ask away, then," Pickering answered affably.

"It's about your friend Dr. Guest."

"Friend!" Pickering snorted. "Neither friend nor doctor, so far as I'm concerned. A real doctor would leave his deathbed to tend to his patients."

"Your colleagues in India spoke glowingly of his dedication."

"He wouldn't be the first to weave a reputation out of whole cloth."

"I'm interested in an earlier time. Do you know anything of his family in Ireland? Whether any of them came here with him?"

"Oh! Well, he's not actually Irish, you know. He was born and raised right here in London."

"And how does one acquire an Irish brogue in the heart of London?"

"The mother died in childbirth, I believe. He was raised by an Irish nursemaid out of County Clare. Bridgid or Cathleen O'Something. Five younger brothers and sisters she brought with her, I think. All swarming about the environs."

"Father dead, too?"

"Never at home. Chief clerk to a solicitor. One of the old praetorians. Counted some of the highest in the land as clients, at least that's what Guest claims. Utterson, I think the solicitor's name was. Higgins would know."

The detective's nostrils quivered visibly at the mention of Mr. Utterson. Even I recognized that here could be no coincidence. Utterson was a friend of Jekyll. Jekyll had murdered Hyde—or been murdered by him, if one discounted Nancy Kelly's story. Now we had the son of Utterson's clerk. It meant something. Unfortunately, I had no idea what. Holmes looked at me archly. "So we can eliminate brotherhood as a motive. Which leaves us with blackmail, eh, Watson?"

I may have mumbled a reply of some sort. A moment before, Martha Pearce had looked up and seen me watching her through the door. The blood rushed to her cheeks. I mumbled something again by way of making my excuses to the gentlemen and slipped into the dining room.

As soon as I was near, Mrs. Pearce flung herself upon me, burying her face in my shoulder. I was entirely unmanned. Her cool facade was broken, baring the soul beneath as she grieved for Freddy; I could only love her for her weakness. I would speak my heart, which I had not known till that very moment. Once again there would be a Mrs. Watson to grace the table at Queen Anne Street.

But I could not simply declare my affections then and there, not as Hill Barton, secretary to a Mafia chieftain. I would have to confess my true identity to her first. There could be no deception between two minds in congruence. It would mean betraying the confidence of Sherlock Holmes. It might bring all his efforts to naught. What was that to me?

Without realizing it, I had taken her hand. She looked up at me, tremulous. The maid vanished into the kitchen. This was our moment.

Then Higgins popped in the door, with the ladies in tow. Mrs. Pearce fled like a wraith. "If we're not safe here, we'll go abroad until they've caught this fellow," Higgins was saying. "We'll go to Italy. Eliza will adore Italy."

I stood there in a daze. Higgins took a plate and began helping himself to the cold tongue. Pickering and Holmes filed in, Holmes's eyes full of curiosity and concern.

"You won't adore it. You wouldn't last a week in Italy, Henry," said his mother reprovingly. "You wouldn't last a week in Scotland. I don't believe you could survive anywhere further than a twenty-mile radius from the Monument."

"Pickering, you'll come with us to Italy, won't you? You'll find more dialects there than the entire damned subcontinent."

"Higgins, have you forgotten you have a student?" Pickering asked, nodding toward Holmes.

Holmes chimed in: "We're just hittin' our stride, Henry."

Higgins darted him a murderous look. "In point of fact, Mr. Morello, no matter whether I voyage to Italy or Timbuctoo or the British Museum, it is my intention to discontinue your lessons as of present date. You and your strong-arm man may clear out, as they say in America, where I doubt you have ever set foot. I don't know if your client is the Duchess of Wurttemberg or the Princess of Waldeck, but you can tell whoever it is that Eliza is not for sale to the blue-blooded boobies of old Europe. I fashioned her for better things than that. If you'll start packing your bags now, you can be gone before tea."

"Henry, you're talking gibberish," said his mother.

"I understand the strain your boy's been under lately, ma'am. I'm sure it'd do him a world of good to take the waters at Bottom-Bottom or wherever. But we got us a contract, and in the good ole U.S. of A., when we sign on the dotted line, we stick to it, or the lawyers start mixing it up. I expect it's the same way here in the land of John Bull. Least that's what my solicitor says."

For a moment, Higgins seemed vanquished. Then he strained a smile through his lips. "You're absolutely right, Mr. Morello. I was forgetting myself. On the other hand, I'm sure you'll agree that a contract is only binding so long as both parties are actually who they claim to be."

Holmes gave a benevolent nod. He took out a cigar and inhaled its aroma.

"In which case I shall be rid of your company by five o'clock at this afternoon. Please do make yourself available at that time, sir."

I couldn't guess what Higgins had in store for Holmes, but the threat seemed real enough. Holmes, however, remained unperturbed. He leaned over to Mrs. Eynsford-Hill and asked, "You got a light, sister?"

The lady blushed like a schoolgirl.

Chapter Twenty-Five

"**W**ell, Watson, time we started packing, eh?"

"Then it's true? Higgins has the means to force us out?"

"He certainly seems to think so. I think we can assume that his pet private detective is ready to share his discoveries. It should be an entertaining performance."

His bravado was cold comfort. "So we are destined never to discover the truth about Eliza Doolittle!" I mourned. "When we were so close."

"Be of good cheer, Watson. There may be other avenues of investigation still open to us."

I found Robert in our shared quarters, sitting on the bed, looking forlorn. "Well, old 'un, appears our fellowship is come to a untimely end. No more into our breeches, dear friend, and hanged be him wot first cries old enough!"

Apparently this was his way of acknowledging the writing on the wall. I was bewildered by the sense of it but touched by the sentiment. Then he added, "Pack yer bag for a tanner."

It was five o'clock on the dot when the front doorbell rang. Mrs. Higgins had packed up the Eynsford-Hills and taken them to tea. Holmes and I were in the laboratory with Pickering. I had attempted several times to broach the subject of Higgins's detective, but neither man evinced the slightest concern in the matter. Holmes had been expounding on the joys of beekeeping instead, which Pickering seemed to find a fascinating topic. The door flew open and Higgins entered with his avenging angel.

The detective wore the same costume I remembered from our first encounter, including the deerstalker cap, which he seemed no more inclined to remove from his head than the meerschaum pipe from his lips, but he was an imposing figure for all that. Higgins seemed to glory in his aura of unyielding authority.

"Gentlemen," he said, "I would like you all to meet someone you may only know from the newspapers. This is the world-famous detective Mr. Sherlock Holmes."

It was an astonishing statement. Pickering and I sat forward in our seats. "Mr. Morello" leaned back comfortably, as if ready to hear a marvelous tale.

Higgins continued. "From the moment I met you, Mr. Morello, I was convinced that you were not who you claim to be. Your American accent is good, but not good enough to deceive the ear of Henry Higgins."

"Then why invite me to bunk here?"

"The best way to deal with a spy is to keep him close to the vest. In light of my suspicions, I sought out Mr. Holmes here to investigate you and find out your true identity. He has now completed his investigation. I'm sure you'll be interested in his conclusions."

"Sounds like a humdinger. Fire away, Mr.—Combs, was it?"

"Sherlock Holmes, thank you, sir. Immediately upon the check clearing, I began the investigation Mr. Higgins requested. I contacted certain parties in the United States, specifically in the area of New York City. After an exhaustive inquiry conducted in both America and Great Britain, I can now confirm that this gentleman is indeed

Giorgio Bernardo Morello, born in Corleone, Sicily, emigrated with his family to New York City at the age of nine. Indicted three times for extortion, twice for conspiracy, twice for grand larceny, once for murder. Acquitted on every occasion. President of Morello Importers, with annual profits of—"

"Wait!" cried Higgins. "I'm not interested in G.B. Morello. I want to know about this fellow, the imposter. You must have uncovered his true identity."

"I'm afraid this fellow is the real Mr. Morello, sir. If you'd care to examine these newspaper clippings with his photograph, you'll see for yourself. Mr. Morello, I am convinced, is a fugitive from justice, and certainly from rival crime families, in his adopted country, but his passport and papers are in perfectly good order, and no extradition has been requested by the U.S. government."

"This is impossible! I tell you this fellow is no more American than I am!" Higgins's face was purple with rage.

"All the evidence speaks to the contrary, Professor. If he is not Morello, I am not Sherlock Holmes."

A sentiment that no one there could deny.

"Just listen to his voice, man! Can you not hear that Sussex accent?"

"Perhaps your ear for accents is not quite as reliable as you suppose, Mr. Higgins," said "Sherlock Holmes."

"Now that you mention it, Mr. Holmes, I'm not at all certain your accent is authentic! Have you ever lived abroad?"

"Higgins, this is preposterous! Are you going to question my accent next?" wailed Pickering.

Higgins's confidence seemed shaken. He pointed a finger at Pickering. "This is your fault! You recommended him. You said he was infallible."

"Oh, I don't think I could have used that word. No one is infallible, Higgins. Excepting yourself, of course."

"When's our next lesson, Henry?" asked Holmes blithely. "We could get in some work before dinner, what d'you say?"

Higgins snarled and stormed out of the room.

Holmes rose to shake his doppelganger's hand. "Thank you, sir. Your assistance has been invaluable. I am deep in your debt."

"The honor is mine, Mr. Holmes. You have been and always shall be an inspiration. And Dr. Watson! I think of you as my writing partner." He shook my hand, though I was dumbfounded. "Now, gentlemen, I must take my leave. Curtain's at eight."

I must have still looked befogged after the detective made his exit. Holmes and Pickering both burst into laughter. "It was the colonel's idea," said Holmes.

"When Higgins asked me who he could hire to investigate Mr. Morello, the first name that came to mind was Sherlock Holmes. But that, of course, was impossible. Then I remembered Eliza telling me all about the play she and Freddy had seen at the Adelphi."

"I confess I am no wiser," I said.

"Watson, I'm disappointed! Have you never seen the American actor William Gillette play Sherlock Holmes on stage?"

"He's seen him now, playing Sherlock Holmes right here in this room!" said Pickering, laughing again.

I had never been fond of play-going. Sherlock Holmes himself in all the many roles he had impersonated in the course of our investigations had been enough theatre to last a lifetime, though I confess to a fondness for Gilbert and Sullivan. But from that moment on, William Gillette became my favorite thespian. Although I never quite understood the reason for the deerstalker cap.

"I'll have to tip the boy to unpack my bag again."

"Save your money, Watson. Tonight you will sleep in your own bed. It's time we made a move in any case. Continuing on here can only restrict our freedom and hamper our investigation. Professor Higgins's timing is advantageous for us."

"Then we're never to find the real Eliza?" Pickering asked.

"On that score"—Holmes pulled a paper from his pocket and handed it to me—"I received a wire from Wiggins this afternoon. Watson?"

I opened the telegram and read aloud:

MISS LAVER HOME FOR FEMALE ORPHANS
ST JOHNS WOOD 6 P.M.

"That's all?" I asked, bemused.

"Wiggins was always a young man of admirable economy. I assume that if we want to find out more, we must be in St. John's Wood in fifteen minutes."

Mrs. Pearce entered. "Mr. Morello, your cab is ready. Robert has put your luggage inside."

"Thanks, Mrs. Pearce. You've been a doll."

She avoided my gaze. Perhaps she regretted our moment of intimacy. I was already half-convinced that I had been saved by fortune from committing a grave error. I have wondered ever since if my error was in walking out of that house that day without unburdening my heart.

Pickering came out to the cab to see us off. "You're coming with us, aren't you, Colonel?" asked Holmes.

"Well, but what do I tell Higgins?" He cast a look back toward the windows of the house, from one of which no doubt Higgins was watching our departure.

"We're about to find out if the girl in that bedroom up there is truly Eliza Doolittle. Shall we wire you the answer?"

Pickering joined us without uttering another word.

We arrived at the Home and dismissed the cab, sending the bags on to Queen Anne Street, where I had already alerted my housekeeper of my homecoming. The Home for Female Orphans had stood in Lisson Grove for over a century. Its matron, Miss Laver, had run the place for forty years; the costume she wore that evening might have been the same she was wearing when she first walked through the doors, all crinolines and stays and lace trim everywhere. Her office was devoid of luxury. Pickering sat down in the chair across from her desk before he noticed there were no other chairs, and was mortified when neither Holmes nor I would let him give it up.

"Mr. Holmes?" She looked over her spectacles at him as if he had been sent up for some dire infraction of the rules.

Holmes bowed. Miss Laver's eyes dissected him swiftly.

"I remember you, Mr. Holmes. Your name was once in all the papers. But I don't believe I've read an account of a new case since the nineties."

"I've retired."

"I can't imagine a man such as you retiring."

Holmes declined to answer.

"Your associate Mr. Wiggins told me to expect you. Mr. Wiggins is another private detective. And these gentlemen?"

"Friends of Miss Doolittle's." Holmes introduced us.

"Is Eliza in trouble?" Miss Laver was not a woman to mince words.

"First, I must ask. The girl in the picture is Eliza Doolittle? You're certain of the fact?"

Miss Laver glanced down at the photograph on her desk. Something in it made her smile. "Certain. I haven't seen her in nearly two years, but it's Eliza, all right. She looks well."

"She was under your care here?"

"Oh, no. She wasn't an orphan, you see. Our rules are quite strict here. Though her papa did try to pass her off as an orphan, and more than once. I think he and Eliza both came to wish fervently that it were the truth."

"Then how did you come to know her?"

"The first time she came to us I was tricked into believing she truly was alone in the world. She was here for several months before the deception was exposed. By then she had burrowed her way into my heart."

"She was a model child, then? Nothing...out of sorts...with her?"

"Far from it. There was everything out of sorts. She was a change-ling."

Pickering broke in. "Changeling? You mean a . . . a . . ."

"A fairy child, left by fairies when they steal human children away. Well, they're not really children, are they? They look it, but they don't act it. They make the milk go sour and the knives go dull. But they bring gifts, too."

"Madame, are you telling us you believe in fairies?" Pickering asked, incredulous.

"I don't know, Colonel. I only know there are more things on heaven and earth than are dreamt of in our philosophies. I know there are children—girls are what I know, really—who simply have no place in this world of ours. They're oddities, misfits. Every hand is against them. Nurse calls them woebegones. They're always coming to her because they fall down more, get knocked down more, try the patience of the world more than other children. Where do they belong? How came they here? I don't know. But they are harder to love, so we must love them all the more."

"But you threw her out," Holmes pointed out. "Did she return?"

"Once she had found us, she was always in and out, stealing food from the kitchen, stealing books from the library. We turned a blind eye, as much as we could. Sometimes she stole a nap in the very chair you're sitting in, Colonel."

Pickering patted the arm of his chair affectionately.

"I wish we could have done more. But the orphanage depends on subscription, and our benefactors, kind as they are, are always quick to believe that orphans are liars and pickpockets out of Mr. Dickens's books. Eliza had to make her way in the world when she was far too young, in the teeth of the wind, with no help from the father. Yet she was bound and determined to survive, and more than survive." She consulted the photograph fondly once more, and then put it away in a drawer of her desk. "Now perhaps you'll tell me: is she in trouble?"

Holmes spoke carefully. "She's in danger."

"Ah. Well, that has always been true. Never before has she had Sherlock Holmes to rescue her. Or do you do that, now you're retired?"

There was no reason to prolong the conversation, which only threatened to become more awkward. We had what we came for. We made our farewells and hastened away. To satisfy some perverse whim of Pickering's, we hailed a motor-cab for the return trip. I nearly expired from the fumes.

"Well, Colonel, you have your answer at last," said Holmes. Miss

Laver has made a positive identification of Eliza based on an acquaintance of fourteen years. There is and always has been only one Eliza Doolittle—"

"Well, I'm glad of that," said Pickering. "I've grown quite fond of her."

"—and I fear she has been in danger from the day she met you."

"But then Higgins was right! Wouldn't Eliza be safer in Italy, or anywhere on the continent?" Pickering asked.

"Perhaps. If she were spirited away in the dead of night by the dark of the moon and then bricked up in the deepest dungeon of some haunted castle in the Outer Carpathians. But that is not the Grand Tour as Higgins envisions it. Hotel dining rooms, train stations, public streets? No, travel of that kind would be a hundred times more dangerous than remaining here in Higgins's house with the faithful watchdogs of the British constabulary at the door."

"Then you do think Hyde will return?"

"The answer lies in this question: why did Hyde break in to begin with, and what did he achieve?"

"But Mrs. Pearce swears nothing was taken from Eliza's room," Pickering pointed out.

"Nothing that Mrs. Pearce knew was there. But there were these." Holmes pulled two glass ampoules from his pocket. I recognized one, which the inspector had found in Hyde's room. Holmes had never returned it to him. The other one was alike in every way, save that it still held a few drops of some blood-red liquid.

"Where did you find that?" I asked.

"In the rolltop desk."

"You didn't hand them over to the police?" Pickering asked.

"Scotland Yard is searching for Edward Hyde. The contents of these two ampoules will not help them. But if I can extract a viable sample from each of these, it should help me understand the connection between Miss Doolittle, Mr. Hyde, and Dr. Guest."

"Eliza? What's she got to do with this blighter Hyde?" asked Pickering.

"I discovered this on her floor last night." He produced a used syringe from his pocket. "I believe Hyde injected its contents into Miss Doolittle's blood. If the residue matches that found in Hyde's flat—"

"Eliza and Hyde are using the same drug," I said.

We dropped Pickering at Wimpole Street and decamped to my rooms in Queen Anne Street. Holmes was relieved to shed the skin of Mr. Morello. He kicked off his boots and stretched out in a chair before the fireplace. "I've had little chance to visit any of our old haunts since this case began, Watson. Fritz Kreisler is playing tonight at Queen's Hall. I think we might indulge ourselves in Elgar, if you'll join me. Tomorrow, I intend to see a doctor."

"Dr. Strachey in Harley Street?"

The notion seemed to stop him in midthought. Then it clicked into place. "Should not be overlooked. If you could pay him a visit, Watson, he might be more inclined to share secrets with a fellow medico in confidence. As for me, I shall visit Dr. Stamford at Bart's."

Chapter Twenty-Six

I rose the next morning at seven. Holmes had already left. My
housekeeper seemed a bit put off by my sudden return, with guest
in tow. The dust on the mantle was proof that she had not been the
most conscientious steward in my absence. I will confess that I helped
myself to a leisurely breakfast. I had not realized it, but playing the role
of Hill Barton, secretary, for so long, had worn upon my nerves.

The newspapers were still full of Freddy's murder, but they offered
little in the way of hard facts. The whole mystery of Eliza Doolittle
seemed more muddled to me than ever, though I sensed from Holmes's
restless energy that he was close to the truth.

Around ten I called Dr. Strachey's office and spoke to an assistant.
I explained that I was Dr. John Watson, and I hoped to consult with
Dr. Strachey about a patient named Gabriel Guest. I was instructed to
come around after three.

Dr. Strachey's establishment in Harley Street put my own poor
squat to shame, with comfortably upholstered Sheraton chairs, a fireplace of Carrara marble, and the latest prints by Sargent and Whistler
and Sisley—at least I hoped they were only prints. The young lady who

greeted me was so pleasingly upholstered and so gracefully shaped that she might have been a Sheraton herself. She knocked on the door of Strachey's consulting room and announced me.

Strachey's inner sanctum was as impressive as the outer precincts, with a mahogany desk as deep as a cricket pitch. There was no question of our shaking hands unless one or both of us climbed on top of the desk to reach across it. A wall full of morocco-bound volumes guarded his back.

Strachey himself rather reminded me of a comic opera tenor. He had a fine prominent forehead, a gold-framed pince-nez perched daringly on his nose, and a lanceolate beard.

"Dr. Watson, is it? I've been expecting you," Strachey said.

"You have?" It occurred to me that Guest might have warned him against me already.

"Perhaps not in person. But I knew someone would come. I have his file right here." He pushed across a fat file folder tied up with a red ribbon.

"This is more than I could have asked for," I said, straining across the desk to reach the folder.

"Not at all. If you're going to treat Gabriel Guest, you'll need every iota of information on his condition. Sit, sit!"

I planted myself in the chair before his desk and untied the ribbon on the folder.

"You're no longer treating him, then?" I asked.

"I made that quite plain to him weeks ago, whatever he may have told you."

I opened the file and began skimming through it. There was so much German terminology scattered through it that I might have been reading a Wagner libretto.

Strachey became impatient. "I've diagnosed his condition as *folie circulaire*."

I could not hide my bewilderment.

"*Folie circulaire*! Manic melancholia. What kind of a psychiatrist are you, sir?"

I mumbled something about the Vienna school, which was the entire sum of my knowledge of psychiatry.

"And you think you'll be able treat him merely with analysis?"

"What do you know of his antecedents?"

"You won't find much on that front. The condition is often hereditary, but it seems his father was the most placid type of fellow, law clerk to old Utterson, if you remember him. Represented half the doctors in Harley Street. A most somnolent pair of fellows when they were together."

"What was it that made you part ways with him?"

"You haven't noticed it yet? The damn fellow self-medicates. And I don't just mean lithium salts. He's concocted one of the strangest witch's brews I've ever come across. Said he perfected it experimenting on soldiers in India. Can you imagine? Ought to have his license voided."

"What, he experimented on malaria patients?"

"On mental patients."

"Well!" I shut up the file folder and pushed it back across the desk. "In view of what you've told me, I don't think I'll be taking him on, either."

He was nonplussed by my sudden turnaround. "Well, I don't want to influence you unduly. Perhaps you want to take some time to review the file—"

I rose from my seat. "No, I'll leave that with you for the next fellow who comes around. I'm sure some young fellow will be eager to take him on. I can't thank you enough for your counsel. Life's too short, eh? Good afternoon to you."

In lieu of shaking his hand, I knocked on Dr. Strachey's mahogany desktop like an aboriginal drummer sending signals from one village to the next. Then I said goodbye to Whistler and Sargent and Sisley and the Sheraton girl.

I decided to stop at Bart's and see if Sherlock Holmes was still there. St. Bartholomew's was the oldest hospital in London, indeed in all of England. It had been a second home to me during my years in medical school. Yet by some strange twist of fate, I had not crossed the threshold of the old place since the day I had been introduced to Sherlock Holmes there all those years ago. Even stranger was the fact that after I climbed the stairs to the second floor, the first face I saw was that of Stamford, my former dresser, who had introduced us. I had not seen him since that day, either.

"I'm in charge of the place now, believe it or not," he said, shaking my hand enthusiastically. "I should have expected you, eh? Where goes Sherlock Holmes, there goes Dr. Watson."

I did not bother to point out that Holmes and I had largely gone our separate ways for the last ten years. Stamford escorted me to the chemical lab, where Holmes was absorbed in his analysis of the contents of the two ampoules and the syringe he had found. It was a cavernous room with a high, arched ceiling. A long table was crowded with flasks and beakers and the long, jetting flames of etnas.

"How goes it, Holmes?"

"Ah, Watson! Having the devil of a time. Come see. Stamford, be a good fellow and find us some tea?"

Stamford was now a greybeard and the chief of chemical research at St. Bart's, a position of some prestige, but at Holmes's request, he hesitated only a moment before he muttered, "Of course," and headed off to wait upon us as if he were a nineteen-year-old assistant.

"Have you been able to identify your samples?" I asked.

Holmes frowned. "The contents of the syringe from Eliza's room and the ampoule from the wardrobe appear identical. Some sort of powerful depressant. I expected heroin, but it's not that. Nor any other opioid, apparently. Nor a cannabinoid. No drug I've come across before. But the sample is so small that I don't expect to discover much more. The red liquid from the second ampoule would seem to be more promising, but also far more complex. There's a phosphorus-based stimulant, but there are some puzzling elements involved. At any rate, the two compounds seem almost to be polar opposites."

"Like a poison and its antidote?"

"A fair analogy. But you don't give poison to one fellow and the antidote to another."

I asked whether he had found lithium salts in either compound.

"An interesting question. Why do you ask?"

"I had a talk with Dr. Strachey. It turns out this Strachey is a psychiatrist, and Dr. Guest suffers from a mental condition—"

"*Folie circulaire*," said Holmes.

"If you already knew, why did you send me to talk to the man?"

"I didn't know, but it was indicated by Guest's behavior, and by your mention of lithium salts. I am glad to have confirmation."

"I'm a practicing doctor, and I've never even heard of *folie circulaire*."

"How would you describe Dr. Guest's character?"

"I'm not sure I could. One moment he's excitable and enthusiastic, and the next he's in the grip of the deepest torpor."

"That, more or less, is *folie circulaire*. Periods of mania alternate with periods of melancholy. There are also periods of lucidity, especially under the palliative of drugs like lithium."

I told him what Dr. Strachey had said about Dr. Guest's tendency toward "self-medication."

"If this is the stuff he's treating himself with, he may have a delicate mind, but he has the intestinal fortitude of a Percheron."

"He experimented on mental patients in India."

"His experiments continued in London."

Stamford returned with our tea. He had even managed to scrounge up a few biscuits, though I suspect they were actually meant for himself. It was rare for Holmes to taste anything when deep into research.

"By the way, you fellows owe me your thanks," said Stamford, pouring the tea.

"We appreciate the tea, old fellow," I replied.

"And the use of your excellent facilities," Holmes added.

"You are welcome any time. But I wasn't speaking of that. Have you forgotten it was I who brought you two together thirty years ago?"

Holmes grinned. "You introduced us, but it was not you who brought us together, Stamford. It was fate."

Chapter Twenty-Seven

Holmes assured me it would be hours before he had any conclusive results, so I returned home alone. After my meeting with Dr. Strachey, I felt I could do myself good by going through some of the latest medical journals. I found something interesting in the *Lancet* on the symptoms of impending apoplexy, and settled into a chair before the fire.

I awoke in darkness. The heavy drapes admitted only a thin mist of light from the streetlamp outside. I could not tell what had woken me, but I felt the hair on the back of my neck prickle with fear. I sat up, trying to brush away the cobwebs of whatever rancid dream still tugged at my mind. There was a draft, that was all.

For the front door was standing open.

The face that shuddered out of the shadows was inhuman. One word oozed from its blackened lips:

"More!"

I moved only just in time. The poker slammed into the back of the chair where my head had lain a moment before. I rolled across the floor and struggled to my feet, putting the chair between us. The poker swept round again, tearing a button from my waistcoat, sparking against the hearthstone.

"Stand still, damn you!" The voice was a guttural whisper. Had I heard it before?

"Hyde?" I gripped the back of the chair, but he grabbed the arm and sent it skirling across the room to smash into the wall. There was nothing between me and him. He seemed to stretch and grow, inhabiting every part of the room at once.

He lunged. I snatched up the fire screen as a shield. I was driven back against the wall, but the poker jammed in the screen. He roared with frustration, tore the screen from my hands, and threw it and the poker across the room. I tripped and fell, which was all that saved me. I was on the floor, crawling on hands and knees, dodging and scurrying like a rat, as he groped for me, blind with rage. He caught a hank of my hair and jerked me to my feet, nearly snapping my spine. Then my hand came against something cold and solid. Admiral Nelson. I grabbed hold of the bust and swung it upward awkwardly. It glanced off his temple and flew from my hand. He swayed for a moment, then dropped like a stone.

I staggered to the lamp and turned up the gas. I gazed down in horror. The man on the floor was not Edward Hyde, but Sherlock Holmes. The flesh of his face was taut against the skull and his color was a dead white. He seemed huddled and shrunken in his clothes. But then the whole room felt shrunken with him lying there. I moved to help him, but he stirred and I drew back in panic. His eyes opened like two lamps of fire. He got to his knees, groaning.

"Holmes? Holmes, my God, man, what's happened to you?"

He looked up at me, his features twisted like a corkscrew, staring as the wolf stares at the lamb. He said once again:

"More!"

—and groped for me. I stumbled back. I knew not what madness had him in his grip, but I had to help him without letting him murder me. He lurched to his feet and rumbled toward me. I turned and ran. I made it to the surgery in time to bolt the door behind me. The door shook as he slammed his fists against it. The lock would not hold against a determined assault, I knew that. I looked about wildly for some kind of weapon. The blank eye sockets of the surgery skeleton stared at me. I thought of my scalpels.

The pounding on the door continued. There was blessed silence for a moment, and then the head of the poker splintered the wood in the center of the door. He didn't need to break the lock. He was going to come right through. And I could hear him under his breath, "More—more—more—more—"

Then a roar: "*Moriarty!*"

The door burst open. The first thing Sherlock Holmes saw was the casement window standing open and the light from the street. The second was the fingers gripping the window ledge, white in the light from the street. He crossed to the window and looked down at the shape of a man, hanging from the ledge, draped in a long dark coat. He grabbed both wrists and yanked.

There was the clatter of bone on bone. Empty eye-sockets leered at him. He tottered backward, baffled to find himself hugging a skeleton when he had expected a man. That moment of confusion was my one hope. I leapt on his back and pressed the ether-soaked towel against his face. He whirled round the room like a typhoon, smashing tables and cabinets, trying to throw me from his back. I clung to him like a drowning man as the room eddied round. With a giant heave, he threw me across the room. I crashed to the floor with my shoulder under me and felt it sing with pain.

He was coming at me, slower now, lumbering, but my right arm was dead. I couldn't get up, could only squirm helplessly. I traded the towel to my left hand. He grabbed me by the throat and raised me above his head as if I were a rag doll. I jammed the ether-soaked towel against his nostrils and prayed. The world broke against me like surf against a seawall and went black.

I woke moments later, lying on the floor. Holmes lay next to me. He had finally succumbed to the ether.

My right arm was numb. I couldn't move Holmes from the floor.

I stuffed a pillow beneath his head, then bound him as best I could. I had nothing but surgical tape to do the job. I wound yards and yards of it around his wrists and knees and ankles. If he woke in that same state of rage he might snap them in a moment. I mended his cuts and bruises, and then my own. The unnatural color and striction slowly left his face. I took that as a good omen. I laid a blanket over his sleeping form, turned out the light in the surgery, and returned to the chair by the fire, this time with a large brandy, hoping to calm my shattered nerves.

I woke some time around four in the morning. Sherlock Holmes was standing over me, looking at me curiously. "My dear friend John," he said, "why did you tie me up on the floor of your surgery? Why is your arm in a sling? And what have you done with Admiral Nelson?"

The admiral lay upon his side on the floor, doughty as ever, but with his nose badly chipped. My housekeeper would ask me about the bust the next day, along with the smashed surgery door, the twisted fire screen, and the general ruin of the house. She did not receive the same explanation I gave Holmes.

"Do you remember any of it?" I asked, after telling him the story.

"I remember being filled with a wild energy, and deciding to walk here rather than take a cab. I remember a feeling of nausea coming over me near the Langham Hotel."

"You sampled the red solution, didn't you?"

"Of course not! At least . . ." He stood stock still, going over every action from the preceding day in his mind. Then he held up one finger.

"I cut my finger on the pipette as I was transferring the solution to a slide. I remember swearing at Stamford. It seemed an insignificant cut."

"But there was blood?"

He nodded. "There was blood. I should have taken better precautions. But only think!"

"What is it I'm thinking about?" I said, yawning. I could think of nothing but sinking into my own bed.

"Hyde resorts to this drug on a regular basis."

"He must be somewhat inured to the effects."

"Somewhat is cold comfort when talking about a drug a drop of which turns a rational human being into a slavering ape. Miss Doolittle is in more danger than I had judged."

"Perhaps Higgins should take her to the continent after all."

"I suspect that was the whim of a moment. And no matter where she goes, Hyde can follow. We must find a way to keep her safe until we can bring him to heel."

"Does such a place exist?"

Holmes touched his temple and winced. There was a purple bruise beginning to bloom there. "That, my friend, is a three-pipe problem."

Chapter Twenty-Eight

"Call Pickering," he said. "Tell him we must meet Eliza for breakfast at the Criterion. Nine o'clock. It is imperative that she be there."

He must have gone out for the morning papers. They lay in heaps around him like drifts of snow. Had he found an answer to our problem there?

I placed the call. Luckily, Pickering was up, and he was able to communicate with Eliza. "She says she already has a breakfast date with Mrs. Higgins." I relayed the message to Holmes.

"Then she can bring her along. This is a matter of life and death."

The Criterion was a grand restaurant facing Piccadilly Circus. It was in the Criterion bar all those years ago that I had run into my old friend Stamford, who had subsequently introduced me to Sherlock Holmes. Besides the main restaurant, there were a number of rooms available for hire. It was to one of these rooms that Sherlock Holmes steered us when we were all met for breakfast that morning. It seemed to be an event for some sort of ladies' group, but open to the public. The room was already filling up as Holmes commandeered a table for the five of us. The ladies were curious, nervous, perhaps even suspicious.

"Who are these people?" Mrs. Higgins asked no one in particular. Pickering shook his head, signaling ignorance.

"Please do be seated, ladies," said Holmes, as he surveyed the room.

"Mr. Morello? What's happened to your accent?" asked Eliza. "Have you had a breakthrough in your lessons?"

"Miss Doolittle, I am sorry to say I have deceived you. My name is not Morello. It is Sherlock Holmes."

"Sherlock Holmes? You mean like the fellow in the play? Running about after villains in a deerstalker cap?" Eliza was sure he was larking somehow.

"Exactly like the fellow in the play," Holmes answered gravely, taking his own seat.

"Wait, you're a character in a play? I don't understand," said Mrs. Higgins.

"I am a private detective, Mrs. Higgins."

"Of no little repute," put in Pickering.

"Not American?" Mrs. Higgins was still trying to follow.

"Entirely English, thank you."

"Well, that's some relief."

"I told Freddy he was real! He used to capture all the bad men in London, but then one day he fell off a cliff and died." Eliza looked at Holmes. "You don't look dead, Mr. Morello."

Holmes gave me a sour look.

"In fact, he did not die, Miss Doolittle," I said diffidently.

She looked from his face to mine, and then to Pickering. There was no doubt to be had that we were all three in earnest.

"So . . . you're not an American millionaire on the run from his gangster cronies? What a shame!" Eliza said wistfully.

"Then what were you doing in my son's home, Mr. Holmes?" Mrs. Higgins asked, climbing her high horse.

"Spying," Holmes answered flatly.

Pickering looked uncomfortable. "I hired Mr. Holmes," he admitted.

"Because you thought I was in danger?" Eliza laid a hand on Pickering's.

"Let's put it that way," Pickering mumbled.

We were interrupted by a platoon of waiters, dancing about with tea and buns. At the same moment, a woman began speaking from the dais, welcoming a roll call of distinguished guests and introducing an honored speaker. We took no notice, but we were obliged, after being shushed by surrounding tables, to lower our voices to just above a whisper.

"Miss Doolittle," said Holmes, "you have been associating with an extremely dangerous man."

"More than one it seems. But I suppose you're talking about Edward."

"You know what it is that makes Edward Hyde so dangerous, don't you?"

"He—Dr. Guest, I mean—had compounded a drug which—"

"Which he tested on Hyde. Which Hyde became addicted to."

She seemed loath to admit it. "Edward would never harm me," she insisted.

"Who are these women?" asked Mrs. Higgins. She was apparently the only one listening to the speaker. The speaker seemed to be saying something not very complimentary about the prime minister and Mr. Churchill. A waiter scooped kippers and fried eggs onto our plates.

"You first met Dr. Guest when Colonel Pickering had a relapse of malaria?" Holmes was saying.

"It was before that, just a few days after I first came to Wimpole Street. You were out that day, Colonel. Professor Higgins brought the doctor in to examine me. He said he didn't want any "Lisson Grove plagues" invading the house with me. I nearly ran out the front door."

"Why was that?"

"All that poking and prodding and questions about my privates? It didn't seem decent to a girl like me who'd never seen a doctor before. And then he stuck a needle in my arm and took blood from me."

"You were perfectly healthy, but Dr. Guest insisted you needed some sort of inoculation."

"That was when Colonel Pickering took sick. Dr. Guest said it would keep me from catching what the colonel had. But that was a lie, of course. Dr. Guest lies."

"It was a powerful, durable sedative, which acted on your nervous system for weeks at a time."

Eliza hesitated. "At first. But as time went on, it became necessary to take the drug more and more frequently."

Mrs. Higgins leaned over to confer with one of the ladies from the next table. She came back to announce, "She says they're with the WSPU. What is that?" Pickering was busy applying himself to the kippers and pretending to be deaf.

"Suffragettes," said Holmes offhandedly.

"Suffragettes! How horrid! Bomb throwers, you mean! These women tried to blow up the House of Parliament! Eliza, we must leave at once."

"I'm sure these aren't the same women, Mrs. Higgins," said Pickering soothingly.

"They are the very same women," said Holmes.

"Oh, dear," said Eliza.

"The drug altered your behavior and bearing so drastically that Pickering almost believed you were a different girl," said Holmes.

Fear came into her eyes. "I . . . almost was. It was meant to keep me docile. Like a lady, he said. I wanted so desperately to be a lady. At least at first."

It was then I noticed a grizzled old fellow in a dark suit standing by the door, and recognized him. Inspector Newcomen! I stood and waved to him. If he was here, it could be no coincidence. He must have come to see Sherlock Holmes. He didn't notice me, however, or at least he did not look my way.

"Holmes!" I said. "It's Newcomen. From the Yard."

Holmes ignored me. He went on inexorably, questioning Eliza. "Hyde came to you because the drug you were given counteracted the effects of the one he was given."

"It weren't—it wasn't Edward's fault. He and Guest had had a . . . a falling out. Guest was trying to poison him."

"You took pity on him. You shared what little you had, what you could beg from Guest."

There were three other men in dark suits, I noticed then, each standing by one of the doors. They were all staidly dressed, with blank official-looking faces looking at nothing and measuring everything. Scotland Yard men they must be, I thought. But why were they here?

"Mr. Barton, please sit down! You're attracting attention," Mrs. Higgins scolded.

"My name is not Barton, ma'am," I said, aggrieved.

"Not Mr. Hill Barton? Who are you, then?"

"I am Dr. John Watson, Mr. Holmes's associate."

"Isn't anyone who they say they are?" She stared at Colonel Pickering.

"I am Colonel Hugh Pickering, ma'am, in case you have any doubts."

Eliza glanced up at me. "You weren't in the play."

"Nevertheless."

"Miss Doolittle, it is necessary for us to destroy these dangerous drugs," said Holmes urgently. "Do you know where Guest keeps his store?"

"I warned Henry that man was nothing but a social climber," threw in Mrs. Higgins, apropos of nothing.

"None of the antidote remains. After the first time he tried to break in, I became angry. I slipped into his laboratory and adulterated his supplies."

"Wouldn't he simply manufacture more?" I asked. Neither Holmes nor I felt it prudent to inform her that the first burglary was actually engineered by the intrepid Wiggins.

"One of the components is a drug that comes from India. It's called argo—ergo—something—"

"Ergotamine?" asked Holmes.

"Yes. Some special strain of it that can only be found in the Punjab.

The ship that carried his supply went down off the Goodwin Sands a few weeks ago. It may be months, even a year before he can get another shipment."

"None left?" Holmes kept driving at her. "Then why did he break into your room the second time?"

"I . . . I don't know. He must have thought I still had a supply. I wish to heaven I had never fallen prey to the drug, Mr. Holmes. I won't touch it again. I don't care if it kills me. I only want to be restored to myself, even if that means I'm a Drury Lane flower girl without a friend in the world."

There was the sound of a whistle, high and clear, answered by more whistles. The hall suddenly went silent, then erupted into chaos as constables poured through the doors.

"Colonel Pickering, I shall never forgive you if our names get into the papers!" cried Mrs. Higgins.

As the constables moved through the room, the women—ordinary, middle-class women though they appeared—rose up against them, in a terrific show of resistance. Out of handbags came stones, and even hammers. Cutlery was turned into weaponry. The speaker on the dais was urging the women to fight, and fight they did. The police, who it appeared had come only to arrest a few known malefactors, were unready for such an assault. The result was tumultuous.

As the din rose around us, Holmes's voice became urgent. "Three names, Miss Doolittle: Betsy Chubb, Nancy Kelly, and Susan Wallace." Eliza was on her feet, looking about anxiously. The Scotland Yard men were calling out names and charges, making arrests, ignoring the chaos on every hand. There had been a bombing of some sort, they said. But Holmes repeated the three names, commanding Eliza's attention.

"I never met them," she said, but she looked sick with terror.

The room had descended into madness, screaming and clawing, some women on the attack, others being dragged away in handcuffs, the constables wielding their truncheons with a right good will. Then Newcomen was with us, and a group of constables. I expected him to reassure us, but that was not his aim. He pointed to Eliza. Two constables grabbed hold of her arms. "Christabel Pankhurst, I arrest you on charges of conspiracy to assassinate the prime minister," he announced.

Under duress, Eliza reverted to her old Cockney ways. "'ere, get your mitts arff me, you!" she yelled. She stomped hard on the foot of one of her captors. He hopped away in agony, but his partner was still able to slip the cuffs on Eliza.

"Inspector, unhand that young lady!" said Mrs. Higgins in highest dudgeon. "Her name is Miss Eliza Doolittle, and she has done no wrong! I shall write a letter to the minister about this appalling behavior."

"And who might you be, eh?" Newcomen asked gruffly.

Sherlock Holmes interposed. "I believe this is the mother, Mrs. Emmiline Pankhurst. You have a warrant against her as well, do you not, Inspector?"

"Like mother, like daughter, I always say. Take her, you men."

"Have you taken leave of your senses? Colonel Pickering, tell them who I am!" Holmes caught Pickering's eye. Pickering turned away guiltily. "Barbarism!" she cried as the handcuffs were clamped on her tiny wrists. "This would never have happened under Mr. Gladstone!"

Holmes again, almost chanting it: "Betsy Chubb. Nancy Kelly. Susan—"

Eliza let it out in a sob. "She came to me. I hadn't seen her since we were children. She came to warn me."

"About the effects of the drug."

She shook her head. "About the effects of withdrawal. I refused to listen."

Then it came back to me, that itch I couldn't scratch. Betsy Chubb and Nancy Kelly had shared rooms in Angel Court with another girl. Eliza's last address before she came to Wimpole Street had been in Angel Court! Eliza was the third girl!

Holmes nodded to Newcomen. Eliza and Mrs. Higgins were dragged away through the roiling mass of women and police.

"My God, Mr. Holmes!" breathed Pickering. "Please tell me how that was necessary."

"We wanted Eliza safe from Hyde. He won't be able to get at her in gaol."

"But Mrs. Higgins, man!"

"Will look after her like the lioness with its cub."

I said nothing. It was arguably a disgraceful thing Holmes had done. But it was unarguably necessary.

"Higgins will kick up a furious row," I warned.

"Undoubtedly. But it will still take him a few days to get the ladies out of custody. Newcomen will see to that. In that time we should be able to track down Hyde."

We made our way out to the street as the police were hustling an ever-growing crowd of arrestees into the vans, surrounded by jeering suffragettes and a sea of gawkers.

"I suppose I'll have to follow them to Holloway. I don't look forward to facing Mrs. Higgins," Pickering lamented.

"I must ask you to do one thing first, Colonel."

"Name it," said Pickering.

"Search the girl's room. We must find her store of the drug."

"But she said she destroyed it," I said.

"She was lying."

Pickering was appalled. "What? Rummage through a lady's boudoir? Absolutely not."

"Not to save her life?"

Pickering thrust his hands in his pockets and stared down at the pavement. He had the look of a man struggling with his soul. Finally he looked up, nodding. "You are the serpent in the garden, Mr. Holmes. I will do as you ask."

With that, he parted from us, walking off disconsolately, looking for a cab. Holmes and I took to the streets. I had no idea where our steps were directed, but Holmes's face was urgent with purpose.

"How do we proceed?" I asked.

"We return to Montague Street. We must try Dr. Guest again. Guest is the key to finding Hyde."

But there was no trying Dr. Guest. When we arrived at his home, his man greeted us with the news that the good doctor had removed himself to a sanatorium in the Swiss Alps, to help complete his cure. He offered to give us the address. His face was bland and unreadable.

We retreated across the street and took up a post behind a plane tree, which afforded us a view of the house from relative concealment.

"Look at those windows, Watson. What's behind those curtains? Is someone watching us?"

There was nothing to be seen, of course, even with Holmes's keen eyesight, but his gaze was so intense one would think he could burn a hole through the curtains—even through the walls.

"You think Guest is still in there?"

"Guest may have gone abroad. But that still leaves Hyde."

"What about his flat in Greek Street?"

He shook his head. "The police watch it. And the landlady knows better than to help him, even if she were so inclined." Holmes considered for a moment. "Wire Wiggins. Ask him to stretch his contacts. Anyone who knows Edward Hyde. Anyone who's heard of him or anyone like him. Tell the Irregulars the hour of need is upon us."

"What about you?"

"I shall remain here. The servant must go out sometime during the day. When he does, I propose to have a look behind those curtains."

I remembered when Holmes burgled a suspect's house before. It had nearly ended in disaster and arrest. "Take care, Holmes," I said.

I did not see him again until the next morning. I rose just after dawn to a clatter in the kitchen. Holmes was at table, wolfing down whatever comestibles he had foraged from the larder. From the state of his dress, he must have just come in. He had used to be all fire and dash when on the scent, but in the grey light of early morning his face was etched in disappointment. I put the kettle on.

"Any word from Wiggins, then?" he asked.

I had no news for him. "Did the curtains ever move?"

He shook his head. "I handed over the watch to the Freddies."

"The Freddies? You mean—?"

"Yes. Von Stetten offered me their services. He's also posted a man at Wimpole Street, and another at Hyde's. Our erstwhile foeman is now our valued ally."

"Pickering telephoned. The police are still insisting that Eliza is actually Miss Pankhurst, in spite of all evidence to the contrary."

"That's Newcomen's fine hand," Holmes said with a grin. "He'll gum up the works as long as he can. Higgins will have a hard time getting round him."

"Higgins does not intend to lift a finger. He thinks Eliza and his mother are getting their just desserts for associating with suffragettes. Pickering wisely has not mentioned your role in the proceedings."

"Guest was using Hyde and Eliza both as human guinea pigs, just as he did with those poor soldiers in India and the three girls driven to murder when the drug was withdrawn. He hoped to find a cure for his own madness, but he was not so mad as to test the cure on himself."

"So a simple case of addiction is at the source of all our mysteries? It seems an unsatisfying answer somehow."

"Because it's not the answer, Watson. Not the whole answer."

"Then what is the answer?"

"We still have not arrived there. But I am certain the girl was not telling me everything. She was holding back, holding back something terrible. How did she ever fall under the eye of this man?"

"Didn't she tell us? She and the Kelly girl were childhood friends."

"Nancy Kelly came here from Ireland when she was thirteen."

"Have I got it muddled? She must have meant one of the other girls." I handed Holmes a cup of tea. He gulped the hot stuff down as though his throat were forged of iron.

"Susan Wallace was raised in Manchester," he answered. "Chubb is from Surrey, which might as well be the steppes of Russia to Lisson Grove."

"Then who grew up with Eliza?"

Sherlock Holmes did not answer at first. His eyes were opaque, his body still as a statue. Then a shudder went through his whole frame: "My God, Watson, what a fool I've been!"

"Holmes, what is it?" I cried. His face was pale as death, terrible to behold.

"Doolittle, Watson. We've got to get to Alfred Doolittle!" He slammed his teacup down, sloshing Oolong all over the cloth.

The urgency of his utterance was like a steam hammer. I accepted it without murmur.

We were throwing on our coats. "He won't be in Scotland still, I'm sure," I ventured. "Perhaps he's returned to London?"

We pounded down the stairs to the street. "We'll get a wire to Wiggins. Have him shake the trees in the man's old haunts," Holmes said.

I whistled up a cab. Holmes's mind was still racing. "He's a public lecturer. He must have some sort of booking agency." He put his foot on the floorboard of the cab, wavered for a moment, then shouted "Langham Hotel, driver!" as I scrambled in beside him.

Holmes had once had connections in the theatre world, but the Langham hardly seemed the place to find a booking agent. Still, when Holmes had his quarry's scent in his nostrils, it was folly gainsaying him.

As soon as we arrived at the hotel, Holmes advanced like Hannibal's legions across the empty lobby. The denizens of the beau monde were not yet abroad. Having gained the ramparts of the reception desk, he waved for a clerk like a conqueror ready to give terms. "Mr. William Gillette, please," he intoned.

The clerk pinned him with a supercilious stare that plainly said a guest like Mr. Gillette was not at home to riffraff off the street. But his actual words were more diplomatic. "Who may I say is asking for him?"

"Sherlock Holmes."

The clerk was dubious. Perhaps he was among those who thought Holmes had met his end at the Reichenbach Falls. Perhaps he had never heard of Sherlock Holmes at all; he was young enough. But the frost of Holmes's gaze chilled him to such a degree that he picked up the house phone and made the connection.

It was the briefest of conversations. Gillette's voice carried through the earpiece wonderfully, as though he were hitting the third balcony. He was not gentle with the clerk. *What kind of nincompoop would make Mr. Sherlock Holmes wait like a peddler on the stoop?* he roared. Scant seconds later we were in the lift, ascending toward Gillette's floor.

He must have been asleep when we called; theatre folk do not rise with the chickens. But he was already making his toilet and ordering breakfast for three when we were ushered in to see him. His valet was laying out his clothes. He greeted us as warmly as if we were bosom friends rather than mere acquaintances. In his dressing gown, stripped of the fore-and-aft cap and meerschaum pipe, I decided he did indeed resemble Holmes.

Holmes laid out the problem quickly. Gillette responded with equal celerity. In moments he was on the line to his own agent in London, who promised to track down Doolittle's handlers posthaste. He begged the grace of an hour. Reasonable enough—still Sherlock Holmes bridled at the delay, pacing the floor like a lion in his cage. He sent his wire to Wiggins, and ordered up the morning papers. He stood still barely long enough to scan the headlines.

"There's been nothing in the papers yet. Pray God we are not too late," he said, more to himself than us. Of course he had not yet vouchsafed the slightest hint as to why he wanted Doolittle, nor why it was so all-fired urgent. I had not asked, knowing him to be close as an oyster when events were building to a head in one of his cases. Was Doolittle somehow involved in the persecution of his daughter? Were he and Hyde confederates? From my own observations I would have said that few men knew or cared less about Eliza Doolittle than her father. Further, I would have said he was not the kind of man to expend the effort to harm anyone, much less his own daughter. If he were indeed involved in a conspiracy, he was just as likely entirely unaware of the fact.

I had hoped that Gillette would ask all those questions I was reluctant to broach myself. But the actor seemed perfectly happy to follow Holmes's instructions without question. The whys and where-fores seemed of complete indifference to him, so long as he could be included in the hunting party. Or worse—and I could not shake the impression—as if he were able to divine all Holmes's purposes without being told, as if he had cut a backdoor key to the detective's ratiocination. The idea was infuriating. I did my best to tamp down my jealousy, petty as it was. I cannot claim complete success.

When breakfast arrived, Gillette served us himself. Holmes of course ate next to nothing. He was deep into his second bowl of shag by that time. Our hour's wait had stretched to two hours. We were all ready to jump.

The phone rang. I choked on a kipper. Holmes pounded my back as Gillette strained to hear over the noise. He hung up the receiver just as I recovered myself. We both turned to him, barely daring to breathe.

"He's giving a lecture this evening in Birmingham."

Holmes knocked the ash from his pipe. "When does the next train leave Euston, Watson?"

There was a time when I would have been able to answer without hesitation, but now I was tongue-tied. "The concierge can tell us," said Gillette, coming to my relief. "Just give me a moment to dress."

I believe Holmes and I raised eyebrows in unison.

"Yes indeedy, gentlemen," said the actor, grinning. "When Sherlock Holmes comes to me with the game afoot, you think I'm not going to join in the chase? You said you were in my debt, Mr. Holmes. Well, I'm calling in that debt."

"What about your performance tonight?" I asked.

"My understudy has dreamed of this day."

Thus I found myself on the Birmingham train, sitting across from not one but two Sherlock Holmeses, both sporting a restless, distracted gleam in their eyes, both keyed to the highest note. The very sight of them like that unnerved me. I spent the bulk of the journey trying to read my novel, which had serendipitously been waiting in my coat pocket since my Scottish odyssey.

We were delayed at Oxford for what seemed an eternity. An RFC aeroplane had crashed near Wolvercote that morning, killing both airmen, we were told, and the whole of Oxfordshire had risen up to see the wreckage. No excuse for the delay, Holmes snapped at the conductor. He vowed to write a scathing letter to the president of the line. We arrived at Birmingham New Street station almost an hour late; I had not advanced a page into the lost world of Professor Challenger.

Doolittle's agent had apprised us that the gentleman was scheduled to give his lecture at six that evening in the lecture theatre at the university. It was the very stroke of six when we came tearing off the train. Thus we set our sights on Old Joe, the handsome old bell tower that lords it over the grounds of the university, and indeed the entire city. We arrived at Aston-Webb Hall at six fifteen, to find the theatre bursting at the seams and the crowd in an uproar. Mr. Doolittle had not begun his lecture. No one could tell us when he would begin. The students were certain that Mr. Doolittle was being denied the podium. He was, after all, a well-known socialist agitator. The Birmingham city fathers, steeped in capitalist orthodoxy, grown fat on the strawberries and cream of capitalist benefice, frowned upon agitators of any stripe, and socialist agitators in particular. The students, for their part, enjoyed being agitated more than anything.

It took us some time to find someone in authority who could tell us what was actually going on, only to find out that no one had the slightest idea what was going on. We found the university provost engaged in heated conversation with a professor of English literature in an alcove outside the theatre. The provost was responsible for the welfare of the hall; the sounds of students clapping and stamping their feet upon wooden planks filled him with fear. The professor had invited the distinguished Mr. Doolittle to speak. All either one was certain of was that Doolittle had never arrived at the venue. The professor suggested the possibility that his speaker had been waylaid by individuals unknown to anyone with the possible exception of the provost. The provost offered to beat the professor to a pulp unless he retracted his invidious accusations. One of the college stewards had been sent to Doolittle's hotel, to ascertain whether the man had ever arrived in Birmingham at all.

Finally a nugget of useful information! "What hotel is Mr. Doolittle supposed to be staying at?" asked Holmes.

Queen's Hotel, we were informed, and Holmes beat such a hasty exit that we were fairly spun around in his wake. Queen's Hotel, of course, is actually incorporated with the New Street train station. You can practically step off the train and find yourself in the main lobby. So it was back along the exact route we had come, and Holmes grumbling under his breath about the slowness of Midlands coachmen. We were nearly out of breath when we fetched up at the front desk to find out what room Doolittle was in. Then we bolted for the lift.

The lift, of course, was out of service. We mounted the stairs, two and three at a time, my heart pounding in my chest. (And did I not hear, from the bottom of the stair, the clerk cry out behind us?—*As you value your life or reason, keep away from the fourth floor!* To this day I'll swear I did.) We arrived at the fourth-floor landing and heard the din.

There were four men standing in the hall, all shouting Doolittle's name, all hammering on his door to be let in, though they could barely be heard over the thundering from inside the room, and the blood-curdling screams of a female in distress. The four men, we learned in short order, were the hotel manager, the hotel detective, the lift operator, and the college steward sent to collect Mr. Doolittle.

"Why do you wait upon the threshold?" Holmes asked the manager. "Surely you have a key!"

The key, alas, had been mislaid, the manager divulged after much hemming and hawing. The chambermaid might have taken it home in her apron, lamented the house detective. A silly woman. A very, very silly woman.

Gillette strode forward. "Then stand back, you pikers!" he cried. "There's a lady in danger of her life!" The actor rammed his shoulder against the door. The door quivered, but held. He stormed it again; the lock splintered, the door flew open, Gillette's momentum carried him into the room. We would have lost one of the foremost thespians of the age had I not fortunately been in place to pull him back as the axe just missed grazing his skull.

There she stood, in bedraggled pink silk with a scarlet bow at the waist, bosom heaving, ostrich-plume hat dangling from her curls, fire-axe in her arms. Fanny Pritchard would have appeared comical save that in her eyes was madness and murder. She swung the axe again, and this time it was I who narrowly missed being unseamed from the nave to the chops.

Then Sherlock Holmes took charge of the fray, snatching up a chair by the door and advancing on the girl with it like a circus lion-tamer. Her face clouded with confusion, but she took a game hack at the chair and sent one of the legs splintering across the room. Holmes drove her to the wall, pinning her between the chair-legs so she couldn't swing the axe. She screamed like a wildcat, and flung the chair back with that inhuman strength granted by Guest's unholy drugs.

But she had dropped the axe. The hotel detective dove for it, displaying the kind of pluck one rarely sees in hotel detectives. He got a kick in the head for his pains that must have had him seeing stars, but the rest of us were able to rush the girl. In the end it took four men to subdue her. Then, when she saw she was bested, she went limp, and fainted dead away.

We all seven stood, breathing heavily, staring at one another, a brotherhood that had fallen down the rabbit hole and found our way back to daylight.

"Where's Mr. Doolittle?" asked the college steward.

Holmes pointed. In the corner stood a wardrobe, of walnut or some other dark wood. The doors were scored and smashed in from the strokes of the axe. From within emanated a mewling like a kitten's. Gillette went to the wardrobe and wrestled the doors open. Alfred P. Doolittle lay huddled at the bottom of the wardrobe, his hands covering his eyes. He was shaking all over like a meringue.

"You're safe now, Mr. Doolittle," said Gillette, holding out a helping hand. Doolittle looked out from between his fingers at the man standing over him.

"Sherlock Holmes!" he gasped. "I been saved by Sherlock Holmes!"

It hadn't been Susan Wallace who had come to Eliza with a

warning, then, or Betsy Chubb or Nancy Kelly. It was her childhood friend, Fanny Pritchard, who must have met the Kelly girl when they had both "trod the boards." She had probably met Gabriel Guest there, too, lurking backstage, and caught his eye. Fanny Pritchard, the fourth girl. She would never again be the merry, thoughtless lass I had met in Edinburgh. But thanks to Sherlock Holmes, at least she would never be hanged for murder.

Most of this was simply conjecture at the time. Fanny hadn't merely fainted: she had retreated into catatonia. Whatever solid information she might provide on the good doctor and the hellish drugs he prescribed was locked within her brain. There would be no questioning her for weeks to come.

Alfred Doolittle never made it to the university that night. He canceled his tour then and there and returned home to the sheltering arms of his wedded wife. Whether he has ever strayed forth again, I cannot say.

We returned to London that night as well. Gillette was exhilarated by his half-day excursion into real-world detecting. I'm told that his performances for the remainder of his London run were extraordinary. But for myself and Holmes, the satisfaction of preventing another murder was thin gruel so long as Edward Hyde remained at large. Freed of Henry Higgins's yoke, Holmes combed the streets of London, looking for Hyde. He had the help of Newcomen and the Yard, Von Stetten and his bravos, and the remnants of the Irregulars. Yet the days passed, and we came no nearer our quarry.

Chapter Twenty-Nine

F reddy Eynsford-Hill was laid to rest the following Saturday. There was a very moving service at St. Paul's, followed by an interment at Highgate. Miss Doolittle and Mrs. Higgins were in attendance, having just been freed from prison, in spite of Holmes's efforts to keep them incarcerated for at least one more day.

Sherlock Holmes and I were not in attendance.

Professor Higgins had not wanted to go, either, and said so, loudly, to anyone who would listen. But no one would; between his mother and Colonel Pickering, he was chivvied and cossetted and finally forced to go. Part of that persuasion was that the entire household staff was given the morning off to attend the funeral. Freddy had been popular with all of them. If Higgins didn't want to go, his mother warned, he could sit home alone and ring the bell, but no one would answer his summons.

The house on Wimpole Street was therefore deserted—except for Sherlock Holmes and myself. We had let ourselves in quietly by the kitchen door with a purloined key mere moments after the last servant had left. Pickering had made a desultory search of Eliza's room and found nothing, but Holmes was sure the girl had not told the truth when she said there was no more of the formula hidden in the house. The empty house presented the ideal opportunity for us to make a thorough search without fear of disturbance. Even the constable who had shadowed the house since the morning of Freddy's death had gone to the funeral.

We ascended to Eliza's room. Pickering had searched there and found nothing, but his scruples made him a less than ideal detective. I felt a qualm about going through the girl's private things in her absence, but Holmes was convinced that there was another cache of Guest's formula hidden there somewhere, and finding it was a matter of life and death. He had no scruples about throwing open cupboards and rummaging through drawers. And yet we found nothing.

"Nothing here," I reported, going through the drawers of her vanity. "Not even face paints. Our Miss Doolittle is a natural beauty."

Holmes continued searching for a minute. Then he stopped cold and looked at me. "No powder? No rouge?" I shook my head.

"This wardrobe." Holmes riffled through the clothes. "Barely half full. And the drawers. Where are her gowns, Watson? Where are her shoes?"

It seemed to me there were plenty of clothes in the wardrobe, but ladies' dress habit is hardly my area of expertise. "Perhaps Pickering took her some dresses when he visited her in gaol," I suggested.

"Pickering went to see her?"

"Every day. Poor fellow felt so guilty."

"Of course!" Holmes cried to himself. He flew from the room and ran downstairs to Pickering's quarters. I followed dutifully. When I caught up, the wardrobe was already open, the drawers pulled out, even the window stood open to the elements. Holmes was waving a dog-eared Bradshaw's guide to steam navigation, and nearly struck me in the face with it. "Never let me tell you Pickering is anything but a cunning old fox," he said.

"Did you think he had flown away?" I asked jokingly, pointing to the open window.

"I did not open that window."

Then we heard a sound: a crash of furniture, and the thud of something heavy falling full-length upon the floor.

"The laboratory!" hissed Holmes. "He was here before us! You have your service revolver?"

I patted my coat pocket. "What about you?"

He brandished his stick.

"Why don't you ever carry a gun, blast you?" I asked as we roared down the stairs.

"One such weapon is enough to provide discouragement. Two is an invitation to bloodshed."

When we reached the laboratory we discovered Dr. Guest, stretched out full upon the floor near the piano, unconscious. The piano bench was open, sheet music strewn across the floor. Upon the piano itself was a small case holding a hypodermic syringe and six ampoules of the clear solution. One of the ampoules was empty.

"He must have been here all along, hiding, waiting for everyone to leave."

"Addicted to his own poison!" I exclaimed, holding the ampoule up for Holmes to see.

"No. Hyde was here. Master and man seem to have had a falling out, and the doctor got the worst of it." He pointed. "His footprints there, and there."

"And there," I pointed, "his boots!"

Holmes looked where I pointed, beneath the settee. There was indeed a pair of boots there, small, but wide enough for Hyde's splayed feet.

"This is curious indeed," he said, "for observe the doctor's feet."

I looked. The doctor had no shoes on. "Hyde must have taken them," I said.

"And left his own?" The queerest look of puzzlement came into Holmes's face.

"Let's get him up on the settee," I said. Holmes seemed not to hear me. He stood staring at Hyde's boots as if he expected the man himself to spring up out of them. I saw to the doctor myself. Guest let out a groan as I lifted him. He was conscious, then, or drifting in and out.

"The boots, Watson, the boots! At last I begin to see the light! The boot-*prints*!"

"What the devil are you talking about, Holmes?"

"Hosmer Angel."

The case came back to me in a flash. Hosmer Angel had been affianced to Miss Mary Sutherland. He was entirely devoted to her, and would have made a most loving husband, except for the fact that he had never existed. Hosmer Angel had been invented and personated by James Windibank, Miss Sutherland's stepfather, for the sole purpose of keeping her unwed and at home so that he would continue to have the use of her independent income. It was a hoax most daring and most cruel. And it was clear what Holmes meant by uttering that name.

"Edward Hyde . . . is Hosmer Angel?" The enormity of the idea nearly unhinged me. "But Holmes! I saw him myself!"

"You saw what Guest wanted you to see, or more like what he wanted Freddy to see. A rival so fearsome it would send Eliza's gentle lapdog trembling under the furniture. A monster fashioned from greasepaint and spirit gum meant to terrorize the matinee crowd."

"Then we were hunting a phantom?"

"While the real monster hid behind the drapes on Montague Street."

Guest sat rocking back and forth on the settee with his head in his hands, muttering to himself.

"Dr. Guest! Can you hear me?" asked Holmes.

Guest lifted a finger to acknowledge.

"Your stay in Switzerland seems to have been less than salubrious," Holmes continued. "I see your associate has been here as well. Yet he has departed in his stocking feet."

"Who?" Guest asked groggily.

"Let us have no more deceptions, Dr. Guest."

"Hyde came. He attacked me."

"You seem to have fought him off."

"I'm ill. I must return home at once." Guest attempted to rise, but had not the strength.

"Doctor, if you would?"

I examined the man. "He has a high fever, that's certain. And his pulse races."

"Who are you?" asked Guest, still in a daze. "Not who you said."

"I am Sherlock Holmes. And you are the man who murdered Frederick Eynsford-Hill."

"No. No. Not I. It was Hyde . . . he's coming back. He might return any moment."

"Scotland Yard is not idle. There are men concealed all over the neighborhood. I need only open the window and whistle and you shall be in their hands. But first there are a few points I wish you would enlighten me upon."

Guest's face was suffused with fear. Sweat poured off his forehead. "Hyde is coming back," he croaked. "You must go. You must flee." He made a feeble attempt to rise, but fell back upon the settee.

"Watson, I think a spot of brandy would do the man good."

I went to the sideboard and poured a glass. I brought it to him and put it carefully to his lips. He knocked the glass from my hand.

"Hyde is here! Run!" he roared.

What occurred in the next few moments was the most nightmarish thing I have witnessed in all my years with Sherlock Holmes. I near fainted with fear. Nor was Sherlock Holmes any less affected. His face was white as the winter moon. All his theories were as ash on his tongue.

Guest was bent double on the settee. His face was purple. His eyes bulged almost out of his head and his mouth twisted. His whole body shook with agonizing paroxysms. He fell to his hands and knees on the floor. His body writhed, seeming to shrink and grow at the same time, as if his flesh were melting wax. The veins stood out like black snakes beneath the skin. His hands became gnarled like old vines. His skin shrank and coarsened till it looked like old parchment stretched across the skull. When he looked up at us, his eyes were no longer those of

Gabriel Guest. They were the mad yellow eyes of Edward Hyde. Once again there hung over him like a cloak that foulness that suggested something beyond the grave.

"My God," whispered Sherlock Holmes, "what hast Thou wrought?"

"He warned you, didn't he?" rasped Hyde, baring his teeth in a simian grin. "The doctor warned you, but you wouldn't listen!" His laugh was like the shredding of rotted canvas. "Now you must take your medicine!"

He was on his feet quick as a flame. I was nearest him. I tried to retreat, but he clamped a hand on my forearm and sent me windmilling across the room. I tumbled over the settee into the fireplace, landing on my side in the fender. The pain shot up my arm like a thunderbolt.

Holmes's stick whipped across Hyde's shoulders. The creature howled in pain. He spun round and lunged for the stick, but Holmes sidestepped like a toreador and dealt a blow that opened up a welt below the left eye. Hyde turned and charged again. There was Holmes, whirling, kicking, slashing with the cane, driving in to land sting after sting. For a man his age, Holmes was still swift and unexpectedly strong. His old skills at single stick had not deserted him.

But they were only stings. Hyde seemed to take no real harm from the blows. He was younger than Holmes, his strength fueled by a monumental rage. He landed a wayward blow against the side of Holmes's face. It was only a slap, but it sent Holmes staggering. He dodged the next hammer blow only through sheer instinct. Recovering his stance, he laid on with the stick again, pushing back in upon Hyde, but more cautiously, step by miserly step. All I could think of was the image of Hyde bringing a horse to its knees with one blow.

Then I remembered the gun in my pocket. I had to reach it, but my right shoulder, where I had landed, was numb once more. I grappled across my body with my good arm.

Holmes looked to have cornered Hyde, laying on at will, opening up fresh wounds upon his face and hands. Hyde seemed bewildered. Then with a snarl he leapt straight up onto the bookshelves and hung there like a giant spider, dripping with malice. Then he plunged toward Holmes. Holmes sprang away, but Hyde landed on his feet behind him. Pivoting, he drove an elbow into the detective's kidney. Holmes gasped and hit the wall, nearly cracking his skull against the doorjamb. Before he could gather himself, Hyde planted a kick in the back of his knee. Holmes fell to the floor in a thunderclap of agony. Hyde's foot came down and would have cracked Holmes's spine had he not squirmed away. The foot came down again, but Holmes caught it and threw him back. Hyde crashed into the piano bench, smashing it into toothpicks beneath him.

Holmes swayed to his feet, sobbing for breath, his strength nearly drained. Hyde sat up, grunted, and spat blood, little the worse for a good sparring. Any fool could see the final outcome of this mismatched battle. But for the briefest moment, Hyde's attention flickered. I saw it. Holmes saw it, too, his one chance at leverage. Even as Hyde scrambled toward the piano, Holmes swept forward with his stick. It came down, not on Hyde but on the hypodermic case, smashing one of the ampoules. Hyde howled in anguish and grabbed for the case, ignoring the blows Holmes rained upon him. He snatched up the case, shut it, and stuffed it inside his coat.

"Little good will it do you," Holmes said softly. Hyde cast a look upon him full of despair. "How long did the first dose last? Five minutes? Your body has become resistant to the antidote."

Hyde sank to his knees, one hand over his heart where the case was secreted. "This is my only salvation," he whispered.

"Then you are utterly damned," replied Holmes. He set the point of his stick at Hyde's throat.

For a moment one could almost glimpse the eyes of Gabriel Guest looking out from behind the mask of Hyde. But Guest was lost forever. Hyde growled and grabbed the end of the stick. The two men wrestled for control. Holmes held on like a bulldog, but Hyde, mounting slowly to his feet, had mastery, marching Holmes backward until he was pinned against the wall. Demosthenes tumbled from his shelf and shattered on the floor. I fumbled for the gun again. Holmes's stick snapped like a twig. Hyde flung the pieces away and slammed a fist full into Holmes's face. Holmes rocked and dropped to his knees, stunned. I could feel the gun wadded in the folds of my coat. My fingers sought the trigger. Hyde seized the phonograph from the table and brought it down on the detective's shoulders, knocking him flat on the floor. He followed with a savage kick to the ribs that nearly lifted Holmes from the floor. Another such kick might kill him. I couldn't tear the gun free.

I fired.

Hyde spun, staring in amazement. Had I hit him? Left-handed, through my coat pocket, my hand shaking like the palsy, had I hit him? Holmes groaned. Hyde took a step forward. A wetness spread through his waistcoat. He reached in and drew forth the hypodermic case. He whimpered, opening the case. Shards of glass tinkled onto the floor, and the spent bullet. Hyde wailed like an animal mortally wounded. He dropped the case. It had saved his life and lost it both.

In that moment I pitied him, I did. But I feared him still. He moved. I fired again. But he was no longer there. There was a crash and spray of glass. Hyde was gone through the window, into the street below.

"Watson," Holmes voice croaked. He was propped against the wall, staring at me. His face was a mass of bruises. "You are a man of miracles."

In a sudden burst of relief, I laughed, almost crying. Holmes joined me in laughter. He hauled himself to his feet, hobbled to my side, and helped me stand. "Good old Watson. Are you all right?"

I nodded. "You?"

"I wouldn't like to go another round on the canvas with that devil."

We heard a police whistle outside. And another.

"Those gunshots should bring half the force at the run," said Holmes. "Let us join them."

Chapter Thirty

We limped out into the street. Hyde was nowhere in sight, but the rumor of his passage was everywhere. There were police constables running, children chasing behind them, and fat nursemaids wheeling crying babies in their prams, all in the same direction. There were barrows and carts lying in the middle of the road, their contents spilled from one curb to the other, their owners hurling curses to heaven. Carriage drivers were shouting at each other and automobile horns were honking. We moved down the street in Hyde's wake.

Further on, we found a four-wheeler overturned in the middle of the street, its driver battered and bruised, surrounded by policemen barking questions. It seemed Hyde had torn the horse out of its traces and ridden off, bareback. A young fellow in a two-seater automobile was trying to get past, honking his horn incessantly, as if he could clear the street with noise.

"Watson, our quarry is mounted. We must secure transport." Holmes turned and pointed to the young man in the auto. "That will do nicely."

I approached the auto. "Good afternoon, sir," I said to the young man. He wore a cloth hat and duster, with the requisite goggles over his eyes, which to my mind always gives motorists the appearance of giant toads.

He greeted me with a vapid look. "Officer, could you please persuade this fellow to move his vehicle with all due speed? If I'm not at my aunt's country house by six, I'll be banished from the dinner table."

I cocked my revolver and pointed it at him. It spoke volumes.

"Here, what are you doing? Help—!" The word died on his lips as I poked the gun in his ribs.

"Move over," I said. The young man complied with all due speed. I got in the car next to him, pushing him into the passenger seat.

"Can you drive this machine, Watson?" Holmes asked, leaning over the dash.

My experience as a driver had been confined to the two-street stretch after we dismissed our driver on the day we had first come to Wimpole Street. Even that would not have deterred me, but—"My shoulder," I said. There was still no feeling in it.

"What a nuisance. Push over. I shall drive." I squeezed up against the young man till he was almost in my lap, as Holmes took the wheel. I was fairly certain I had two streets' worth of experience over Holmes as a motorist. He gripped the wheel tightly. "Now what?"

As quickly as possible, I shared my scant knowledge with him regarding gear shifting and foot pedals. The young man in goggles and duster appeared to be trying to contribute, but was only able to utter the words "bup-bup-bup" repeatedly. I had not removed the gun from his vitals.

"Excellent! I have the gist of it," said Holmes. The gears ground, the car jumped, and the young man groaned. We were off. Our progress was closer to that of a wounded rabbit than a gazelle of the African plain, but Holmes learned quickly and the grinding of the gears became less horrendous as we bucked down the road.

It was not hard to guess what route Hyde had taken. Boys were chasing down the street, wild with excitement. Then we saw up ahead a crowd of police constables around a man on a horse. There was no question it was Hyde: the man was not seated astride the horse, but standing on its back like a circus rider, lashing it with a coachman's whip as it reared in a frenzy. Then the horse broke through the crowd at a gallop. Holmes attempted to follow, but a crowd closed in behind wherever Hyde went. Holmes wove in and out of traffic, spinning the wheel like a helmsman in a storm, but we could gain no ground on our quarry.

"Can this machine go any faster?" Holmes yelled over the roar of the engine.

The young man's vanity gave him voice. "My good man, you're jolly well behind the wheel of a Widgeon Seven. It can reach speeds up to fifty per!"

"We have to catch that man on the horse!"

"That madman? Who are you geezers?" the young man asked.

"Sherlock Holmes and Dr. Watson!" I cried.

"What, like in the play? Ripping! If you'll let me drive, we can catch this bally villain without killing ourselves in the process."

Holmes slammed on the brake. We all spilled over the dash, and then Holmes climbed over me one way and the young man climbed over me the other way, and presently I was crowded against Holmes with the young man at the wheel, zipping in and out of traffic. Down Oxford, through Regent Street and Coventry we pursued our prey, till we came into the Strand. Here we happened upon an amazing sight: two autos had actually collided head on. Steam rose from their crumpled bonnets, and the drivers stood in the middle of the road, threatening each other with hellfire and perdition, near ready to come to blows. They blocked the road completely, but our pilot took the ruin in stride, simply hopping the curb up onto the sidewalk. Pedestrians dove out of our path as Holmes slapped the driver on the back, congratulating him. There was no question he was a skilled pilot, but the growing mass of people in the Saturday streets made it ever more difficult to maneuver.

"We'll never catch him this way, guv'nors both!" said the young man.

Holmes nodded grimly. "Turn right at the next street. We'll take the bridge."

"You mean to abandon the chase?" I protested.

"I mean to waylay our quarry. We shall not lose him."

I had my doubts, but forbore to voice them. The young man, on the other hand, seemed ready to place absolute confidence in the name of Sherlock Holmes. We crossed over Waterloo Bridge to the Surrey side and were soon threading our way among the wharves and warehouses, Holmes shouting directions to the driver at every knot in the road. It was an amazing piece of navigation when you remembered that Holmes had barely set foot in London for ten years. Still, with every mile I feared Hyde was further and further away. Holmes must have read my thoughts.

"Never fear, Watson. He'll stay close to the river through Fleet Street and Cheapside. We'll catch him before he makes the Isle of Dogs."

"How do you know where he's headed?"

For answer, Holmes waved at me the Bradshaw he'd found in Pickering's room. "Left here, young Phaethon, left!" he cried to our driver.

We had gone far out of our way, but there was no denying the traffic was thinner on this side of the river and we were making good time. Soon we were shooting out onto Tower Bridge and crossing the Thames once more. The below-bridge steamers seemed to hail us with their horns. We continued up Little Tower Hill to Smithfield, between the Dock House and the Mint. There Holmes directed the driver to slue the car round broadside of the street, cutting off any chance of Hyde escaping to the east. It was an eerily quiet corner, as if some great disturbance had passed and pulled the flotsam of London along with it. Holmes looked anxious. We shaded our eyes to gaze up Tower Hill, hoping we were not too late. To our left rose the shining white tower that had been the city's first bastion against barbarous invaders. The driver drummed his fingers upon the dash. A long, nervous moment passed.

Then we heard the hoofbeats. Presently we spied Hyde galloping down the avenue, bearing down on our barricade, throwing terror in the hearts of passersby. He had left his pursuit far behind. I drew my revolver.

"No, guv'nor, you'll kill the horse!" cried our driver.

Holmes stayed my hand. "He cannot pass."

But Hyde showed no signs of stopping. He came thundering along, flogging the horse furiously. At the last moment our driver dove from the car, Holmes threw himself beneath the dash, and to our wonder, the horse took flight, sailing over our heads, its last hoof knocking the hat from my head. It cleared the car, hit the street with a spark, and continued onward.

The young man let out a whistle. "I'd like to put twenty quid on that bally Pegasus in the steeplechase!"

"He'll kill the horse beneath him," I said.

"He'll have to halt soon," Holmes replied.

"Doesn't look as if he's in a hurry to slow down," said the young man. He took his seat, put the car in gear, and spun it around, and we started our pursuit once more.

"We're almost to the docks. It's Brunswick Wharf he's making for. That's where the steam packet sails for India." Holmes opened the Bradshaw between us, the wind whipping the pages. The dog-eared page was a timetable for ships embarking from Brunswick. One ship, the *Abydos*, had been circled on the page.

It wasn't long indeed before we came upon the abandoned horse, standing in the middle of the street, its tongue lolling and coat covered with foam. The poor beast was surrounded by a group of boys who seemed to be wavering between throwing rocks at it or hanging garlands of flowers upon its withers. The young man braked the car and hopped out. He strode up to the horse and threw his coat over its back.

"One of you lads fetch me a bucket of water and there's half a crown in it for you," he said. The boys dispersed like a swarm of flies, racing for the nearest pump.

"Gentlemen, take the car if you need it!" he called back to us. "Leave it on the pier. I'm staying here with Pegasus."

"You're a man of heart!" I called back.

The young man was crouched beside the horse, checking its hooves. "Heart? I'm going to buy this ruddy steed and race him in the Grand National."

The streets ahead were so packed with humanity, on foot and in every kind of conveyance, that Holmes and I opted to walk. Walk he called it, at least, but I soon found myself at a near trot trying to keep up with him. We could have wished for the company of Bert and Toby both, I thought, but Holmes seemed like a hound himself with the scent in his nostrils, moving ahead unwavering. I thought I glimpsed Hyde a number of times ahead of us, bowling over innocent passersby in his advance, but when I pointed, Holmes barely acknowledged me. He was focused on his target. We came at last to the wharf itself, so engorged with humanity that we could barely move forward, but Holmes betrayed no frustration, only clear-eyed determination. It was easier slogging through the crowd than I anticipated. I wondered if Hyde had blazed a trail for us. At last we burst into daylight, the sun sparkling on the Thames, the smoke from a dozen smokestacks rising toward heaven.

"We're looking for the *Abydos*, remember, Watson. And that," he pointed south to the end of the pier, where a steam packet was blowing its horns "—will be it, I think."

"They're raising the gangplank!"

"Yes. The question is, has Hyde already boarded?"

Now we sprinted. Yet even as we ran, the answer revealed itself. There was a black figure hanging from one of the boat's mooring ropes. From a distance it could almost be mistaken for a rat, but as we closed, it became evident that it was a man, climbing hand over hand up the breastline toward the ship's foredeck. We were hardly the only ones to see it. There was a crowd at the rail shouting and pointing, and they had already won the attention of a couple of deckhands.

"Should we find the harbormaster and have him contact the captain?" I asked.

"I have no doubt the police are already taking that step. Let us try something more direct."

He ran to the bollard that held the line. It was a thick rope and taut. Holmes attempted to pry the rope off the bollard. I ran to his side to help. The wharf hand in charge of the line descended upon us in wrath, but after a hurried explanation he joined our efforts. We pushed and pulled and grappled with it till we were red in the face, but all at once the rope sang free, almost snapping us in the face. We watched the rope sway out across the pier and slam against the hull of the ship, with Hyde still holding on. For a moment it seemed he would lose his grip and fall, but then he was pulling himself up hand over hand toward the bow rail.

"He's not a man, he's a python!" cried Holmes, exasperated.

Hyde climbed over the rail into a knot of sailors armed with blackjacks. Whether they were trying to help him or harm him we couldn't make out, but the next moment he was knocking them aside, tossing one over the rail screaming into the river. A moment later he was climbing the superstructure toward the upper deck. A crowd of hands and passengers gathered beneath him, a couple of sailors waving carbines, but no one seemed inclined to shoot. Another crowd formed on the deck above, but as soon as he reached it, he scattered them like ninepins and continued his climb.

"What can he be thinking, Holmes? There can be no escape."

"He does not seek escape, but revenge."

As he spoke, a porthole opened above Hyde, and a small face looked out. I seemed to recognize that brave face; my heart beat faster. I pulled my gun out and tried to aim, but I found my left arm shaking so damnably that I dared not shoot. There was something hypnotic in the man's jerky, swaying ascent, as if he were the bob of a pendulum. He would surely reach his goal; he was almost there now. There was a sudden glare, which made me turn my eyes, and then the crack of a gunshot. I looked up again to see Hyde still hanging by one hand from the rail. Then he fell like a stone.

"Who fired?" I asked, looking about wildly. The crowd seemed to sway as everyone turned toward where the sound of the gunshot had come from. "Who fired?"

"Ah, John." Holmes's eyes were not on the ship but on the far shore. "That we may never be able to say."

The gangplank was let down again, and the police bustled aboard in short order. No one on deck seemed to have seen who fired. Sherlock Holmes identified the dead man as Edward Hyde, the murderer of Frederick Eynsford-Hill. There had been such a white-hot pitch of life in the man that even now, gnarled and twisted, he seemed more alive than most. Yet there was no question he was dead. There was a bullet through his heart, as well as one through the right shoulder, though witnesses had heard only one shot. Neither Holmes nor I felt it necessary to volunteer any information about the shoulder wound. Once Holmes had identified him, he seemed to show little interest in the corpse. He searched out the purser instead, to ask him a question.

"Purser, when do we sail? Can't the police take this fellow and go?"

"I'm sorry, sir. It won't be long now," the purser replied.

"The gentleman in cabin eight invited me to cards this evening. He's not one of those seagoing card sharpers, is he?"

The purser consulted his manifest. "Colonel Pickering, sir? Nothing to fear there. I met him when I came aboard. Retired army. Returning to India."

"Certainly is blessed with a beautiful young wife."

The purser coughed discreetly. "His niece, sir. Miss Elizabeth. In cabin ten. You won't see much of her, I'm afraid. Took sick as soon as she came aboard."

"Ah, well, thank you, Purser. One can't be too careful these days."

As soon as the purser was out of sight, I exclaimed. "Pickering and Eliza? How can that be? I'll be dashed if I understand anything about this case, Holmes."

"I think we'll find the answers in your rooms. Let us repair there."

It was Holmes at his most enigmatic, but I was too exhausted from the frenetic events of the morning to ply him with more questions.

The throng on the docks had become a sea of people. Crowds of the curious, who had already heard of the shooting on the *Abydos*, swelled in among the usual crowds of leave-takers and well-wishers.

Holmes and I moved against them as against a great tide. Then a tall fellow in an astrakhan coat and a Tyrolean hat collided full on with Holmes, nearly knocking him down. I bent to help Holmes, who'd had the wind knocked out of him, and thus only caught a glimpse of the man before he was swallowed by the crowd. "Holmes!" I cried. "That looked like Colonel Von Stetten!"

Holmes only grunted and leaned upon my shoulder. We ground our way through the boiling mass of humanity. At last we got hold of a cab and went home the slow way.

Chapter Thirty-One

We were in my rooms, sitting before the fireplace. Neither of us had mustered the energy to light a fire. For the longest time we neither spoke nor smoked nor even looked at one other, but only sat leaden and dispirited, staring dumbly at the ashes in the grate as the evening grew chill round us. The day's events had unsettled me profoundly. Once again I looked to Sherlock Holmes to set the world in order, but he seemed as lost as I. Then at last he roused himself and turned to me. "I expect a communication of some sort from Colonel Pickering. I hope it will shed light on this affair."

I nodded, unbelieving.

"You are a medical man, Watson. What devil's brew could affect a man of parts that he is so transformed—?"

"Blasphemy" was all the answer I could muster. "Blasphemy."

Holmes put a hand to his cheek and winced. I had applied liniment, but the bruises would take weeks to heal. "Your arm?" he asked.

I lifted my right arm slowly. The feeling had come back into it, but it was a mixed blessing at best. "I could not shoot him, Holmes. Even seeing what he was, I could not shoot him."

"No. You are too decent."

"He would have killed Eliza! And the colonel. But for the intervention of some man not so decent."

"Go into the hall. Bring me what you find in my coat pocket."

I brought back a heavy object, tied up in a woolen scarf. Holmes unwrapped it. "A Mauser C96," he said. "Recently fired. This is the weapon, I think, that was used to kill Edward Hyde."

Where had Holmes got it from? Then the answer came to me, plain as a pikestaff. "Von Stetten," I said.

"Yes, it was he. As you said, he ran into me at Brunswick Wharf. No coincidence there. He must have followed us, or Eliza. He had no intention of letting her come to harm. And then he planted the murder weapon on me."

"He tried to frame you!"

"I think not. He couldn't chance being found with the weapon in his own possession. It would have created an international incident. But who would search Sherlock Holmes? In Von Stetten's eyes, I am an entity outside and above the law. We have your case histories to thank for his impression."

We heard a light step in the hall, and a timid rap on the door. "Our messenger!" cried Holmes. He strode to the door and flung it open before there was another knock.

"Oh!" cried the messenger, frightened by his suddenness. She looked up at us, fragile as a canary.

I recovered myself first. "Mrs. Higgins. Do come in, ma'am."

She was still dressed in mourning. She walked in, bird-like and querulous, casting sidelong looks at Sherlock Holmes, but we persuaded her to take a seat and some refreshment. Once her nerves were calmed, she regained some of that air of authority that was her natural armor.

"Colonel Pickering asked me to come," she said. "He gave me a letter for you, Mr.—Watson, isn't it?" she said, looking at me. "I'm not accustomed to dealing with persons of your . . . trade. You should know that my son is devastated by what has occurred, although he is of course in no way to be considered responsible." She produced a thick envelope from her bag, and handed it to me. Then she composed herself, aquiver with anticipation. Apparently she expected to hear the contents of the letter. Considering the trials we had put her through in the last few days, it was difficult to deny her the right. I glanced at Holmes. He gave an almost imperceptible nod.

I took a penknife from the table and slit the envelope. Inside was a short letter in Pickering's hand, and still another envelope. I unfolded the letter and read aloud.

MY DEAR JOHN,

As you read this, I will have set sail for India. I do wish I could have made a proper goodbye, but some secrecy has been necessary for our preparations. I'm afraid that long years of service to the Raj have rendered me unfit to enjoy the free and easy ways which are now the custom of the capitol. I am of the opinion now that the heart of the empire is closer to Calcutta than London.

I do not return alone. Miss Doolittle accompanies me on my voyage. Over the course of the last months, she has become dear as a daughter to me. After her interview with Mr. Holmes, Eliza revealed certain facts to me that I found frankly astonishing, but they did not alter my fondness for the girl one iota. Her story and its consequences, I think, should make it impossible for her to remain in England, so I offered her the opportunity to take up a new life far away from her old haunts. She has accepted unreservedly. I cannot say what alterations may occur in her in the near future, but she will always be Eliza. I have you and your Mr. Holmes to thank for assuring me of that. Enclosed you will find a letter from her which should clear up any lingering questions you may have regarding her role in the events of the past months.

London is a great city, Wobbly, but it's cold and grey and

wet. If ever you find the wind digging into your bones as it did mine, remember that you have friends in sunnier climes who would welcome you as family.

Your old comrade,
HUGH PICKERING.

The second envelope was addressed to Sherlock Holmes, but he requested that I read it aloud as well. It was from Eliza.

DEAR MR. HOLMES,

I have asked the colonel to take down what I say, since no one ever taught me to write so well as Professor Higgins taught me to speak.

I was always what you might call a spitfire, or as some would say, a shrew. I had no mum to teach me better. And then my deformity told against me with those who might have been kinder. My father was an amiable old scoundrel, but took no more notice of me than he would a pet parakeet. He tried more than once to shove me into an orphanage. Miss Laver at the Home would have taken me in, but the subscribers wouldn't abide it. So I went my own ways. The first time a man spoke to me kindly was Colonel Pickering. The first time a man paid attention to me was Professor Higgins. He took down my words. My words! As if something I might say could be worth listening to and remembering. Learned men they were, anyone could see. You wonder that I made my way to their door the very next day? Henry Higgins turned my head; not with chocolates or dresses or taxi rides, but with the attention he poured upon me. He scolded me and cursed me, but he never ignored me.

I never suspected I had sold myself into bondage. I let them take me in and try to bend me and shape me into a middle-class lady. But at first I could not learn what Professor Higgins wanted to teach, because no one had ever taught me how to learn anything. I was a failure. I would always be a failure. Professor Higgins was beginning to lose patience. Soon I would be out on the street again.

That was when I met the devil. Gabriel Guest was the first doctor I ever met, and a gentleman, too, it seemed, so when he told me I needed an injection to keep from catching chills like Colonel Pickering, I never doubted him. And when I came up so sick after, I thought I'd got my medicine too late to save me. I came over weak as a lamb, and I was off my head for what seemed like weeks, though it was only a few days. When I came round again, I knew something was wrong. Colonel Pickering tells me he feared the real Eliza had been spirited away and replaced by a new girl. He wasn't far wrong.

I could only wonder at the cause of it. The sickness, or the cure? The fever had burned through me like fire in a dry wind, lighting my flesh, turning my bones to kindling. Everyone around me noticed the change, how could they not? But no one said a word, no, not even me. Every time I tried to speak of it, my tongue grew unaccountably heavy, my heart pounded, and my lips felt as if they were sewn shut. I was looking out at the world through the bars of a prison. A terrible fog settled over my mind, while my heart rattled like a tambourine.

Slowly it dawned on me that I was being treated differently. Tradesmen were more at ease with me. Professor Higgins smiled upon me. Even Mrs. Pearce unbent toward me. At first I thought it was only sympathy for me after my illness. Then I began to realize it was due to the alteration in my appearance and bearing. My deformity had slid from my shoulders. I began to grow more confident as the professor became more lenient, and that made my lessons easier. Everything became easier, at least outwardly. I began to think of myself as two women, the old contrary Liza and the new Miss

Doolittle, the professor's pet. Liza was always there, dark and brooding beneath the deep layers of the drug, and oh! how she hated Miss Doolittle and all her pretty little ways. Miss Doolittle was worshiped and adored, but she was no more than a porcelain doll upon a shelf. Miss Doolittle was the cage Liza was confined to. And whenever Liza shook the bars of her cage, along would come sidling Dr. Guest with his needle.

He told me quite brutally that the change in me was due entirely to the injections, that I would degenerate—that was the word he used—to my former condition without a steady schedule of them. If I obeyed him, I could become a true lady, he claimed, not just on the surface but in the blood, "fit to be the helpmeet of a gentleman." Else I would be reduced to the streets once more, this time to the very lowest dregs of society. The picture he painted was so terrifying that I let him dose me again and again, till I practically became a prisoner locked inside my own body. There were times he took liberties with me, and I could not summon the old will to fight. For the first time in my life, I needed a protector. I wanted to reach out to the colonel, but I was too ashamed. Then I found my knight in shining armor, the last man you would think: Edward Hyde.

You'll say Hyde is a monster, and that's true. But so I am a monster. When first I met him, I knew only that he was the doctor's factotum. I soon learned that Guest exercised some power over him that made him a prisoner, even as I was. In our private moments we plotted together how we would rid ourselves of our gaoler. Even when I came to realize what Hyde was, that his prison was the face and form of Gabriel Guest, I never thought of them as the same man. If Guest withheld the poison from him, Edward would be snuffed out like a candle. If he withheld the antidote from me, I might wind up like Betsy Chubb. I was too cowed to fight.

Not Edward. He began to test the bars, to force his way out of the cage even when Gabriel refused to take the formula. He claimed it was his soul that properly owned the shared body, that Gabriel Guest was only an empty shell. He fought tooth and claw. But eventually he would find himself exhausted, or on the run, and then he needed the antidote. He did not trust Guest's servants in Montague Street, or the landlady in his Soho rooms. He asked me to keep a small cache of the antidote with me. There were occasions when he would contact me, desperate, begging me to bring him a dose, in whatever hellish corner of the city he might be hiding. I accepted this trust, but I loathed seeing him transformed back into the smirking doctor.

Then the cargo ship *Mahratta* went down off the Goodwin Sands. Gabriel was terrified. Without the Punjabi strain of ergotamine, he could manufacture no more antidote. He sent Edward to carry off the cache he had entrusted to me. He failed, as you remember, but then I felt doubly betrayed. I struck back in anger. I arranged to meet Edward, promising him all of the antidote I possessed. Then when he was gone from home I stole into Gabriel's laboratory and adulterated his supply. I vowed to take no more myself. That was when I took to my bed, and allowed no one to visit me. Over the course of the next few days, my body began to stir and change again, and the face in the mirror hardened into that old familiar face that I had discarded so wantonly. I didn't know if I would survive the change. I knew what had happened to Betsy Chubb and Nancy Kelly. I kept a vial of the antidote by my bedside. That cowardice was my undoing.

Edward came to me again in the night. He found me in the throes of delirium and injected me with the antidote. He must have meant it as an act of mercy. What cruel mercy! Again I was torn apart body and soul by the hellish drug. I feared I would never have the strength to fight again.

And then they told me my poor Freddy had been killed. It wasn't Edward's fault. It is his agony that makes him lash out, I know, but what good is it to say it? No one around me is safe anymore. My guilt has become insupportable.

Most of this you had already gleaned somehow. Perhaps I should have confessed it all, but would you have believed my story? Can you believe it even now? I have confided in the colonel instead. He took me at my word. He is the only man on earth I trust.

Thank you for showing me what I must do, Mr. Holmes.
ELIZABETH DOOLITTLE.

We sat in silence for a time, each trying to absorb the facts of Eliza's confession. Then Mrs. Higgins rose to her feet. "Well, it appears my son's faith was misplaced. His naiveté and sentimentality have betrayed him as they did his father. Still, I had hoped for more from Miss Doolittle, and especially from Colonel Pickering. Indeed, since you were obviously deep into my son's counsels, I will admit that I had entertained the possibility I might one day call the girl my daughter. But one cannot make a silk purse from a sow's ear, no matter how convincing the illusion. As for that fellow Guest, I never cared for his manner."

That was her final word on the subject. She made ready to go. We exchanged pleasantries as though her errand had been a mere social call, and we would all meet again at the vicar's for tea. Then she looked us up and down. "Imagine two old men playing detective among respectable people!" With that burnt offering to the temple of her vanity, she departed.

I turned back from the door. Holmes was standing with his back to me, staring into the fire.

"Holmes! Eliza is aboard that ship without a drop of the antidote! Will she survive the crossing?"

"Damn Eliza," said Holmes quietly.

I strained to hear him aright. "What did you say?"

"And damn Pickering and damn the *Abydos*, may it sink to the bottom of the sea as surely as the *Mahratta* and the *Titanic*."

I knew that his nerves had been strained to the breaking point. Once a case had reached its conclusion, Holmes often subsided into melancholy or worse. "You don't mean that, Holmes."

He turned to me as if nothing had gone before, and said, "Watson, could you check Bradshaw for me? I must return home in the morning. I have responsibilities." He said nothing more, but went off to bed. When I woke the next morning he was gone, having left a note on the breakfast table.

WATSON,

Unable to sleep. Taking the midnight train from Victoria. Please excuse my outburst of the evening. My appetite for the uncanny has never been robust.

Yr Comrade in Arms,
SHERLOCK HOLMES.

I breakfasted alone. The workmen would be in soon to replace the surgery door. Admiral Nelson was retired to my bedroom. The skeleton went into a cupboard. In the afternoon I would see patients.

Chapter Thirty-Two

That was the unhappy note the affair ended upon, or so I believed at the time. The Great War came and went, taking the lives of a generation of young Englishmen, leaving a nation bereft of its future. It was on a bitter winter day in 1919 that I received a visit from an unexpected, unwelcome guest. He stood on the icy step, dressed in a soldier's greatcoat with the badge of the Royal Fusiliers, holding his wasted frame up on crutches.

"You don't remember me," he said.

"Can't say I do." I had assumed that he was collecting subscriptions for wounded warriors.

"My name is Mead, sir, Cyril Mead. I was for a time valet to a Dr. Gabriel Guest. You attempted to question my master once in connection with a murder investigation. You and another. Mr. Sherlock Holmes, I believe it was. I turned you away."

I remembered him then. He had never looked young, but now he seemed almost a specter. "What is it you want from me?" I asked gruffly. I did not want to feel pity for the man.

"You wanted information from my master at the time. My master was a very secretive man, and I was not in his confidence. But one sees. One suspects. One wishes one could . . . atone, even though one has committed no actual crime, do you see, sir?" There was a shine in his eyes, in spite of the cold.

"You're not here to ask forgiveness, are you?"

"I'm here to give you the information you asked for." He withdrew a bundle of papers bound up with twine from inside his coat. "I warn you, sir. It is terrible."

"What do you want for this information?" I asked, still suspicious.

"I hope to sleep at night."

I took possession of the bundle from him and he went away in ghostly silence, his crutches leaving pockmarks in the snow. I never saw him again. I hope he has found the peace he sought.

I sat down before the fire and cut the bundle open. I began to read.

My name is Gabriel Guest, a physician by profession, a scientist by avocation. My father was a grey little man in a grey little situation, clerk to a solicitor named Utterson, himself the greyest of all the grey men ever called to the bar in grey London town. My mother was no more than a shadow. She vanished in the noonday sun.

There was but one figure in my childhood who stood out from the dreary fogs of my youth, one of Utterson's clients, a tall man with flashing eyes and a face that shone like hot coals. His name was Henry Jekyll.

As I read, the evening shadows began to gather round me, and the fire died down. I found myself listening to the sounds of traffic in the street, rendered alien and remote by the soft hissing of the snowfall and the steady beat of wind upon the glass. There was the rustling and scratching that might have been mice in the walls or something more, and the creak of floorboards announcing a visitor who never arrived. I found I had read through several pages of Guest's writing without the slightest idea of what they contained. It seems childish now that

I report it, but the advancing shadows had returned me to that night when the face of Sherlock Holmes, contorted by the Hyde elixir, had leered at me out of the darkness, and I'd had to fight for my life against my best-loved friend. I set aside the documents, rose, and built up the fire. I turned up all the lights in the house, trying to chase away the phantoms of the past. I tried to settle in and pick up where I thought I had left off:

> *Higgins planted the thought in my mind: what effect might it have for a subject to take the antidote without ever having been subjected to the formula? Test subjects were near at hand. The Women's Hospital is just down the street from the rooms I had picked for Hyde. I chose women because they would be more easily manageable than men, and less likely to have any defenses. Young single women are a disposable commodity in London, as are soldiers in India. I sought out the lowest of the low, and the streets of Soho yielded them up to me. Nancy Kelly, Susan Wallace, Betsy Chubb, Fanny Pritchard.*

No. I stopped and put the papers away. The awful story of Guest and Hyde was not one meant to be read alone on a storm-tossed night in London. There was more in the bundle: a letter from old Utterson, and some sort of testimony from a lawyer named Lanyon, but they were concerned with Henry Jekyll, the first Hyde, the originator of the cursed formula. There was a lengthy *apologia* penned by Jekyll himself. Finally there was the formula, printed out by itself on the last page, as neat and innocent as a recipe for apple strudel. All of it could wait. I would go down to Sussex, and see my old friend Sherlock Holmes. We would read it together. Spring would be knocking at the door in Sussex.

I had not seen Holmes since just before the war. Strange rumors had come to me through various channels of a drastic change in the great man's habits. He dabbled in spiritualism, some said. There was talk of séances and experiments in psychic phenomena taking place under his roof. It was even said that he had placed an article in *The Strand* arguing the veracity of the Cottingley fairy photographs. In public I dismissed such stories as idle gossip, but privately I had been troubled. We had not spoken of the Doolittle affair in all that time, and I hesitated to remind him of it. I sent him a wire to broach the subject. The reply came swiftly:

COME AT ONCE.
HOLMES

There was little to mark the passage of years in Sussex. It was a bright afternoon when I arrived, though a chill breeze still combed the grass on the downs. The garden seats before the villa had gone green with moss. Ivy stirred upon the kitchen wall. There was a fountain plashing in the middle of the courtyard now, with a mermaid perched atop it, a bit of whimsicality that seemed out of character for Sherlock Holmes. But the bees were loud as ever and the sitting room was the same cheerful mess. Holmes still gazed at me with those same probing eyes and sardonic smile. When I handed him the bundle of papers, he touched the twine as fondly as if it were a violin string.

"How are the colonel and Miss Doolittle?" he asked me.

"They survived the voyage, if that's what you're asking."

He laughed. "Forgive me, Watson. I was angry when I spoke those words. Before that day, my practice had always been confined to the realm of the possible. My deductions were straitjacketed by logic and probability. I was wearied almost to death by the trivial puzzles presented by the mundane crimes you so faithfully documented. The resolution of the Doolittle case opened an abyss before my feet that filled me at first with terror. But in time I came to realize that the realm of the supernatural afforded me broad new scope for investigations. My pulse has quickened once again."

"The supernatural? You don't mean séances and ghost photography and all that parlor spiritualism, do you?"

"Call it what you will, Watson. We march together hand in hand with those who have passed before us. I have seen them myself, communicated with them myself, here in this very room beneath this roof. There is no death, only a transformation. It was Edward Hyde who first drew back the veil for me."

"But there was nothing supernatural about that!" I protested. "That was science! Twisted, perverted in intent, but science all the same. You analyzed the formulae yourself. We both witnessed the effects."

"We witnessed a man shed his outer skin and a gibbering ape step forth. That you call science. But every day men slough off their physical forms to liberate their spirit bodies. That you call superstition. It is all one to me."

I did my best that day to dissuade Holmes from his newfound enthusiasms, but he was as serenely confident in his explications of the spirit world as he had once been in his powers of observation and deduction. And I could not deny that the old eagerness that had once fueled his greatest successes as a detective had returned with a vengeance. He was once again the hound upon the hunt, though the malefactors he hunted were all beyond the grave.

He drew a chair close to the fire. I followed suit. He untied the string and leafed through the pages. At one point he stopped and put his hand palm down on one of the pages, as though he were probing for a pulse. Then he smiled, shook his head, and tossed the entire manuscript into the fire.

"Holmes! Are you mad?" I cried. I started toward the fire, but he held me back as the flames took it hungrily.

"What need to read it, John? This manuscript bells at us like a pack of hounds." Holmes smiled serenely. "Shall I tell you what I hear? Do you not hear it yourself? The voice of Gabriel Guest, a motherless boy who despised his plodding father, Utterson's clerk, and worshiped Dr. Henry Jekyll, a perfect stranger, but a man so full of dark purpose that his face was a palimpsest of corruption for those who could trace it. Jekyll disappears, the father dies, Utterson dies, and still the boy burns for that dark purpose. Somehow Jekyll's papers come to him, all his secrets laid bare. But the mightiest secret of all, the one he cannot decipher, becomes the lodestone of his future. It leads him to the study of medicine and chemistry, leads him to the army and India. It spawns the grotesque experiments on the soldiers under his charge. And once he has the key, once he has the formula, it leads him back to London to reenact the debaucheries of Edward Hyde. He even adopts the same name in homage to his private Baphomet. And like Faust before him, he believes he can control the demon he has summoned."

Moriarty on the windowsill started cawing at something outside and would not be quieted till Holmes took him up and set him on his shoulder. I watched Guest's papers blacken and curl away in the fire.

"But Eliza?"

"I fancy it was Higgins who first put that in his mind, or at least fanned the flames. What could the antidote effect by itself, they wondered, in the absence of the formula? Could they not turn a girl of the streets into a drawing room angel? Guest worked upon the four women, Chubb, Kelly, Wallace, and Pritchard, and he was gratified by the results. But he cast them all aside when Higgins found Eliza Doolittle."

I could do no more than stare open-mouthed. Every word that Sherlock Holmes had spoken rang true. It was either the finest piece of deduction he had ever propounded, or the manuscript indeed had spoken to him from the fire. For sanity's sake, I chose the former proposition.

Holmes moved to the door and took his coat from the peg. "Come away from the fire, Watson. It will take time for the miasma to dissipate. I think we could do with a stretch of the legs, eh?"

We stepped out of the house, and the wind from France hit my face. Then a sense of loss welled up in me like a stone in the heart. "But you've destroyed any proof!" I wailed.

"Who shall we prove it to, John? Our poor England, indeed all of Europe, has known such atrocities in the last few years as neither Guest nor Jekyll could summon from the iciest depths of the Infernal. They need no proof. The poison gas, the zeppelin bombardments of helpless cities, the submarine murders, the scattering of disease germs, are they not proof enough of the atavism of the human race?"

His words were full of despair, but he spoke as dispassionately as a chemist detailing the results of his latest researches. He stretched his arms and cracked his knuckles together.

"Shall we walk down by the shore? Climactic conditions should be excellent for mermaid sighting."

The afternoon sun beckoned on the cliffs, and the wind promised to wash away all nightmares. I followed him down to the sea.

Chapter Thirty-Three

There was one more thing I had to do. Holmes had not asked me to, nor had Pickering. I did not do it for Eliza, or for Freddy. I did it for four young women whose lives had been thrown away, whose names were no more to me than yellowing newsprint.

It was a biting March day when I knocked on the door at Wimpole Street. A rather frowzy housemaid whom I had never seen before answered the door.

"Who shall I say is here, sir?"

"Er, is Mrs. Pearce at home?" I stumbled.

"Martha Pearce? Cleared out before the war, I heard tell, and all her people with her. If you're wanting Mrs. Pearce, you'll have to run down to Ipswich. Except that's not her name any more. Married some fellow, I heard. Only been here six months myself."

"I wanted your master. Professor Higgins still lives here, does he not?"

"He does indeed, and keeps us all at sixes and sevens. A right slave driver he is, sir, and I don't care who knows it."

"May I speak with him?" I gave her my name and she left me

standing in the hall. I stood there a good long time, recalling all that had happened in that house. I wondered if I had been forgotten. Eventually Higgins appeared, in an old smoking jacket and slippers, scowling at me.

"What the blazes do you want?" he asked.

"We have never been properly introduced. My name is Dr. John Watson. Do you remember me?"

The shock of recognition curdled his face. Though we had never returned to Wimpole Street after Pickering and Eliza set sail, Pickering had left a letter with Higgins explaining what he could of the matter, as well as a check for Higgins's tutelage of "Mr. Morello." Holmes himself had sent Higgins tickets to *Sherlock Holmes*, when it was still playing at the Adelphi.

"Am I likely to forget the criminal saboteurs who came into my house, stole my peace, turned my household upside down, and turned those dearest to me against me? State your business, sir, and be gone with you."

"I came here to gaze on the face of the man responsible for the death of Frederick Eynsford-Hill."

"Ah, that was my fault, was it? I suppose I'm also to blame for the death of Captain Scott and the Norwich floods, too. Damn your impudence!"

"You knew what Gabriel Guest was when you brought him into this house."

"If I had known what you were, I would have had the footman turn you into the street! Perhaps I should do so now."

I ignored the threat. "You knew what Guest would do to Eliza. You urged him on."

"It's Eliza now, is it? You're on familiar terms with the girl you helped steal from under my roof?"

"The girl you would have broken down till she was fit to be no more than your slave? I thank heaven we were able to save her from that."

"What gentleman of discrimination does not attempt to mold his future helpmeet into a creature that will bring him satisfaction? I had the means at hand and I employed them."

"You could make Eliza talk like a lady, but you couldn't tame her spirit. You needed potions for that."

"Come, Doctor, we're not unlike, you and I. We're men of science, settled in our habits, comfortable in our solitude. Does this mean we must be denied female companionship entirely? I don't mean the sodden harlots of Whitechapel or Soho. I mean young, vital women. But they must be pliant, they must be amiable, they must be disciplined. Between Guest and myself, we were able to turn a girl of the streets into the simulacrum of a lady. Had it not been for Pickering's unfathomable sense of conscience, she could have been an ornament to my household. Have you never wished for such an ideal?"

"And if men, yes, and women, too, die because of it?"

"That was Guest's fault, not mine. He could not rule his appetites. I have no such weakness. And now, Doctor, I must beg you to take your leave. I have other responsibilities to attend to."

He seemed unassailable in his egoism. He turned his back and started down the hall. I wanted desperately to penetrate his complacency.

"At least I know that Miss Doolittle is safely away, and you will find the days of your loneliness stretching away before you." It was an awkward thrust, one I knew had not hit home.

"Oh, quite. An excellent sermon. Good afternoon."

He turned and went into the laboratory. I heard the lock turn. Then his voice, clearly, with perfect enunciation:

"Are you ready to resume your lesson, my dear?"

And a woman's voice—nay, a girl's voice—answered, "Yes, thank you, Professor Higgins."

It is raining today in London as I finish my narrative. Whenever the weather is like this, I think of old Pickering, and his invitation to join him in the tropics. I went out to visit a few years ago, after the war. He had lost the use of his legs by then, but his spirit was still strong, and he had a devoted nursemaid in Miss Doolittle, or Mrs. Parvinda, I should say. She had married one of the native gentleman, a librarian and teacher. She had changed, but no more than could be accounted for by the passage of years and the vicissitudes of climate. She was no longer beautiful as I remembered her in her youth, but she was now something better: she was lovely. Loveliness is a trait of the soul, which shines forth in spite of any outer device. As for deformities, physical or spiritual, she had none that I can report.

Together they urged me to stay and make my home with them, but I was restless. I remembered how Holmes used to say that when he stayed away too long from London, the criminal element became excited. Holmes is in his grave on the green Sussex downs, and Pickering in his on the Malabar Coast. I am retired from my practice; I could travel anywhere I wish. But the grey streets of London have me locked in their embrace. Like old Toby, I retrace every day the footprints I once followed eagerly in the shadow of Sherlock Holmes, remembering the faces and the voices of all those we hunted and all those we helped. There is only one mystery left to explore, and as always, Holmes is one step ahead of me.

Acknowledgments

T hat this book rests in your hands is a bit of a miracle, so it's only right that I thank the miracle-workers. First my infinitely patient editor Dan Mayer and the staff at Seventh Street, especially Marianna Vertullo and Jennifer Do, as well as copy-editor Marianne Fox. I'd like to thank my faithful readers for their incredible kindness and inexhaustible enthusiasm: Laura Roach Dragon, Betsy Hannas Morris, and Pat Shriver. Special thanks to Nancy Bilyeau, Max Epstein, and Patricia Burroughs, who led me through the tortuous maze of publishing. Thanks also to agent Jill Grosjean.

Without my entire family, this book would never have seen the light of day, nor would I be here to see it. My profound thanks and love to my sisters, Nancy Bos Labiak and Beverly Williams Ward, and my nieces Maurna Thornton and Dawn "Sassy" Williams.

Certainly I must acknowledge *i migliori fabbri*: Arthur Conan Doyle, George Bernard Shaw, and Robert Louis Stevenson. I hope you can forgive the liberties I've taken with your characters.

Finally, a thanks to my teacher, Diana Ely, to whom I owe so much.